# I Married An Earthling

# I
# Married
# An
# Earthling

a novel by

**Alvin Orloff**

**Manic D Press**
**San Francisco**

The author would like to thank Mark Ewert, Timmy Spence, Tony Vaguely, Deena Davenport, Tyler Ingolia, Bambi Lake, Jennifer Jazz, Art De Brix, Bryon Fry, Keith Klippensteen, Robbie D., and most especially, Dodie Bellamy and Kevin Killian, for their ideas and/or encouragement.

Cover illustration: Maurice Vellekoop
Cover design: Scott Idleman/Blink

Library of Congress Cataloging-in-Publication Data

Orloff, Alvin, 1961-
    I married an earthling / Alvin Orloff.
        p. cm.
    ISBN 0-916397-64-5 (alk. paper)
    1. Gay youth—Fiction. 2. Human-alien encounters—Fiction. 3. San Francisco (Calif.)—Fiction. I. Title.
PS3565.R5795 I2 2000
813'.54—dc21

                                                    00-008961

Distributed to the trade by Publishers Group West

This book is dedicated to
Jennifer Blowdryer,
who taught me how to live *à go-go*,
and
Michael Collins (aka Diet Popstitute),
who taught me how to revel in perversity.

# Prologue

The night of Veeba's party I wanted to look my absolute best, if not outright most spectacular. I spent hours nervously making up my face, donned a demure yet dazzling wig in sassy scarlet, and slipped into a lavender suit with orange spangles I'd procured just for the occasion. Somehow, perhaps through beginner's luck, I achieved a sort of rough-and-ready glamour which I recognized as a marked improvement over my usual frumpish appearance. Upon entering her exquisitely furnished home however, what little confidence I had disappeared before the intimidating crowd of sophisticated celebrities I recognized from fashion runways, art galleries, and hair salons. Finding an unobtrusive place to stand under a large fruit tree, I tried to calm my nerves by nibbling on a baked ozgruch served by a passing robomaid. Improbably enough, I'd received a personal and entirely legitimate invitation to this astoundingly fashionable soirée from the hostess herself, Her Excellency, Veeba 22.

Just a few days earlier I'd seen an unusually tall woman glide regally into the vid-monitor lounge of the Institute for the Study of Quaint and Primitive Cultures where I'm a professor of Earth Studies. Following closely behind her was Klajo 139, the Institute's chairman, looking resplendent in a pink and silver-flecked chemise.

"So what exactly is it you do here?" she asked him, not sounding like she especially cared for an answer.

"In this room we study broadcasts from uncivilized worlds," Klajo replied grandly. "All transmissions are picked up by interdimensional, transgalactic, subspace probe, recorded and then analyzed by specialists from the appropriate department." He gestured proudly towards the rows of view-screens in front of which sat dozens of academics in comfy chairs happily absorbed by exotic broadcasts.

The woman ambled about the room peering over shoulders. "Why? What's the point?" she queried in a seductively listless tone. I found myself attracted by the dignified features of her rather masculine face which was flawlessly framed by a feather-petalled wig in a charming shade of chartreuse.

"Why?!" Klajo had clearly never been asked this question before. "Well, we have to keep on top of things, don't we? The Boxnogians, Yupgupians, Earthlings, and others won't always be what we technically refer to as 'barbarous backwaters.' When they're ready for contact with the civilized universe we need to know."

"I suppose," she said, peering at the images on various view-screens. "And you *like* doing this?" Her large, heavily mascara'd eyes gazed at Klajo with an alluring intensity as he ran his fingers nervously through his silvery-white hair which he'd set in a mass of gaily scalloped curls. "It doesn't become distressing or tedious?" she continued, examining her reflection in the monitor next to mine which was switched off.

"Tedious? Certainly not!" insisted Klajo, rubbing his hands together anxiously. "The variety of programming is enormous. You just wouldn't *believe* some of the things we see. *Most* amusing!"

"And what does he do?" I didn't turn around, but I could positively feel the woman pointing at me.

"This is Norvex 7, a professor in Earth Studies and one of our brightest stars here." Klajo patted me on the back. "Norvex, I'd like you to meet Her Excellency, Veeba 22. She's thinking of doing my hair."

"An unparalleled pleasure," I said, rising and curtsying as obsequiously as possible. Of course I'd heard the name; Veeba was one of Braxo City's foremost hairdressers and her zany antics were widely featured in the media. Doubtless Klajo, oft referred to as "Old Sensiblepuss" by more with-it professors, hoped to upgrade his dowdy image with a new coiffure.

"What's that you're watching?" she asked, pointing at the screen before me which showed a heavily made-up woman wearing a lavender chiffon evening gown and a blazing red wig with a looped crown waving her arms histrionically. A prim blonde in a flowered housedress stood beside her watching in horror as a man in a blue suit turned into the Earthly bird known as a chicken.

"It's a serial comedy called *Bewitched* in which Samantha, the mate of a high status Earthling named Darrin, possesses occult powers which she forswears to avoid exacerbating his insecurity. Her fabulous mother Endora, groovy cousin Serena, and nelly uncle Arthur, loathe her husband and the plots usually revolve around their tormenting him with their own magic."

"Mother? Cousin? Uncle?" Veeba, perplexed, batted her lashes coquettishly.

"The Earthlings, alas, do not have incubators as we do, and must still reproduce the old-fashioned way. Kinship bonds are extremely important to them, which is the key to the humor. Darrin, as patriarch, expects to be obeyed. The viewers enjoy watching the stuffy authority figure being humiliated."

"How intriguing. It's quite amazing how quickly the Earthlings have become chic," observed Veeba, looking straight at me in a way I found rather unnerving. "You must be ever so pleased."

"Naturally, it's terribly nice to have others share one's interests." As we spoke I was unable to dissuade my eyes from engaging in a close examination of her lean and rather attractive body which was clearly visible through her dress, a transparent silver tulle concoction trimmed with pink fluff. "I began studying back when we only had radio transmissions and didn't even know that Earthlings look just like Zeeronians. Back then we might have been studying transgalactic surveys of waste treatment programs for all the attention paid us by the public."

"Why is Earth so wildly popular right now, do you suppose?" she asked with what seemed like unfeigned curiosity.

"Just recently Earth has entered a state of accelerated cultural development. A lively intellectual skepticism is combining with a playful hedonism to jolt the planet out of its primitive rut. The dead weight of tradition, the chains of morality, and the shackles of literalism are disappearing from the broadcasts. The bland predictable characters one saw a few years ago have given way to sarcastic talking horses, masochistic but vivacious genies, people reincarnated as vehicles, and funny monsters. And it's not just television that's changing. Art, politics, and music are all rapidly..."

Veeba clapped her hands together with delight, interrupting my pedantic spiel. "Oh! I love that Earth song! You know, the one that goes, 'Who's walkin' down the streets of the city, smiling at everybody she sees? Something, something, capture a rainbow, everyone knows it's Windy!'" She had a deep, sexy voice but couldn't hold a note.

"I believe the song is entitled *Windy*."

"Yes, that's my favorite. Maybe you'd like to come and tell me and my friends all about Earth at my next party?"

"He'd be most honored!" Klajo answered for me, still trying to curry favor. I was indeed honored, but gave Klajo a brief, icy glare for his rudeness in accepting an invitation on my behalf without asking me. Unfortunately he was too busy fawning over Veeba to notice.

"I'll have my computer call your computer with the details," she said, giving my arm a friendly little squeeze which startled me with its familiarity. "I'll be looking forward to our next meeting. Now Klajo, let's see some more of your delightful Institute!"

Since that day I'd done nothing but fret. Earth studies might be "in with the in crowd," as the Earthlings would have put it, but was I "in" with it? It seemed too much to hope for. Veeba's circle was the chicest of the chic. Now, as I stood nibbling ozgruch and watching her guests dancing, drinking, and frolicking with abandon, I felt particularly unfashionable. Time passed. Nobody spoke to me and I dared speak to nobody.

While standing there paralyzed with insecurity I was startled by a tap on my shoulder. I turned to behold Veeba 22 in a stunning transparent cellophane body wrap with an arresting orange wig of careless curls.

"Your Magnificence, thank you so much for inviting me! The

party is splendid, clearly you've scored yet another triumph."

"Thank you, Norvex, I think you're right. And I'm so glad you can be here to enjoy it. So *very* glad." Then, holding my hand in her own, she addressed the throng.

"People! People!" Several, but not all, faces in the immediate vicinity looked over to us. "This is Norvex 7 from Earth Studies. He's an expert!" The crowd murmured approvingly. "Give 'em the real dish on Earth," she stage-whispered as she dashed off. There was a brief, uncomfortable pause, during which I wondered how to begin.

"Tell us about *The Beverly Hillbillies* – is it as good as they say?" asked someone to my left whose face I couldn't see.

"Well," I began nervously, clearing my throat and speaking as loudly as possible to be audible over the loud background music. "The protagonists, the Clampetts, are naive rustics plunged overnight into a culturally sophisticated and technologically advanced milieu which they barely comprehend. It's actually a brilliant metaphor for the entire situation on Earth, where the natives have been plunged into modernity virtually overnight. They've had electricity for barely a century, and the camp sensibility not even that long. On the show, the character Miss Jane Hathaway, representing the social superego, is locked in eternal struggle with her boss Mr. Dryesdale, representing materialistic individualism..."

"Did you just say the Earthlings have achieved what we would call modernity?" interrupted a suave man in a mauve body-stocking. He wore a bemused smile and held himself with a confidence I wished I possessed.

"Well...," I gazed out at all the faces hanging on my next word. My throat constricted, and without thinking too hard about it, I replied. "Yes. Yes, they have. They've started wearing fun, kicky clothes, often using day-glo colors and plastics, which more than one Zeeronian designer has used for inspiration. Their music just keeps getting faster and catchier, and the planet's youth are demanding the right to engage in a hedonistic orgy of self-indulgence instead of waging war."

A few faces around me registered shock, but my interrogator just chortled condescendingly. "Allow me to introduce myself. Gazro Mol,

Earth Studies, Multiversity of Planet Mithrib. As an expert in the field, I can't help but note that no world has ever achieved civilization before its twentieth millennium of continuous cultural development. Earth, if I'm not mistaken, only has six thousand years of recorded history, or thereabouts."

"True," I allowed. "But I consider it possible, even likely, that it's following an anomalous course of development. We've all enjoyed the planet's fashion, music, and television. What other barbarian planet has ever had such a vogue? By comparison, the Yupgupians are incurably vacuous and the Boxnogians depressingly unrefined. Actually, I don't think the Earthlings are barbarians at all." I said this realizing full well I was proclaiming academic heresy, but the thrill of entertaining the party guests was far too enticing to resist. Scores of beautiful people were now standing in a circle around Gazro and I, gazing respectfully and with real interest.

"Balderdash!" scoffed my opponent, wagging his neatly manicured finger at me in the intergalactically universal gesture for reproach. "How can a people who still play competitive sports, worship gods, and eat animals be classed as anything but barbarous? And what about *Gunsmoke*? Do you call that civilized?"

"No," I conceded, "and as you suggest, most of the transmissions from Earth are every bit as dreadful as one would expect from a people who've only just invented artificial sweeteners. Still, if one watches their local news programs regularly, which I do, there are plenty of indications that the planet's primitive provincialism is retreating before an exuberant and unapologetic cosmopolitanism."

"If you're reclassifying the Earthlings as semi-barbarous that would make them eligible for trade and tourism," observed a woman to my left. "How do you think they'd react to a visit from one of the civilized worlds?"

"I can't say for sure, but there's a show called *Star Trek* depicting a future in which Earthlings not only vanquish war and prejudice but roam the galaxy looking to meet and befriend alien races while wearing micro-miniskirts and attractive skintight uniforms. Surely that's a hopeful sign."

"You, my dear, are more than too much!" laughed Gazro, grabbing me by the arm and leading me to a mountain of inflatable pillows. As we sat I was glad to see the crowd which had been watching us disperse, leaving us in privacy. "When Her Tremendousness told me she'd found an Earth expert to invite to the party I hardly expected such an enthusiast."

"Do you know her well?" I asked.

"We're just acquaintances," he replied, in his pleasant sonorous voice. "In some ways she's a typical hairdresser: lighthearted, ostentatious, and given to whimsicality. What sets her apart is an unusual penchant for risking public humiliation with her unfashionable behavior. Once she failed to show up at a party and the next day claimed to have spent the evening home *alone*."

"Gracious, that is odd. I don't know how you do things on Mithrib, but here stylists accumulate power by collecting their clients' confidences. Few are willing to brave social ostracization."

"My sources tell me that it's part of a well thought out act. Veeba feels that people will confide in her all the more if she plays the fool, since compared to her public social gaffes, no one could possibly consider their own secrets the least bit embarrassing."

"Fascinating strategy," I observed. "The hairdressing field is highly competitive here on Zeeron due to the enormous influence our beauticians wield."

"Oh, I'm quite aware of the power which you Zeeronians invest in your stylists. On Mithrib we don't even have to curtsy to our hairdressers, only blow kisses to their navels."

"Every planet has its own conventions," I said tolerantly, helping myself to some more ozgruch from a passing robo-maid.

Gazro peered into my eyes. "You seem to truly adore Earthly culture."

"I find it most fascinating. Just today I deciphered some rather cryptic Earth humor. Perhaps you've heard of it, 'Tee many martoonis.' It refers to the amusing habit Earthlings have of scrambling their words when they've ingested recreational toxics."

"How delightfully daffy!" said a voice from behind my head. I turned around to behold Veeba, whom I surmised from her composed and harmonious face, had only just arrived and not overheard our discussion of her. "I just knew you two would hit it off. But now, Gazro, I'm afraid I'm going to steal Norvex from you. The stress of the party has been magnificent and I feel the need to make love immediately." Veeba pulled me by the hand to a beautiful fake-fur lined nest in the center of the living room and proceeded to ravish me. I could feel the envy of the party guests as they gazed upon our passion. In my wildest dreams I had never imagined scoring such a social coup!

Dear Diary,                                              Thursday, Sept. 5

Will my agony never cease? Am I going to spend the rest of my life being tormented by an insanely cruel world for absolutely no reason? It's bad enough that after a nice summer of reading and watching old horror films I have to go back to high school for my senior year, but my little brother Kyle is starting 10th grade, so he'll be there too. He returned to the family homestead a couple of days ago after spending the summer filming in L.A. He walked in the door, saw me, and said, "Hi Fatso!" I ask you, is that any way for a little brother to talk? Kyle wasn't always such a creep, but ever since he got cast as Devon on *Hangin' In There*, becoming a heart-throb to millions of love-starved teenage girls, he's really become a monster. Fame has gone to his head and driven him insane.

Drusilla - Dad's fourth wife (her real name is Beverly, but Drusilla seems like a better name for an evil stepmother) - made me clean the house, a total ordeal because, as usual, everything was already so clean I couldn't figure out what to do. I mean, the maid was in two days ago! After an hour of mopping spotless floors and dusting gleaming surfaces I told her I'd finished. She ran around pointing to nonexistent specks of filth and shrieking, "What about this? Have you done anything at all in here?" Housekeeping has driven Drusilla insane.

The moment Kyle got back he took over the living room, blasting his horrible rap CDs and yammering away on his cell phone. In retaliation I went to my room and started playing Diamanda Galas at top volume, but his boombox is so much more powerful than mine I couldn't drown him out. Come dinnertime he refused to eat the lasagna and chocolate mousse Drusilla slaved away over because – get this – his personal trainer has him on a diet! He's never been fat a day in his charmed little life!

After heated negotiations, dinner was frozen and Kyle took us all out to eat, his treat, at the new Uzbekistani restaurant downtown. The place was all done up in rustic central-Asian decor with giant photos of yaks, mosques, and yurts. Our waiter, by contrast, looked like Swedish ski instructor: tall, blond, and carelessly handsome, with broad shoulders and an easy smile. I guess they couldn't find any Uzbekistanis. Kyle ordered a salad, which at least gives me the hope that he's developing an eating disorder, while the rest of us ate pomegranate chicken with something called Samarkand pilaf which, if I'm not mistaken, is flavored with small rocks.

As usual, Kyle was going on about his glamorous life in the Hollywood fast lane, his only conversational topic. "Colby Summers and I went cruising in this awesome T-Bird convertible he got so he could research his part for this historical drama about '60s surfers."

"Is this the same Colby Summers who was arrested for brandishing a loaded pistol at the Emmies?" asked Dad suspiciously.

"No, that was *Ashland* Summers, his older brother," answered Kyle sounding exasperated, like you'd have to be crazy to ever confuse Colby and *Ashland* Summers. "The car is totally sweet. It has this red vinyl interior..." He caught the disapproving look in Dad's eye. "Colby's a really good driver. Real safe. We both had our seatbelts on." Kyle's been wanting a car for the longest time.

I accidentally dropped a chicken wing on the floor and was bending over to pick it up when Kyle turned to me. "You still don't have a driver's license, do you, big brother?" I didn't bother to answer. He knows full well I don't.

"Why are you wearing dark sunglasses?" I asked him once I'd hidden the wing under my salad plate.

"Why are *you* wearing dark sunglasses?" he countered.

"I *always* wear dark sunglasses," I replied. "Light hurts my eyes."

"Light never hurt your eyes before you became a Goth and started dressing like an S&M vampire," he shot back.

"Kyle!" barked Drusilla. She'd like to pretend fifteen-year-old boys don't know what S&M is.

"I wear dark glasses so my fans don't recognize me," explained Kyle, obviously pleased with himself.

"That is *so* pretentious!" I replied.

"I want you both to take off your sunglasses right now," ordered Dad. "This is a restaurant."

The second we did take off our glasses these two girls from across the room came up to our table and asked Kyle for his autograph. After they left, giggling and intoxicated with prepubescent lust, he acted like it was this big trauma to have had to sign his name. Poor baby!

"See," said Kyle after they left.

"You may put your sunglasses back on," said Dad to Kyle.

"They recognized him before he took them off," I pointed out. "I saw them looking over here."

"That'll be enough, Chester." Parenthood has driven Dad insane.

"Yeah, leave me alone, Fatso," sneered Kyle.

"I may be plump, but at least I don't play some demented middle-aged scriptwriter's idea of an every-teen on the worst sitcom to ever disgrace the television screen."

"Stop it *now*," barked Dad.

"You're just jealous of my thesbian ability," said Kyle.

"I believe that's thespian, dear," corrected Drusilla.

"Don't encourage him to be pretentious," whispered Dad. I didn't say anything to Drusilla, I just gave her an I-told-you-so look. "Kyle!" screamed Dad.

"Please, Dad, you're embarrassing me. This is a restaurant," I muttered.

"I can't afford to be associated with this sort of controversial behavior," said Kyle. We all stared at him. "Well, my publicist says..."

"I don't think we need to discuss your publicity right now," said Dad. "Let's just finish our food."

For the rest of the meal we all glared at each other, family-togetherness style.

I'm not exaggerating, *Hangin' In There* really is vile. The so-called jokes are all snappy put-downs. Anytime anyone says anything, the next line will be an insult. It doesn't matter if you're a nun, a grandmother, or on your death bed, you have to be sassy and irreverent at all times. The show was originally family-oriented, but when it became apparent that Kyle had that certain something-extra that makes him a star, the focus shifted to him and his bland adolescent traumas. As "Devon" his tag line is, "This... *cannot* be happening to *me!*" which he says real slowly and ironically with clenched fists and closed eyes whenever the plot complication kicks into gear. Once, when he came home for the weekend we got into an argument about his borrowing my boombox without asking, he actually used the line in my presence, forcing me to sock him in the arm.

I guess I should have known publicly dissing *Hangin' In There* would make everyone think I was jealous, but it's just *so* offensive I can't resist. At school, where I'm easily the most unpopular student ever, people say things like, and I quote, "Poor Chester, he's totally freaked out that Kyle's cute and successful and he's a fat, ugly fag." Jealous? *Ha!* The show's poofy soap-opera style hairdos alone are enough to make me run screaming. My brother, however, is totally thrilled by every second of his stardom.

Dear Diary,                                              Tuesday, Sept. 10

Today Mr. Waxman, my Current Affairs teacher, held me as a political prisoner. I got detention for being what he called "flippant." Our assignment was to write an essay about fiscal responsibility, an issue close to his miserly heart. I turned in a brilliant original piece for which I was cruelly persecuted. I submit the work itself as evidence:

*A Brief Meditation on Foreign Policy & National Security*
*in the Age of Fiscal Prudence* by Chester Julian

I was recently shocked to discover that the United States spent $291 billion dollars on defense last year. If this huge expenditure brought our nation prestige and authority abroad it would be money well-spent. Sadly, it does not. Our enemies can still oppose our national interests by waging sneaky guerrilla wars or brandishing nuclear weapons. Even worse, foreign intellectuals smugly dismiss us as militaristic barbarians and say unkind things about our nation at their universities and cocktail parties. For that kind of money, one expects a little more.

I immediately set about thinking of ways to cut the budget without jeopardizing our national security. We've already wasted far too much money on expensive armaments, stationing soldiers in horribly overpriced Europe and Japan, and just *thinking* about Star Wars has cost untold billions of dollars. Still, we can't unilaterally disarm or hostile invading armies might descend upon American soil to rape, plunder, and pillage, causing unspeakable humiliation and inconvenience. True, the collapse of the "red menace" leaves only a handful of nations with anything remotely resembling open hostility towards the American way, but we'd better be prepared just in case. The North Koreans, Iraqis, and Cubans could be deciding to gang up on us even as I write!

I suggest that it would be far cheaper to bribe than to fight the enemy. Despite their interesting accents and unusual clothes, foreigners are, at heart, a lot like Americans. They just want to live their lives, go to work, watch T.V., do a little shopping, what have you. If we ply them with gifts they'd become genuinely loyal to their generous benefactors in no time.

I call my plan "Operation UNCLE SAMta Claus," and it would work like this. Every year the State Department could release a list of naughty and nice nations. The former will get rewards in the form of desirable American consumer goods; the latter, lumps of coal. If we're afraid the naughty nations might use the lumps of coal for fuel we could give them Chia Pets, handkerchiefs, or other completely undesirable gifts. Nations falling in the middle would get nice cards wishing them happy holidays. The whole world would spend the year trying to get on our good side so that come Christmas they'd get nice presents. Governments whose representatives called us dirty names at the U.N. or who taught their schoolchildren to chant "Death to The Satanic Zionist Yankee Imperialists" would be overthrown by angry mobs when their citizens realized they were getting stale fruitcakes for the holidays while the residents of nearby pro-American nations were getting attractive Timex watches or Amana Radar Ranges.

Assuming we kept $91 billion for the military (plenty enough for a few marching bands and nuclear bombers), and cut $100 billion out of the budget (saving every American approximately $400!), that would leave $100 billion a year for Operation UNCLESAMta Claus. In a world with almost six billion non-Americans that might not sound like much, but even in the highly unlikely event that every nation on Earth were good one year, we could still spend $17 on each gift - quite enough to dazzle a Dominican or inspire an Indian. Naturally there would be shipping and handling fees, but these would be more than offset by the discount the government would get for purchasing in bulk. True, pleasing the relatively upscale and notoriously finicky western Europeans would pose a problem, but then they're the least likely to hold serious grudges against America anyway.

Let's consider the effect of this program on one of America's most feared enemies: Iran, population 62 million. The Iranians might wake up one morning after a year of toning down their anti-Americanism and discover that we'd left several giant giftwrapped boxes at the border. Inside would be 10 million toasters (approximate cost: $250 million), 20 million pairs of comfy slippers ($300 million), 5 million backgammon sets ($50 million), 20 million fruit & cheese baskets ($600 million), and 10 million Farsi-English dictionaries (to help with the thank you notes; $200 million). The total cost would be a mere $1.4 billion, well within our budget, and quite enough to win the affection of a nation where the average wage is about $50 a week. Why, in no time at all Teheran would be overrun with American tourists lured by the warm friendly natives.

Operation UNCLESAMta Claus may sound utopian, but it's based on solid principle: you catch more flies with honey than with vinegar. Greed would replace fear as the guardian of our national interests, allowing us to strike a convincingly peace-loving pose and scoring a great public relations coup. No longer would we have to labor under the embarrassing stereotype of the "Ugly American." You may ask, "Dare we try this?" I can only reply, "Can we afford not to?"

After praising a few students who allegedly turned in well done essays and mocking a few who failed to do the assignment, Mr.Waxman turned to me with a frightening look. "Mr. Julian, your entire essay was a joke. You may be clever, but if you don't take my assignments seriously you're just wasting my time, the class's time, and your own time." He slammed his hand on the desk for emphasis. "I want to empower you to hold meaningful opinions about important issues of the day, and you handed in a joke. I'll see you in detention." Everyone cackled. My peers will side with even the most hated authority figure for a chance to laugh at the class scapegoat, yours truly. Well, what can you expect from spoiled mall rats who dress like gangsta rappers? Only eight months, two weeks, two days, and eleven hours till graduation.

Dear Diary,                                    Wednesday, Sept. 11

Kyle is so obnoxious! Today he asked me, "Have you tried anything for your acne, Fatso?" Is it my fault my skin resembles the surface of a rotting pizza and I have the physique of the Pillsbury Doughboy? Luckily, I'm a Goth and can hide my hideous complexion behind a full face of makeup, and wear all black clothing which I'm told has a slimming effect

"I'm seeing a competent dermatologist," I replied. "Have you tried anything for your spiritual bankruptcy?" Kyle acts like being handsome is a good idea he had that I'm too stupid to think of; as if having pouty lips, golden skin, and high cheekbones with piercing green eyes is evidence of inner virtue. His vanity should make him less appealing, but instead it gives him a self-assurance which instantly marks him as an alpha-male, making him even more attractive. Last year he was voted the handsomest teenage boy in America by *Girl Talk* magazine. Everyone (parents, teachers, children, dogs) loves him on sight, even when they don't know he's a star.

Dad's friend, Joe Cromwell, came over for dinner last night. When he saw Kyle and me together he made a totally tasteless joke. "I can't believe these two are related. You sure your first wife didn't have a thing going with the milkman? Har, har, har!"

"What's a milkman?" asked Kyle.

"They used to deliver ice and milk to people's doors in the old days," explained Drusilla.

"Oh right," he smiled, "and all the bored housewives would have affairs with the delivery guys."

"I'm sure that's just a myth," said Drusilla.

I looked at my biological mother's picture smiling down from the mantelpiece, oblivious to the slander against her virtue. Since she left, several wives have asked Dad to remove her beaming image, but he refuses out of duty to his sons which is actually sort of noble of him since she ditched him for a glamorous Argentine cattle rancher. Of course he can afford to be high-minded since he's had no trouble replacing her with a series of sporty blondes. Joe once joked that Dad got them all from a clearinghouse in Nebraska. Har, har, har!

After dinner, Joe and the whole family went to the garage to look at Kyle's new car. He's not old enough to drive, but he found a good deal on a vintage convertible. Mr. Lopez, Kyle's manager, has convinced Daddums that Kyle should lead the lavish lifestyle appropriate to a budding media star, so Kyle's always buying expensive toys, games, clothing, and sports equipment. To avoid charges of exploitation, Dad puts everything Kyle doesn't spend into a savings account, excepting the money for our lovely house and a maid. Has this led to any sort of favoritism? Absolutely, positively. Kyle is everyone's little angel. The one person who never benefits from his obscene Hollywood salary is me. I'm reduced to babysitting for pocket change.

"You could have a car like that if you worked for it," said Dad, who doesn't consider babysitting work, at least not for a boy.

"This horseless carriage fad is on the way out, Dad." I reminded him, "Anyway, I'm going to live in Manhattan where there's no parking."

"What is it with you and Manhattan? It's dirty and crime-ridden. I ought to take you there and show you."

"I can be packed in an hour!"

He ignored my offer. "Joe can get you a trainee position any time." Joe runs a nanotechnology company and his second wife, Yvonne, is my godmother, so I have a standing offer to join the cyberworld. I strongly suspect Dad just wants to make sure I'm employable so he won't have to support me for the rest of my life. Unfortunately, for him anyway, my distaste for mechanical things is matched only by their distaste for me. I can crash a computer faster than you can say, "Exciting career opportunities in the high-tech world!"

"Microcomputers are the new frontier. Right, Joe?" asked Dad. Joe nodded, then looked away embarrassed. The last thing in the universe he wants is for me to contaminate his crisply efficient business. "You've got to have some ambition in life," said Dad while caressing Kyle's car obscenely.

"My ambition is to be left alone," I revealed with a quiet, dignified flourish, and retreated to my room. Through my window I could see Kyle, Dad, and Joe peer knowingly into the car's engine while Drusilla sat on a lawnchair finishing her lime Jell-o. Kyle caught me looking at them, put on an expression of mock horror and made the sign of the cross. He started doing that when I went Gothic just to irritate me. Shutting the curtains I blasted Thrill Kill Cult on my stereo and tried to forget my troubles by reading more of *Miss Manners' Guide to Excruciatingly Correct Behavior,* but had trouble concentrating.

Dear Diary,                                                   Thursday, Sept. 12

Drusilla wants me to go back to my therapist, Dr. Bushman. I told her, "No way," but she just peered off into the middle distance and said we'd talk about it again later. Of Dad's four wives she has got to be the creepiest (though Dora, the New Age one, used to get pretty spooky with her Ouija board, and Hannah, the German one, could make my spine tingle with her scary bedtime stories). I guess we got off to a bad start. Last summer when she married Dad and was moving in (she was the real estate agent who showed him our house), I did a little snooping through some of her boxes. Underneath a bunch of dull stuff (matching faux-marble and gold toiletries, expensive beige clothing bestsellers) was a photo album from the '80s with a shot of her at age fifteen as an entrant in a Madonna look-alike contest held in a Michigan shopping mall. I thought it was a scream, kind of cool even, and was laughing when I showed Dad. He started cracking up too, then she walked into the room, snatched the picture out of Dad's hands, ripped it in two and started crying. Dad took her into his room to console her and I accidentally-on-purpose eavesdropped a little.

"It's bad enough that Kyle ignores me, but Chester hates me, I can tell," she said between sobs.

"No, he doesn't," said Dad. "He's just at that age."

"Do you know he writes down everything we say? I've seen him. He keeps notebooks."

"I'm sure it's just a phase. And what's so wrong with keeping a journal or a diary?" he protested. "Lots of kids do it."

"I think he should see someone." The way she said "see" made me cold with fear.

"You mean..." Dad is always a little slow.

"A counselor, or a psychologist," she sniffled. "You think it's normal the way he dresses and acts?"

"Well, I'm not sure what you mean," Dad said warily, "but the nail polish has me a bit worried."

The next day they told me they wanted to send me to a shrink. Needless to say Kyle was not asked to see a therapist since he is obviously a happy, well-adjusted, and, oh let's come right out and say it, a *perfect* child. Since I didn't have much else to do I agreed to go. My social life is pretty limited since my peers, with the exception of my one friend, the equally detested Daphne, all basically hate my guts. I was actually sort of curious and looking forward to it.

Dr. Bushman's tidy office looked like a family room lifted from the pages of a particularly sterile *Better Homes and Gardens*; lots of floral print and pastels. Drusilla would have loved it. The doctor herself was bland and professional with a newscaster's forced smile. Maybe it's a fault of mine, but I really think you can judge a person by how they dress. Her tan skirt-suit with pearls and stiff, frosted hair screamed clueless; definitely in touch with her inner Stepford Wife. She asked me to take a seat in the overstuffed armchair and tell her about myself, assuring me that nothing I said would be repeated to my parents.

"What's to tell?" I shrugged. "I'm an average seventeen-year-old genius with a slight weight problem and bad skin."

"Why are you here, do you think?" Dr. Bushman shifted in her chair.

"I'm precocious and maladjusted. Guys like me are always misunderstood and persecuted as teenagers, then we move to New York and become famous artists or playwrights or whatever and get revenge on all the conformists from their stiflingly insular and oppressive hometowns by dissing them in *Newsweek* or *Artforum*. You have to expect to be unpopular if you're smart though, because most people are stupid."

"And you keep a journal, or record, of all the things people say to you?" she asked, shifting in her seat.

"Among other stuff." I picked away at the nail polish chipping off my thumbnail.

"I used to keep a diary," she said with a bright smile. "I think it's healthy. Now, your father tells me you have a girlfriend..."

"Daphne's a friend who's a girl," I corrected. "I don't swing that way."

"But no male friends," she continued. "He's worried that you're unhappy."

"Of course I'm unhappy!" I snapped at her. "Not only don't I have a boyfriend, I'm forced to get up at the crack of dawn and go to school with a herd of moronic sadists."

She took a few notes, then looked at me over the top of her glasses. "You're obviously intelligent, Chester, and I'm sure once you think about it, you'll realize that we can have a much more productive relationship if you speak from your heart. I'm here to help you. There's no need to hide behind witty banter."

I decided that I hated Dr. Bushman. As far as I'm concerned, anyone who doesn't like witty banter doesn't deserve to live, let alone practice psychology. I should have left, but having nothing else to do I put my sarcasm on hold and went through with the session. Afterwards I rewarded myself for surviving my first visit with a package of assorted fat-free donuts. Really good fat-free desserts almost make life seem worthwhile.

Dr. Bushman got to know me pretty well over the next few months, but I didn't learn much of anything about her or what she was thinking. All she ever said was, "How did you feel about that?" or occasionally,

"How did that make you feel?" I was beginning to wonder if it wouldn't be cheaper for Dad to train a parrot for me when she changed routine and I figured out she was a total quack. She asked me if I'd ever experienced sexual feelings towards Kyle!

I told her I hadn't, but she kept asking me again in different ways. It turned out she had this insane theory that I'm not really gay at all. In her twisted mind I want to sexually dominate Kyle to overcome my own sense of inferiority, but the incest taboo forces me to project those "longings" onto other boys. It depressed me that even in therapy I couldn't crawl out from under Kyle's shadow. I told Dad I wasn't going back. He asked why, but I just said the therapy wasn't going anywhere. Fortunately, he didn't press the point, probably happy not to shell out the hundred dollars a week. Still, I wonder what, if anything, she actually told them.

Since then I've been officially declared a PROBLEM, and my loving parents talk about me in the third person even when I'm in the room, which I consider the height of rudeness, if not outright child abuse. Now with Kyle back home I guess they really want me to shape up. I have no intention of going to any quack shrink of theirs though. I plan to be extremely firm about that.

Since Kyle got back there's been a constant stream of popular jocks and pretty girls over to the house. At school these same people taunt and jeer at me, but here they usually pretend not to see me. Today though, I answered the door and found Erik Federico, who asked, "Hey faggot, is your brother home?"

He had'nta ought'nta said that!

Dear Diary,                                        Friday, Sept. 13

Tonight we ate dinner in the living room so we could watch the season premiere of *Hangin' In There*, which was a total entertainment atrocity. Drusilla, Dad, and Kyle's friend Howie, who was staying for dinner, all put on this big show of how excited they were. As I tried to eat the inedible roast beef (which Kyle skipped in favor of ChocoBuff, this new super-advanced, protein-enriched, muscle-building milkshake) I had to practically strangle myself to keep from criticizing the show.

Before Kyle got on T.V., if I pointed out how stupid some show was he'd agree with me, but now dissing sitcoms is a federal offense as far as he's concerned.

The episode started off with Kyle, looking frumpy in a patterned sweater that just screamed *Cosby Show*, overhearing a new boy, Joe, ask his girl, Kiera, to an upcoming dance. He's sure he'll be dumped since Joe has a car and is on the football team, so he runs off to ask another bimbette, Veronica, to take her place. Veronica agrees, but surprise! Kiera doesn't like super-perfect Joe and turns him down flat. Horrors, Devon has two dates! He seeks advice from his pals Benny, the dumb jock, and Oscar, the smart nerd. Hilarious hijinks too nauseating to mention ensue. Throughout the show Mom, Dad, and Howie laughed out loud, and asked Kyle all sorts of stupid behind-the-scenes questions. I didn't have anything nice to say, so I said nothing at all, which I could tell really made Kyle really mad. My reaction had nothing to do with being a blood relative of the show's star attraction, but how can I expect anyone to believe that?

Dear Diary,                                                                  Monday, Sept. 16

I must suffer from delusions of grandeur. Why else would a boring nobody like me with no life experiences bother to keep a diary? The only news is that Kyle gave me $20 for Ninja Pit Bull 4, this ultra-violent videogame I got from Aunt Megan on my last birthday. He revels in mindless escapism, though what he has to escape from is beyond me. If I had his looks and money I'd be busy going on a mad spree breaking hearts and buying CDs and I don't know what all. Anyway, I took my $20 and spent Saturday with Daphne roaming the thrift shops, of which lovely Saint Dymphna has four – a good number for a small town populated exclusively by the affluent. I didn't find any good clothes but did score a cool Henry Mancini record. When I can't irritate Kyle with Goth or Industrial (sometimes he gets off on the machismo and starts punching the air and saying "Yesss!"), there's nothing to drive him crazy like playing lounge music on Dad's old Hi-Fi in the living room. The only drawback is that Drusilla loves it and waltzes around the house humming the tunes. I hate to think I'm giving her reason to hope I'm developing into the mature, tasteful, lobotomized person she'd like me to be.

I almost forgot, one of the little old ladies at the Our Lady of the Sacred Bleeding Heart Thrift Shop actually crossed herself when Daphne came in the store! It's amazing how people freak out just because they see someone wearing a witchy black dress, huge pentagram necklace, and *Night of the Living Dead* ghoul makeup.

During the next few years a huge debate raged at Earth Studies departments across the galaxy. I and my friends (dubbed the Terraphiles) advanced the concept of the "Terran Miracle" which posited that Earth had leapt prematurely into a semi-civilized state. We watched with glee as new dance crazes swept the planet, its literature and arts got wackier and zanier, and the first tentative steps were taken to initiate communication with the local plants and animals. More cautious professors (Terraphobes), led by the charming Mithribian Gazro Mol, scoffed at our optimism, claiming Earth's spurt of creative excellence and rapid social progress was only a foreshadowing of a civilization several thousands of years away.

The strongest argument on our side was found in the planet's sophisticated and imaginative television sitcoms. *Green Acres*, for example, explored the conflict between a surreal, aristocratic humanism (represented by Lisa Douglas, played to perfection by blonde bombshell Eva Gabor) and an unimaginative, bourgeois rationalism (represented by her husband, Oliver Wendell Douglas, played with understated elegance by Eddie Albert). Rather than having Lisa's thesis and Oliver's counter-thesis produce a synthesis, as primitive dialectic philosophers would expect, the two engaged in a sidesplittingly funny comedy of manners that kept me in stitches night after night.

Another show, *Batman*, deconstructed the hyper-moralism so common on primitive worlds by presenting a parody of the extreme dichotomy between good and evil. The "heroes" (mythological creatures embodying pro-social values) spent the show battling "villains" (the mythological embodiments of evil, antisocial values), who inevitably maneuvered them into a titillating light bondage situation. The effect was as erotic as it was comical and sophisticated.

As the Earth debate raged, my social life blossomed. I went from attending only dull faculty parties to taking full advantage of Zeeron's varied and exhilarating nightlife, for the first time mixing socially with stylish and prominent citizens. When the Earthlings managed to send one of their own to visit their orbiting moon I organized a gigantic Earth-themed costume party at my house. After watching several cooking shows (no easy task since the Earthlings eat dead animals and I accidentally glimpsed television chef Julia Child handle a bloody chicken carcass) I concocted a typical Earth meal of "lasagna" with "wine" and "garlic bread." We had no idea whether my handiwork even came close to approximating the flavors of the originals, but they were universally deemed "interesting" in both flavor and texture. The party made such a splash I determined to have many more, even going so far as to redecorate my home in the enchantingly zesty Earth style known as '50s Atomic to add thematic spice.

My most spectacular social achievement was without a doubt my relationship with Veeba 22. From time to time after our initial encounter she would ask me out for a date. I always eagerly accepted her invitations, although I suspected dating me was part of her calculated campaign of self-humiliation. She seemed to delight in the amused stares which I (in my dowdy professorish garb) received when she took me out dancing or to a swank party; and my attempts to make fashionable conversation with her stylish friends were, often as not, received with hilarity, for although I'd achieved a small measure of celebrity status because of my peculiar theories, I had not achieved a commensurate degree of respect. Perhaps Veeba found me a welcome diversion from the exhausting frivolity of the rest of her life; someone she didn't need to impress or keep up with. Whatever the truth of the matter, it's to her credit that she tried her best to understand me and my obsession.

"What do you see in the Earthlings, dearest? What makes them more interesting than, say, the origins of Yupgupian rock formations?"

she once asked.

"I've wondered the same thing myself," I admitted. "Perhaps I'm attracted to the exotic because I've never felt I fit in here on Zeeron."

"Why ever not?" she asked.

"Well, Zeeronian society is the most formidable in the galaxy. It can be quite intimidating, especially for a nobody professor. We academics aren't exactly afforded a great deal of respect, you know. I sometimes imagine that if I was an Earthling, people would like and accept me without reservation. On Earth academics are more revered than socialites, decorators, or even hairdressers."

"That's sick," she observed. "Anyway, you're not a nobody professor anymore, you're a kook with a nutty theory now. A *somebody* kook."

"Well, *Your Magnificence,* even *somebody* professors don't receive the same deference as the lowliest of hairdressers. It gets tedious always being socially suspect."

"That isn't the *only* thing that gets tedious." She threw me an icy glare.

More often than not though, we got along swimmingly. The real problem I faced in the ensuing years and decades was that the Terraphiles' position collapsed. I watched the news helplessly as war, tyranny, pollution, stupidity, conformity, and boredom all raged out of control on the hapless planet I'd so grown to love. This sad state of affairs was reflected in the planet's sitcoms. Shows full of whimsy and social allegory like *The Flying Nun, Get Smart,* and *The Addams Family* were canceled and replaced by an endless cavalcade of predictable and unconvincing realism. Every now and again a modicum of fantasy (witch, angel, space alien) would appear, but only for novelty's sake; not one ever disrupted the tedious mixture of smug, apolitical irreverence and earnest moralizing that became the television norm. Every few years something good and fine would indeed come along, *Pee Wee's Playhouse* or *Absolutely Fabulous,* but these exceptions were decidedly rare and generally short-lived.

At first I was delighted when, on Earth, a few shows from the Terran miracle were rerun as "classics." That happy development was diminished by the elevation of horrible dreck to the same exalted status. The Earthlings were perplexingly unable to discern the vast differences in quality between the loathsome buffoonery of *Welcome Back Kotter*, the delightful shenanigans of *The Patty Duke Show*, or the charming, albeit realistic, antics of *The Mary Tyler Moore Show*. A network devoted entirely to old television even ran an ad which featured space aliens visiting Earth to watch Nick at Nite. "Not if you keep showing reruns of *The Bob Newhart Show* we won't," I muttered to myself.

Worse still, the social mutants who had been so popular just a few years before (such as zany beatnik Maynard G. Krebs of *The Lives and Loves of Dobie Gillis* or kooky New Waver Johnny Slash of *Square Pegs*) vanished from the television screen. Punks, ravers, or Goths appeared only in cautionary police dramas or as make-over victims for pro-blandness talkshow hosts. This development particularly dispirited me since, just as biological evolution depends on physical mutation, cultural evolution depends on social mutation. Television was acting to suppress the new subcultures without which there could be no social progress. I was therefore saddened, but not surprised, as over the years most of my colleagues unobtrusively switched sides in the Earth debate or fled the department.

I, however, stubbornly maintained a glimmer of hope, and for my efforts, was soon branded a fool, and even worse, passé. As one might expect, the Zeeronian public's taste for things Earthly waned considerably, depopulating my classes and erasing my hard-won notoriety. Worse, the Terraphobes relentlessly teased me every time we saw another example of Earthly shortcomings: heavy metal music, televangalism, cigar chic. Veeba, who continued to see me, perhaps because I was now less popular than ever, always had the same question. "Still flogging that tired theory about Earthly civilization, love?"

Typical of the bland new style of show was *Hangin' In There*. Normally I ignored such horrendous programs, but one day I gave in to the spaceship crash-like fascination and watched the season premiere. Sitting in mute horror, I watched a love triangle involving two girls and "Devon," the handsome, if wooden, adolescent lead. Thinking the girl he first asked out to a dance no longer liked him, having switched her affections to a new higher status male, Devon asks a second. When the first female lets it be known she still plans to attend with him, he must choose which girl to disinvite. On Zeeron all three would attend together and happily engage in a ménage-à-trois after the dance. The Earthlings, however, would prefer to have someone's feelings hurt than relax their primitive taboo against group sex. After interminable agonizing the boy tells the second female what happened. She understands, forgives him, and attends the dance with the other male. The lead learns an "important" lesson about honesty. From watching the show one would never know that on Earth, as anywhere, social lying is indispensable for the smooth functioning of civilization.

With *Hangin' In There* fresh in my mind, I went to give a lecture on first few seasons of *The Simpsons*, which I felt to be undeniably as good as anything from the Terran Miracle three decades before. Although I tried to focus on my subject, my mind kept wandering back to the travesty I'd witnessed just before class. During the question and answer session after my prepared speech, Zerma 14, known across campus for her trademark silver-sequined body stockings and gold buzz-cut hair, quite astutely pointed out that the show was essentially a send-up of Earthling stupidity.

"Laughing at dullness may be a sign of intelligence, but it's not the same as real innovation or insight. *Green Acres* posited an alternative, or what was it you called it last week... surreal?... world in which the values of charm and zaniness prevailed, without so much refuting, as transcending the rational. The acceptance of two paradigms simultaneously is evidence of advanced intelligence, mere *parody* is not."

I noted that the show in question, although parodic, was not exclusively a sarcastic put-down of social stereotypes, and went on to cite examples, make points, and generally plead my case. A good lecturer, and I flatter myself that I am one, can tell when he's losing an audience, and I'm certain I lost that one. The students, usually apathetic, were suddenly filled with thinly veiled antagonism. They posed question after question about pollution, wars, country music, plagues, poverty, and the continuing popularity of Mariah Carey. My evasive excuses for the Earthlings sounded lame even to my own ears, and I felt my face redden and burn with humiliation.

After the lecture I went to the faculty lounge. The institute has one of the finest in the galaxy, with a carpet made of Vush, a blue legume from Quixbin, and walls covered with a sweet-scented, pink-flowering drugnutz vine from Glaxus Major. There are also plenty of adorable little furry creatures called zachmaps, nervous twitching little things who like nothing better than nibbling pink blossoms and nuzzling the toes of tired academics.

I'd been spending less and less time in the lounge as my academic credibility evaporated, and on that fateful day I hadn't set foot in the place for weeks. The vast space was all but empty as I entered and gazed at myself in the floor-length mirror. Despite the dim, flattering lighting, I looked every inch the undistinguished minor academic. Another drudge in a sensible orange jumpsuit with sensible matching purple thigh boots, belt, and hoop earrings. Was I so *very* sensible in self-presentation to compensate for my senseless theories? There was a certain worried look creeping into my face around the eyes. More than anything else, that scared me. I was 126 years old, and my one claim to fame was a kooky theory about Earth I'd come up with at a party and wasn't even sure I still believed in. Perhaps I should have bowed to the inevitable and given up, but some combination of intellectual vanity, curiosity, and ambition prevented me. Instead, in one madcap moment, I decided to pay a visit to planet Earth.

Dear Diary,                                     Monday, Sept. 16

Why was I born into this insufferable family? I was awakened at seven this morning by what sounded like the storming of Normandy Beach. Bleary eyed and half-afraid I'd be bayoneted by German infantrymen, I managed to crawl to my door and peek outside. To my horror, what looked like an entire Hollywood studio had crammed itself into the hallway.

"Morning, sleepyhead!" chirped Drusilla, peeking around a gigantic spotlight.

"What's going on?" I asked with a sinking feeling in my stomach because I already knew whatever it was would involve Kyle.

"Didn't your father tell you? They're filming part of Kyle's music video in his room, you know, authentic teenage Americana. Isn't it exciting?"

"Have I missed something? Does Kyle play a musical instrument or sing?" I put on my robe and came into the hallway.

"Not yet, but the idea is they'll do this video and test-market it to see if music audiences respond to him as well as television..."

She was interrupted by a man in an expensive-looking Italian suit, his hair in a ponytail. "What's that supposed to be? A Satanic druid?"

"This is my other son, Chester," explained Drusilla. "The black hooded robe is just what he wears in the mornings, it's not a costume or anything." Mr. Ponytail shrugged and walked off, barking orders at various stylists, cameramen, grips, gaffers, and whoever-they-weres. "That's Jody, the director," she explained.

"How exactly am I supposed to sleep with this insane racket going on?" I asked.

"Why not take this inconvenience, this so-called problem, and turn it around," suggested Dad, coming up the stairs carrying a tray of croissants. "Use being up this early as an opportunity to do things you normally can't! Enjoy the morning sun or go jogging."

"How dare you suggest such a thing! And why didn't you at least tell me in advance so I could sleep over at Daphne's or something?" I followed Dad and the croissants into the upstairs den where Kyle was standing in his underpants having full body makeup applied (yet they get mad at me for wearing a tiny bit of neutral lipgloss and eyeliner!) by a beautiful blond woman who slightly resembled Pamela Anderson Lee.

"Great, food!" said Kyle, hungrily eyeing the croissants.

"No food," snapped Jody, poking Kyle's lean stomach. "Don't want any bloat."

Kyle's big green eyes went all puppy-dog. "But I haven't eaten yet."

"Oh honey, quit whining. You can eat later!" said Drusilla.

"Almost finished," declared the Pamela-clone.

"What are you doing?" I asked as she brushed something dark on Kyle's sternum.

"Applying some shadowing so his pectoral muscles stand out more," she explained. "There, I guess I'm done. Jody, what do you think?"

"More ab shadow," he ordered.

Kyle looked stressed out. "But I'm hungry!"

"Nobody wants a fat crooner," threatened Jody.

"Y'know what you can do?" said Pamela. "Chew on a croissant so you get the flavor, but don't swallow, just spit it out into a napkin."

Kyle turned to Jody. "Can I do that?"

"Sure, just don't use your lips, and remind me to check your teeth before we actually start shooting."

As Kyle chewed he was put in a pair of baggy white pants, a baggy white shirt open to the navel, and a thick gold neckchain. For reasons too weird to contemplate he was left barefoot. I went off to the bathroom to splash water on my face, hoping (in vain as it turns out) that I'd wake up and find that this was all a nightmare. When I returned to the hall, drawn by unwholesome curiosity, I saw Kyle in his room doing a runthrough. Cheesy slow-jam music throbbed, blazing lights shone, and a wind machine billowed Kyle's shirt as he clenched his fists to his stomach and emoted like an over-the-top parody of a power-ballad crooner:

> *Baby I know I was wrong, to let you down*
> *To turn your smile, into a frown*
> *Give me one more chance girl, and let me stay*
> *I'll stay with you, both night and day*
> *I love you, love you, love you, with all my heart*
> *We'll stay together, we'll never part*

"He looks great!" said Pamela coming up from behind me as I stood, mesmerized with disgust.

"But he can't sing," I noted.

She looked at me like I was crazy. "Your brother has got *it*. He doesn't need a voice."

"More emotion!" screamed the director.

"And he has nothing to say," I added. She looked at me like I had an infectious disease and inched away.

I grabbed a couple croissants, went down to the basement, turned on the air conditioner (to drown out the music from upstairs), curled in a fetal position, and fell into a deep, troubled sleep.

Dear Diary,                                                    Tuesday, Sept. 17

I've been exiled - banished into the night by the cruel and wicked parental creatures! I'm writing this in the basement of Daphne's house where I've been granted temporary refugee status by Mrs. Van Vechten, Daphne's mom, who said that until things cool down at home I can stay in their rec room. Wreck room would be more like it. The basement flooded last winter and the carpet smells of mildew and mold, and it's become a storage space for surplus junk: a rock polishing machine somebody got as a present and never used, three broken chairs, a ping-pong table with no net on which sit countless unlabeled and unloved boxes of who-knows-what, and not one, but two Nordic Track exercise machines covered in dust.

It all started when Daphne and I were hanging around the house and started watching *Zhandra Phillips*. The topic was "Devilish Moms, Divine Daughters," and the show began with a grave-looking Zhandra, in one of her scary pastel pants suits, pleading with her mongoloid audience to show understanding and respect to the freaks about to be paraded before them for their entertainment.

"Eww, look at those losers!" shrieked Daphne as Zhandra finished her rap and the camera panned to the daughters, four young girls (one in a chador, one in a nun's habit) with pursed, disapproving lips. After a few questions, during which she established that the girls were all virgins who thought their moms were just plain total sluts, Zhandra, her brow furrowed with concern and dismay, called for the offending mothers to come out.

A motley crew of middle-aged seductresses in miniskirts and bosom-revealing blouses sashayed onto the set and sat across from their daughters. "They don't look *too* slutty," I observed. "I mean, they're no worse than, say, my dad's third wife, or your science teacher, Mrs. Radinsky." Just then Kyle appeared in the doorway between the living room and the kitchen.

"Hey Chester," he smirked, "I thought you said television was electronic opium for imbeciles."

"We're watching to see how bad it is," explained Daphne.

Kyle plopped himself down on the sofa, put his Nike clad feet on the coffee table, and began to watch with us. "Oh my God! What is *wrong* with those old ladies?" he asked.

Daphne, champion of all underdogs, rose to the bait. Her face became flushed with anger, though you could hardly tell under her heavy kabuki-like makeup. "Those women look perfectly fine. You don't have to put them down just because they don't measure up to your male standards of correct feminine appearance and behavior."

"They look like washed-up hoes," said Kyle, who must have picked up the term "ho" from all that horrible gangsta rap he listens to.

"And what's wrong with looking like a prostitute?" Daphne wanted to know. Ever since I met her last year in Creative Writing she's been going on about wanting to be a sex worker. "Prostitutes have rights and feelings and..."

I interrupted. "Shhh! I can't hear the show with you two talking! I think the mom on the far left is a stripper." Zhandra slowly shook her head in disapproval as a chesty bleached blonde started doing a bump and grind dance while the audience hooted and hollered. After the woman sat down with a big crazy smile the camera zoomed in for a shot of her daughter who was covering her homely face in a theatrical display of embarrassment.

"Those women aren't good-looking enough to show so much flesh. I mean, if you look like Meg Ryan it's one thing, but *come on.*" Kyle gestured at the screen.

Daphne was still on her soapbox. "Maybe that's how they want to look. They don't need you, or any man's approval for how they dress. They can show their breasts, or pierce their labias, or dress like men..."

"Well, thank *you,* Miss Super-feminist Dyke Woman," interrupted Kyle. I guess he's learned how to be a reactionary as well as an airhead from his Hollywood buddies.

"I wouldn't kick Catherine Deneuve out of bed," said Daphne.

"Chester would," guffawed my darling brother.

"You're so provincial," she sniffed. "Just because your brother is a gay..."

I interrupted again. "I'm not '*a* gay,' I'm gay! You don't say 'a' in front of it. It sounds stupid."

"You two are..." Kyle searched his limited vocabulary for an insult as on screen the nun lunged for her mother's throat and a wild melee broke out, complete with fisticuffs and flying chairs.

"*You* are an instrument of patriarchal oppression," said Daphne, pointing at Kyle rudely.

"Whatever," said Kyle heading back to the kitchen for more ChocoBuff.

"What a dim child," said Daphne, shaking her head sadly.

After the daughters won the fight and were awarded the million dollar prize, we went to my room where we got it into our heads to do a photo-essay on a virginal teenage girl (to be played by Daphne) and her slutty mom (to be played by yours truly). Daphne has a great camera her mom gave her. Mrs. V. is really into photography and thinks her daughter should be the next Diane Arbus or Nan Goldin.

Daphne took the black velvet I hang around my bed and wrapped it around herself like it was a long skirt, put on this wickedly ugly sweater my Aunt Megan gave me for Christmas, and topped it all off with a pair of reading glasses left by my last mother. For myself, I decided to borrow my current mother's hideously tasteless, low-cut, gold lamé evening gown. Sneaking into the master bedroom I immediately found it in her unnaturally well organized walk-in closet which smelled of cedar and sandalwood.

Back in my own room I took off my black tee shirt, black peg-leg pants, and knee-high black patent leather Docs. In the mirror I saw a pudgy, spotty blob. Me. I pulled the hideous excess flesh away from my stomach, imagining myself thin. "Why do they call these 'love handles'?" I wondered aloud. "They ought to be called hate handles. I hate them, and everybody hates people that have them."

Daphne scowled. "Nobody hates you because you have a tiny bit of baby fat. You're too self-conscious. If you'd just engage in more sexual intercourse you'd lose a lot of your body hang-ups. You oughta read Wilhelm Reich."

"You're a noble friend," I said. "And if you can think of any way for me to lose my virginity I'm open to any and all suggestions."

"I'm not being noble. Why do you believe Erik Federico and all those idiots at school when they tell you you're fat, but you don't believe me, a total genius and true blue friend, when I tell you you're not?" She was exasperated so I let the subject drop, but the mirror doesn't lie. The dress was a tight fit, but by sucking in my gut I finally managed to just squeeze in. I applied a full face of makeup, using blue eyeshadow for extra-tacky effect, forgetting till I'd finished that the film was black and white. For a final flourish I took the feather boa Daphne'd given me for Samhain last year and wrapped it around my neck. I've never done drag before, but I think I looked pretty good in a *To Wong Foo, Thanks for Everything, Julie Newmar* sort of way. I practiced making slutty mom faces, trying to be seductive and controlling at the same time.

"We'll have to shoot from the knees up since we don't have the right shoes," said Daphne, affixing the camera to my dad's tripod.

"Do you think my black nail polish will look too dark?" I asked.

"Nah," she said, peering through the camera.

My tangled, over-processed, crimped, blue-black mass of hair refused to lie down and look feminine. "Will you get my Hyper-Hold Hair Spritz from the bathroom for me?"

Just as Daphne opened the door, who should walk by but the handsomest teenage boy in America.

"Va Va Va Voom!" Kyle shrieked, doubling over with laughter.

"Oh, really! Grow up Kyle," said Daphne indignantly.

"Hey, maybe Mom would like to know about this. Since I'm an agent of pakriacal impression it's my duty to tell her."

"Wait!" I screamed.

"What?" he asked, still laughing.

"Um," I replied brilliantly.

Daphne helped me out. "Kyle, you're not using your brain, this could be good publicity for you. There could be a story in *Celebriteen* or *Girl Talk* about how accepting you are of your older brother's cross-dressing lifestyle and photos of you two going to baseball games together. I can see the headline now 'Actor Kyle Julian and his Teen Tranny Brother.' You could help promote tolerance for an oppressed minority group."

"But I'm not a transgendered person," I objected, "and I hate ballgames."

By this point Kyle was in hysterics. He began skipping around the hallway, mincing, flouncing, and maliciously sing-songing, "Chester is a tranny, Chester is a tranny!"

"Afraid of getting upstaged by your brother?" Daphne asked.

Kyle calmed down enough to answer. "No, but I'm not looking for publicity that makes me look, you know, *unwholesome*. My fans do *not* want to see me eating hot dogs with that!" He pointed at me as if I was a thing instead of a living, breathing older brother. Anyway, it's a property rights issue." He turned to me. "Did you ask Mom if you could borrow the dress?"

"Um," I replied.

"Well, it's just like you said when I borrowed your boombox; it's a matter of common courtesy to ask first." He skipped off to the kitchen. I tried to follow but the dress was so tight walking was impossible, I could only slink seductively like an old time Hollywood vamp.

"Come back here!" I bellowed.

"Oh well," said Daphne. "We can do the shoot another time. You look too upset to photograph right now." She began packing up her camera.

"Daphne, this could be serious. Help me get this dress off before my evil stepmother sees me in it. Quick!"

Making no move to hurry, Daphne started to unzip me. "Hold still, the zipper's stuck."

"What!" I shrieked.

"It happens all the time. These dresses were designed by men as a way of keeping women dependent. What if men's suits had zippers in the back that they couldn't reach by themselves and that always got stuck?"

"Hurry!" I pleaded.

"Look, your mother is an Episcopalian, not a Nazi." Just then the Episcopalian walked into my room without knocking and cried out in revoltingly high-pitched indignation.

"What are you doing! You're stretching out my best dress! Do you have any idea how much it cost!?" She started trying to pull the dress off me, her face ketchup-red with anger. I stepped back to avoid her claw-like clutches and tripped over the boa. There was a hideous ripping sound, then complete and completely unnerving silence.

Daphne spoke first. "My mom and I are meeting Aunt Jenny at Wonder Wok for dinner. I'll call you tomorrow, Chester. Goodnight, Mrs. Julian."

Mrs. Julian stared at her like she was Satan's spawn, finally managing to say "Goodnight" in a tone that would have produced frostbite in anyone but Daphne. I shimmied off the tattered gown, and wearing only my underpants, ran into my closet and shut the door.

"You come out of the closet right this minute, young man!" Drusilla hollered.

"I'm practically naked!" I replied, which was true, though probably beside the point.

"Don't think this is over. When your father gets home we're going to want to have a word with you," bellowed Drusilla, shouting much louder than absolutely necessary to make sure I could hear through the door. After she left I put on some clothes and lay on my bed. I probably should have prayed to Satan or God or someone for help, but I've never been religiously inclined.

Five minutes later the phone rang. "Chester, sorry about the fib."

"Daphne! What fib?"

"I'm not really going to Wonder Wok for dinner. There is no Wonder Wok," she confessed. "I don't have an Aunt Jenny. I don't even have an aunt."

"Yeah, yeah, yeah, I get the point. Now what am I going to do? Drusilla is really pissed. She and Dad might make me see a shrink again."

As I spoke, I heard my least favorite sound in the world: the hideously elongated whine of my stepmother's voice calling "Cheeesteeer?" It comes out like a question but it's really a command to appear in the kitchen immediately.

"Gotta go," I said hurriedly. "Wish me luck."

"In a few years you'll look back at all this and laugh," said Daphne. I hung up the phone, threw on some clothes, and went down the steps. Slowly.

Standing at the foot of the stairway was my dad's current infatuation looking grim. "Your father and I would like to have a word with you in private." She stalked into the master bedroom where Dad, just home from work and still in his suit, sat frowning on the bed. "We've been concerned about you for a while now," she began in an artificially calm tone. "You don't seem happy. Your brother is happy, we're happy, but you seem… unhappy. I've often wondered if we've done something wrong. Have we done something wrong?" I honestly think the institution of motherhood should be outlawed.

"No, Mom. You and Dad have not done anything wrong," I said. I was still standing while my parents sat on the bed. It was twilight and the only window illuminated me while they were shrouded in darkness. Chalk one up to my stepmother's staging talents.

"Why were you dressed up like Beverly?" asked my father in a quavering voice.

"I wasn't trying to look like Mom!" He actually suspected me of being a *Psycho* type crossdresser! "I was just using her dress as a costume to play an unrelated character."

"That, at least, is a relief," he said as much to himself as me.

All the same, I was asked, then told to see a shrink. I think they're worried I'm going to want an expensive sex change operation and expect them to cough up the money. Naturally I refused, pointing out that there was absolutely *nothing* wrong with me. They kept insisting and I kept refusing until I was starting to get worried they'd commit me just to get the stupid argument over with.

"Why can't you leave me alone?!" I pleaded. "I promise never to borrow either of your clothes without asking again."

"Things cannot continue this way," said Dad. From the way he was speaking to me while looking out the window I guessed that he was getting as bored with the whole argument as I was.

I extended a tentative olive branch. "Can we just agree to disagree about all this? I'm hungry."

"This teenaged rebellion, I suppose you'd call it, is wearing me out," he admitted.

"It just may be that all this teenage rebellion, as you call it," I was thinking quickly here, "is the result of a delayed reaction to Ritual Satanic Child Abuse. Yes, I'm starting to remember… fire, dancing, people in hoods. And you were there, and you were there…"

"Ha, ha, ha" said Dad. "If anyone in this family has ties to the Eternal Adversary I'd say it's far more likely the boy who asked for the *Necronomicon* for Christmas."

"And sleeps till noon on Sundays," added Drusilla.

"Rather than attending church with his hard-working, long-suffering parents," finished Dad. I could tell he was softening up by the way he was switching into parody mode, like someone who's playing at being an angry father on a sitcom.

"It's not just the Satanism," added Drusilla. "You have no consideration for others. Your *lifestyle* is your own business, but to see my beautiful, lovely gown turned into an article of drag - how could you!?" She was getting all misty eyed, like she was going to cry (over a stupid dress!) which for some reason absolutely enraged me.

"Listen, Step-Mommy Dearest, the only reason I put on your gown was not because it was *lovely,* but because it's so tacky, it's funny!"

I guess that was kind of harsh. Drusilla's face went white with horror and Dad's turned blue with anger, all traces of sitcom Dad disappearing.

"To live under my roof you have to treat everyone in this family with respect. Since you refuse to do that you can just get out of here!" he ordered, pointed to the door.

For a moment I didn't know what to do, then I happily stomped out of the room. I filled a couple of pillowcases with clothes and CDs then went over to Daphne's and told my whole story to Mrs. Van Vechten who sees male homosexuals as a cross between angels from heaven and lovable but naughty lap dogs, and was only too happy to take me in. Unfortunately, she doesn't have a guest room. As God is my witness, Kyle will pay for this.

Dear Diary,                                        Friday, Sept. 20

I had the most amazingly vivid dream. I was on a tropical island with palm trees and a white sandy beach, and then I was swimming in this warm blue water. All these amazing things were swimming around me: starfish and fish that glowed like they were under a black light, big pink corals and bizarre creatures with deelybobbers on their heads. Truly awesome. Then there was this cute blond merman with a tail of iridescent scales, and we swam together like dolphins. After a little while he kissed me but then started swimming away. I wanted to kiss him more so I followed, but was having a hard time keeping up. Then I heard the piercing buzz, irritating bleep, and whining ring of the three alarm clocks Daphne set up around the room to make sure I actually get up at the ungodly hour of 7:30 a.m.

The unpleasant shock of being ripped from hot sexual pursuit in dreamland and plopped back in my own hideous corner of reality was so intense it was almost physical. I felt like one of those cartoon characters who has a sixteen-ton weight fall on them and instead of being killed they crawl out from under it, only they're collapsed like a pancake. As I loped around the room like a wounded animal turning off the alarms I considered going back to bed, but by the time I'd restored quiet my mind was already too disturbed by The Tragedy That Is My Life for there to be any hope of sleep.

I went upstairs to use the bathroom and while brushing my teeth stepped on the scale. Though I'm only 5'7" I weighed in at 153 pounds. I'm a shrimpy blimp. Discouraged and defeated, though the day hadn't even begun, I returned to my basement and searched through my pillowcases for something clean to wear. Dame Fortune smiled on me and I finally found a pair of slightly faded black stretch-jeans and a '70s purple tuxedo shirt with ruffles and an enormous collar. For accessories I chose a black bolo tie with a silver skull, and assorted kinky, black leather studded jewelry. Then I went into Mrs. Van Vechten's room (she was already on her way to work) to use her full-length mirror. I was Gothic looking, but somehow without the vampiric glamour. It was the pants - they'd faded somewhat around the knees and I'd tried touching them up with black magic marker creating an ugly two-tone effect. I went back to my lair and put on a pair of pants that were blacker but way, way too tight. (Have I been gaining weight? Must remember to stop eating.) I eventually wriggled into them, but they made my shirt bunch up so I changed to an oversized Nine Inch Nails tee shirt. It looked like a maternity dress but I was too tired to change again.

Back in the bathroom I stared at my face. Above and beyond the usual repulsion I feel when I see my weak chin and large nose, I was disgusted to count eleven blemishes. I slathered on two coats of foundation but was only partially successful at covering my zits and even less successful at matching my skin tone. For some reason budget foundation comes only in various shades of orange and I looked disturbingly like an Oompa Loompa. I quickly added eyeliner, a subtle purplish lipstick (Provocative Passionflower), and mascara which I also used to darkened my eyebrows. Glancing at my watch I noted it was 8:25. We'd be late for school, but could still theoretically make second period. First though, I'd have to wake Daphne.

I entered her room without knocking. Daphne wouldn't wake up at a mere knock anyway. I'm sure her room has furniture and a rug and all the things a normal teenage girl's room is supposed to have, but I've never seen any of them. All I've ever seen is a mass of black clothing several feet deep, in the middle of which sleeps Daphne, on what is presumably a bed. I started the waking process by shaking and slapping her. Getting no response I got a cup of cold water from the bathroom and poured it on her face. She stirred, but didn't waken. Exhausted by the early hour, I sat down to rest. I must have dozed off, because the next thing I knew I was wakened by the phone. After eleven rings I found the receiver, not under, but actually inside, a vintage ballgown.

"Hello," I grumbled, wondering who'd be calling so early.

"Oh, hi Chester, it's me. Are you two getting up okay?" It was Mrs. Van Vechten who'd probably been contacted by the school as many times as my various mothers about her child's tardiness.

"We're more or less on the way out the door," I lied.

"Well, I won't keep you. You're already a tiny bit late you know, sweety. Have a good day at school and give Daphne my love." She hung up.

"Daphne, wake up, we're late!" I screamed while shaking her cadaverous body. One eye opened tentatively.

"Who are you? What's going on? What time is it?"

"I'm your best friend, Chester, we're on our way to high school, and it's," I looked around for a clock and finally saw its luminous dial swimming on a sea of panties and stockings, "10:21."

She sat up and wiped the sleep from her eyes. "We shouldn't have stayed up so late," she said, slowly falling back down. "Why am I wet?"

"Your mom called. I told her we were on our way out," I said, pulling her back up to a sitting position.

"Okay, I'm up, I'm up," she said, halfheartedly tossing clothes right and left. "Where's my robe?"

"It might help if I turn on the light," I suggested.

"No!" she screamed as if I'd suggested we feed ourselves to the lions at the zoo.

"Anyway, we needed to stay up late to see *The Love Boat*. I mean, it was the Andy Warhol episode!" Daphne and I got turned on to Warhol by one of her collegiate boyfriends, Karl, a film major who was into nudity. Once I went over to his place to pick up Daphne and he even answered his door naked.

"It's sad that he got on and off the boat without finding love, but also kind of admirable," observed Daphne, putting on a robe. "And that wig! What can you say?"

"Only that he was, or is, God," I replied.

Then, locating her CD player by what could only have been instinct, Daphne put on Helen Reddy's *Greatest Hits* and began singing along. "Delta Dawn, what's that flower you have on? Could it be a faded rose from days gone byyyy?!" We used to only listen to dark music but we had to broaden our tastes after a while. You can only hear Dead Can Dance so many times before you get really, really depressed.

After a leisurely breakfast of dried apples with peanut butter (why is there no fat-free peanut butter?) Daphne agreed to get dressed. It was 11:20 when we started the nine-block trek to school, trying as always to avoid any contact with the sunlight, or "deadly solar radiation," as Daphne calls it. After we went our separate ways, I congratulated myself on arriving at school not only before noon, but only mildly depressed at wasting another precious day of my one and only life on Earth.

**4**

Brilliant! A visit to Earth would give me the chance to re-establish the dignity of the Terraphile position and, incidentally, anoint me the preeminent authority on Earth by virtue of being the only Zeeronian to have set foot on the planet. Exceedingly dangerous? Yes. Foolhardy? Probably. Unprecedented? Exactly! Visiting a world full of armed conflict and disease would change me from a vaguely discredited academic into a courageous explorer. I could dine out on the journey for decades! Immediately, before I could come to my senses and change my mind, I went to the vid-phone in the corner and called the *Interplanetary Enquirer* to give them the scoop. The young man I spoke to seemed truly interested and respectful, unlike the alternately sleepy and hostile students who stared in my general direction when I lectured. "This'll be bigger news than Jikpot 4's new pink jumbo-sequined dinner tunics!" he assured me. I thanked him and hung up, making a mental note to see Jikpot about some new clothes before I left.

Before I got a chance to re-examine myself in the mirror to discover if the timid face I'd seen before had been transformed, half a dozen of my colleagues entered the lounge, burbling with jocular camaraderie. Trying not to look too pleased with myself, I casually informed them I'd be doing a bit of research on Earth itself in the near future. Instantly I became the center of their gleeful attention as everyone encouraged me to go, all the while making it clear they full well expected me to meet with an untimely end. Professor Zaxub 9, immaculate in a sparkling green ensemble to complement her flatteringly formal emerald pixie-cut hairdo, congratulated me with sadistic delight.

"Norvex, you'll be the first Zeeronian to visit a barbarous world in decades! Finally, someone willing to lay down his life for science!" she all but laughed.

Gripke-Ulznar 4, a sour heavyset fellow in a silver mu-mu with matching cape and snood, was no more encouraging. "Well, if you're not stricken with a plague, blown to bits by military weapons, or bored to death by primitive philosophical speculation about the meaning of life, you'll return as not just a celebrity but a hero. Won't that be nice for you." Gripke's teasing annoyed me because he'd so quickly detected my self-interest.

"Even if you meet with an untimely end, you'll go with dignity," chirped Zaxub, all feigned smiles and false cheer. "Your epitaph will read 'Martyr For Science,' or some such noble accolade."

I ignored her. "Frankly, I don't feel we can make any intelligent decisions about Earth based solely on their broadcasting. Think of planet Feljmork where the bulk of the population use telepathy to put on extremely fine light opera. For years it was thought they were imbeciles because all we knew about the planet was the holographic programming broadcast by the Yiznerkians who, you will recall, turned out to be their pets."

Gripke put his arm around me in an ostentatious display of what I assumed would be fake camaraderie and led me away from the others. "Listen, seriously, you really want to go through with this madness?" I nodded in the affirmative. "Well, it so happens I think that's fine. Really. No, *really*, really! Your trip will make our Earth Studies department number one in the universe, you can pick up some nice artifacts for the museum, and we can see if it's true, as the planet's authors always claim on talk shows, that Earth's literature is of a higher quality than its television. Zaxub ought to be grateful rather than jealous. Sure, if you make this trip you'll eclipse her and the rest of us, but you'll be putting your life on the line, so you really will deserve any glory you get. If you return, that is." I pulled away, unsure how to take this.

"Thank you all for your kind words of encouragement," I said, backing towards the exit like a cornered animal. "And rest assured, I shall return," I added as I fled the lounge. Irritating though it was, the teasing cemented my decision to carry through with my plan. I would never give my spiteful colleagues the satisfaction of having me pull out due to fear!

The Institute keeps several serviceable spaceships for faculty use, but never having learned to fly, I'd need a pilot. As for the rest of my crew, I'd need a doctor since I wasn't about to trust our health to the natives and, since Earth is an aesthetically-deprived area, a ship's stylist. At a faculty party later that night I asked Zaxub 9 if she knew anyone who might care to accompany me and she laughed so hard she spit out an hors d'oeuvre. Bruglip 14 and Zubnuf 222 declined pleading fatigue which, given their two-parties-a-night schedule, didn't surprise me. The rest of the Earth Studies department also bowed out for a variety of flimsy reasons. Ambition may have overcome my own common sense, but it seemed my fellow academics kept theirs well in hand.

For days I combed all 57 civilized planets trying to find someone to accompany me on my perilous voyage with no luck. The gray monster of despair began to take hold of me. If the trip fizzled out from lack of interest my status would plummet even lower than before.

Finally, about a week later, Runchka Bezoo from the semi-barbarous planet Felkus called. "Norvex, I am a botanist whose wish it is to visit the planet Earth in order that scientific knowledge regarding its plant life may be acquired by the Felkusian Floral Academy. I request the opportunity to accompany you as your pilot. Fortuitously, I am also a qualified physician and hence may fulfill the role of ship's doctor as well. I have calculated that there is a 96.3 percent chance that I will perform my duties adequately." Felkus, I should note, is classed as a semi-barbarous planet not because it's afflicted with violence, superstition, or any of the usual things we associate with barbarism, but rather because the socially-retarded populace is made up of grinds and bores who dress hideously, converse appallingly, and have little or no sense of humor. The operating theory as to why these benighted people remain so uncouth is that they are hermaphroditic and parthenogenetic. Thus, as they mate only with themselves, they have no need to develop the social skills necessary for dating. Although I would have relished a companion with whom I could engage in witty repartee, I was glad to find anyone at all willing to come along and welcomed Runchka to my crew.

The very same night Runchka called I made a date with Veeba, whom I'd avoided since deciding to visit Earth for fear she would mock me as my colleagues had. I arrived at the fashionably offbeat food gallery we liked to frequent wearing a conservative purple body-stocking (exactly the sort of outfit she liked me in because it made be look so "adorably square and professorish") which I accented with an acid-green wig which majestically swooped to one side in a daring dip. The maitre d' took one look at me, sneered, and began leading me towards a table in the back of the enormous cavelike room near a bunch of children engaging in a loud messy orgy.

"I'm meeting Her Amazingness Veeba 22 here shortly," I informed him curtly. He stopped in his tracks, turned, and gave me an astonished look.

"Well, why didn't you say so!" He proceeded to lead me in the opposite direction, towards a raised terrace covered in charming vines with luminescent leaves and little berries which, every so often, would explode with a cute little popping sound. We climbed up a short flight of stairs and I was deposited at a table in the discernibly posher area. Nearby diners looked to be, if not hairdressers, at least party artists, models, go-go dancers, or other high status types. At the table nearest mine sat a young man, nude with silver hair, who, when he caught sight of me, closed his eyes with a groan, as if the sight of such an unfashionable creature as I had overtaxed his aesthetic forbearance.

After an interminable wait, Veeba showed up in a fashion-forward outfit made of clear plastic showing off the slim, tall, boyish figure that never failed to excite me. She also sported a four foot tall mood-wig which made her positively tower over me. At the start of our meal the wig was blue, indicating a calm peaceful state of mind. As I revealed my plans, her wig slowly changed to green indicating envy, then an excited orange. She leaned across the table, her breasts disarranging my salad, grabbed me by my collar and stared directly into my eyes.

"You've found your ship's stylist. Let's go to Earth!" she bellowed loudly enough for the whole gallery to hear. After a moment's apprehension at the thought of straining our relationship with excessive proximity, I told her I'd be honored to have her aboard. I wasn't planning to stay more than a few weeks, so how badly could we get on each other's nerves? Anyway, I was more than a good bit anxious to meet my destiny.

Returning to Veeba's, we were met by her robo-maid, Gropvak, which greeted me with its usual, "And who, or what, are you?" Before I could answer it took my jacket and tossed it on the floor with one arm while slamming the door with another, yawning with its third, and doing absolutely nothing with its fourth, which ought to have been fixing me a drink. Although she knows I find it irritatingly juvenile, Veeba thinks it's cute to turn the sassy-meter all the way up on her appliances. I sat down and demanded my drink, but Gropvak just snorted and began dusting a small tree. "I'll fetch it," volunteered Veeba, dashing off to the wet bar in her reception hall. While she was gone I found Gropvak's control panel and, ignoring its petulant whines of, "Don't touch me, you asymmetrical lump of organic matter!" turned it down to Mildly Irreverent. Then, returning to my seat to await my date, I idly picked up what I thought was a tube of Veeba's lipstick and tried to open it. It was actually a vial of pleasant-partyizer, and I released almost a quarter cartridge of rapture gas before I realized my mistake. I never use the stuff myself, but Veeba is a veritable addict and has a particularly potent brew made up specially by Zulak 3, the chemical artist. As the gas's unmistakable smell perfumed the air with its almost sickening sweetness my skin began to tingle and a numbness crept into the corners of my mind where anger and fear lurked. Then a palpable sense of well-being swept over me, followed by profound elation. Suddenly my toes tingled, my eyes couldn't focus, time stood still, and I felt *extremely* amorous. By the time Veeba returned with my drink, looking radiant in an immodest pink feathered peignoir, I had transformed into a crazed love machine. Our mad passion continued until the wee hours of the morning.

**5**

Dear Diary,                                          Sunday, Sept. 22

I had to go back to the house owned by my biological father to pick up some more clothes and junk. I got there at 11, hoping he and his brood would be at church so I wouldn't have to see them, but for some (ungodly?) reason he and his wife were there lounging around the living room. The woman who refers to herself as my mother stalked into the kitchen, but Dad tried to talk to me.

"Where have you been?" he asked casually enough.

"Out." I started up the stairs, followed by my lumbering parent.

"What have you been doing?"

"Nothing," I said without turning around.

"Your mother and I are very worried about you," he breathed down my neck.

I went into my room, still followed. Dad has this bewildered way of looking at stuff (especially the rubber bats hanging from the ceiling, the wrought-iron candelabra, and the vintage horror movie posters: *Carrie, Elvira Mistress of the Dark, Rosemary's Baby*) that drives me crazy. He has all these unspoken judgments you can see in his eyes. It makes me feel violated, if that's the word.

"Frankly, Dad, I think we should end this conversation right now on the grounds that it's too clichéd. I mean, 'Your mother and I are very worried about you.' That wouldn't even make it into an after-school special. They wouldn't use dialogue like that in an car commercial."

"It disturbs me that you regard our conversations as dialogue to be compared with entertainment. This is not a story, this is reality."

I finished stuffing my wrinkled clothes into a garbage bag. I won't let the maid do my wash because she refuses to use an ecologically sound, biodegradable detergent. Unfortunately, I tend to get behind with my laundry.

Dad cleared his throat. "Chester, are you listening?"

"Sure, whatever," I muttered without looking at him.

"Don't '*whatever*' me, young man! It's time you grow up. You're not even trying to act like a mature adult. You know, you get out of life what you put into it." He crossed his arms on his chest like he was making an important, meaningful point.

"I suppose Ann Frank got out of life what she put into it? Oh yeah, we live in a totally just universe for sure," I replied, searching around the bed for anything I might have overlooked.

"Never mind. I guess it's useless to try and reason with you." Dad's a real quitter, I'll say that much for him.

"If you want me, I'll be at Daphne's," I said, walking out the door. Much to my relief Dad didn't try to follow or stop me. As I stood on the sidewalk looking at my house, the only place I've ever lived in my whole life, it occurred to me that I'd be perfectly happy to never see it again.

Dear Diary,                                     Monday, Sept. 23

This morning Dad called up and demanded to speak with me. He kept his temper but was still totally unreasonable. "Look, I'm only asking for you to come home, apologize to your mother, and see a psychiatrist. We love you and we want you to get well. It doesn't have to be Dr. Bushman if you don't want."

"Great, Dad, because Dr. Bushman isn't a psychiatrist, she's a psychologist," I snapped back at him.

"We just want to spare you a lot of pain. I'm not sure you're aware of the consequences of your actions. Why not try and get along with people?" He was pleading and then lowered his voice. "And this gay vampire thing you're into is very disturbing."

Total exasperation. "What are you talking about?"

"It's time you grow up. Stop with the outfits and the nail polish and acting so effeminate. What about Daphne, you two seem to get along so well, maybe you could..."

"Dad, don't be disgusting!" I hung up. He called right back but I wouldn't speak to him. Mrs. Van Vechten answered and he maliciously made her promise I'd go to school and take my vitamins.

Daphne and I arrived at school in the middle of second period, early for us. I went to my remedial math class (my genius doesn't extend to mere numbers), and no sooner had I settled into my seat, ignoring the glare from Mrs. Glenmore, than Ted Lyons passed me a note.

Chester, I think you should know Kyle told Erik you were a gay transsexual and now they're telling everyone at school your mom caught you jerking-off to an International Male underwear catalog in her best dress and threw you out of the house. I'm really sorry, but that's what they're saying. You'd probably better be real careful because some other guys were saying they were gonna kick your ass. Not like they usually do, but seriously this time. Not just bruises – broken bones and shit. I think what they're doing totally sucks.

Ted

I took off my sunglasses and tried to make eye contact with Ted, but he was busy watching Mrs. Glenmore, who was actually quite a sight in her peach-colored pants suit. After class as I was walking to study hall Ted nodded a little jock nod of acknowledgment, a brave gesture given that he did it moments after Erik Federico spotted me and screamed, "I hope you have insurance, AIDS faggot!"

Could Ted be one of *us*? I've always wondered about him. He's as handsome as Kyle, but in a much less Hollywood way. He's got brown curly hair, freckles, and a little pug nose that's so cute I could positively die every time I think of it. I've never heard of him dating a girl, but then I don't really get to hear of much since (Daphne excepted) none of my peers have spoken to me socially since about sixth grade. Ted's never spoken to me before either, but then he's never picked on me like virtually every other boy in school. Maybe I could convince him to be my lover and run away to Paris with Daphne and me. We'd become a cause célèbre with the glitterati and attend all sorts of exciting parties in honor of human rights. I can't really quite tell because his clothing is so baggy, but I suspect Ted is totally buffed.

My first period teacher Miss Devane caught up with me this afternoon and asked for an essay on tardiness to make up for being late. You don't get graded on punishment essays so I whipped this up to give to her tomorrow:

*Nightpeople of the World Unite,*
*You Have Nothing To Lose But Those Unattractive Bags Under Your Eyes!*
by Chester Julian

Does the sound of the word "morning" (sounds like mourning!) throw you into a state of violent nausea? Do you have a hard time showing up for anything scheduled before sundown? Is your favorite time of day 2 a.m. or later? If you answered yes to even one of these questions, you may well be a member of one of the world's most savagely oppressed minorities - Night People! For centuries we've suffered under the nine-to-five tyranny, but now WE ARE RISING UP TO DEMAND OUR FREEDOM!

Day people call us insomniacs or lazy, perpetuating the vicious prejudice that makes our lives unbearable, or at least, often highly unpleasant. Consider the old saying, "Early to bed and early to rise, makes a man healthy, wealthy, and wise." Wrong! Being awake during the day vastly increases the chances of contracting sunburns and skin cancer! Wealthy? Not only is skin cancer expensive to treat, but waiters make more money at dinner shift than lunch or breakfast. Wise? Who amongst us can really say what wisdom is? Is it "wise" to expose oneself to deadly solar radiation in these times of diminishing ozone layers and astronomically expensive dermatology?

It's not only attitudes and innuendo that oppress us. No sooner have we nocturnals dragged ourselves out of bed when government offices, businesses, churches, stores, and schools start closing. HOW

ARE SUPPOSED TO GET ANYTHING DONE?! In most places (excluding Las Vegas, that oasis of enlightenment) even bars and nightclubs must by law close at obscenely early hours. Worse, daytime noise from construction, traffic, and pesty loved ones is a constant source of irritation to those trying to catch our forty winks. THESE INSUFFERABLE INCONVENIENCES AND INDIGNITIES MUST STOP!

We, the differently awake, must by law show up to school as early as 9 a.m., yet teachers are offended if you try to sleep in class! Adult nocturnals can work as night watchmen or other menial occupations (on the hideously named "graveyard shift"), but most professions are closed to us. Is there no room for night lawyers, night senators, night interior designers? Most nocturnals have to suffer through day jobs, downing endless espressos in the morning and sleeping pills at night. Is it any wonder that we stumble around making too many mistakes, having too many accidents, and missing all the perks which rightfully belong to us but instead go to insipid early-risers with their perky morning patter?

Is any of this our fault? No! Scientific research proves nocturnalism is an innate tendency. We're like left-handed people who were also once scorned and forced to conform to the ways of a cruelly indifferent majority for violating ancient taboos based on ignorance. A civilized people should not demand uniformity from the vast rainbow of diversity that is humanity. The persecution of the unique, the unusual, and the abnormal must cease. Why? Because WE DEMAND IT!

We nocturnals also object to the myth (originally promoted, we suspect, by wicked 19th century robber barons to justify the twelve-hour workday) that humans only need eight hours of sleep a night. Some people need ten or twelve hours of refreshing slumber, yet our somnaphobic society ignores such needs. We nocturnals declare our solidarity with the unrested. TO BE TIRED IS TO BE OPPRESSED!

It's time to stand up (or maybe it would be more appropriate to lie down) and demand that the enemies of nocturnalism *give it a rest*! A GOOD DAY'S SLEEP SHOULD NOT BE A CRIME!

There is no right way to visit a barbarian planet. I once had a colleague who went with a group of Mithribians on a fabric finding expedition to Vachkiss. Although they knew the Vachkissian culture was infected with a rather vulgar and puerile strain of stand-up comedy, the crew was still unprepared for the harsh reality of being subjected to so many glib routines, and in short order became overwhelmingly morose and taciturn. This occurred close to half a century ago, yet many of them suffer from melancholia and uncontrollable fits of groaning to this day. Fearing an equally grotesque tragedy would befall my own mission (or worse, that the Earthlings would just kill us), I consulted Hoznak 4, a fellow Terraphile who'd left the Institute to work as an interpretive dancer. I went to the Braxo City New Theater where he was performing in *Spring Needs No Alibi*, and found him lounging backstage in a skimpy silver toga. After exchanging pleasantries, I explained my plight.

"Are you sure you need to be so worried? I mean, shouldn't we Terraphiles be convinced the Earthlings are advanced enough to welcome alien visitors?" I might have thought he was teasing me, but his large eyes betrayed not a hint of sarcasm. Hoznak is such a sweet person.

"Well, I'd like a plan," I replied. "Just in case."

He stared at his luminous pink fingernails and began applying green dots to them with a small airbrush. "You could be especially polite and sweet to them... No, that might make you look vulnerable.

Hmmm, this is more difficult than one might think."

"If only I had a weapon," I murmured.

He looked up, shocked. "Don't talk nonsense. You couldn't use a weapon if your life depended on it. Wait!" He got a big crazy excited look on his face. "The Earthlings don't know that no planet with weapons and violence has ever become advanced enough to develop interstellar travel! Why not tell them you *do* have a weapon? How would they know you were lying?"

"I'd hate for them to call my bluff. If their motion pictures are any guide, the Earthlings imagine space aliens will be as intent on dominating them as they are on dominating each other. If they mistook me for part of an alien invasion they'd attack no matter what, don't you think?"

"Norvex, they wouldn't dare! How could they risk it? They fear death as much as we do, don't they? Just tell them they'd better not mess with you if they value their lives. Look." Hoznak held up his hands so I could admire his work.

"Nice job. Want to come along? I've coaxed Her Wondrousness Veeba 22 into joining me."

"Veeba? Quite the coup! I'd love to go along, but frankly I'm too busy." He smiled. "The annual Drugnutz Blossom Festival is coming up and I'm putting together an outfit that makes me look like a giant flower."

"Sounds enchanting, you must show me the pictures when I return. I wish you luck."

"Keep it, you're going to need all the luck that's going around, Norvex," Hoznak said sincerely. "Give my regards to Broadway."

Unable to think of a better plan, I decided to try Hoznak's suggestion; I'd intimidate the planet's governments into granting us permission to land with threats of violence. Even with the authorities on our side we'd still be at risk from anti-alien vigilantes, so I'd convince them to protect us by insisting that any attacks upon our person would precipitate intergalactic war. Unlike Zeeronians, who do as they please only within the limits of good taste and fine manners, Earthlings are a feisty, unpredictable lot, and it would behoove us to take every precaution.

Eager to get under way before my traveling companions could change their minds or lose interest, I decided we should leave the next morning. After calling Veeba and Runchka I went for a walk, taking what I hoped would not be a last ever look at my beloved campus. I fed the two-headed lichkiss birds who eat zorj berries right out of one's hand, admired the handsome purple gemstone encrusted buildings, and smelled the sweet spicy fragrance of the frobel flowers. Ah, Zeeron, jewel of the cosmos, what a wonderful life it had given me. I started feeling terribly homesick, although of course I hadn't left yet.

The morning of our take-off was quite chilly which I took as a good omen since I always find it easier to leave somewhere cold. The rocketport was crowded with stylish interplanetary travelers and harried robo-porters, all hurrying this way and that in a great confusion. I lost my way a few times, but finally caught sight of Veeba through the crowd. She was perched on her luggage chattering away to a gaggle of fellow hairdressers, looking the picture of poise. Naturally she'd dressed up and, despite the temperature, was blindingly beautiful in her puce bejeweled hot pants and tube top with matching thigh boots and a green wig of tousled, twining waves. Runchka stood mutely beside her, resplendent in a white chiffon tunic with his/her naturally orange hair done in fab fingerwaves. Several news artists stood at a respectful distance waiting to ask Veeba some questions, and I was slightly miffed she wasn't bothering to speak with them.

"Veeba, Runchka, good morning. Ladies and gentlemen of the press, good to see you!" I sang out cheerily as my groaning robo-porter set down its load of luggage near my compatriots.

"Norvex, that simple yet elegant black A-line sleeveless minidress with silver stockings is quite lovely. Will you be wearing that outfit to meet the Earthlings?" asked a handsome girl whose name-tag indicated she wrote for the Mithribian *Daily News*.

"You'll have to ask my ship's stylist, Her Incomparableness, Miss Veeba 22," I replied.

"No questions. I'm not in the mood. Press conference over," Veeba barked. The news artists wandered away dejectedly.

"My word, Veeba! That really wasn't necessary, was it? I mean, this whole trip is a publicity stunt, in addition to wanting to further science and so forth, and here you are squelching the publicity." Veeba's hairdresser friends talked among themselves, pointedly ignoring the cranky professor in their midst.

"Sorry, love, but do let's get going. I hate waiting around rocketports. All the rushing about disturbs my equilibrium."

"Fine, then," I replied curtly, looking around. "Where's the ship?"

Runchka pointed to our handsome mid-sized saucer on a nearby blast-off pad, and we made our way to the door, arriving just as a few Earth Studies faculty members pushed their way through the crowds to wish me well.

"Have a nice trip. See you soon, I hope!" jeered the malevolent Zaxub 9 with a mocking smile.

"Don't forget to bring me a present!" called out Gripke, waving.

"Have a ball!" Hoznak cried encouragingly while giving me a hug.

"Thank you all. If I'm not back by Intergalactic Makeup Day, come and get me!" They all laughed and I waved goodbye.

Entering the saucer, the living quarters of which resembled a comfortable but somewhat overwrought drawing room, I noticed a gleaming silver metallic figure ineffectually hiding behind a Kaxamian fruit bush, the ship's only vegetation. "Can I help you?" I asked in my least helpful voice.

The figure straightened up and peeked around the leaves. "Hi Mr. N!" chirped Gropvak. Obviously Veeba had set its sassy meter down low to avoid antagonizing me. "Mind if I hitch a ride with you to planet Earth?" I'd specifically asked Veeba to leave it behind since our quarters were already cramped.

"Hmmm." I was trapped. I could hardly make it disembark and be humiliated in front of all the news artists, hairdressers, and academics whom I could still see outside the porthole, waiving and blowing kisses. "I don't see why not, Gropvak. You can stay here and mind the ship while it's in orbit and we're on Earth - make sure it's not hijacked or something."

"The thing is, Mr. N, I was sort of counting on going down to the planet to help pick up after Miss Veeba. Nobody knows how to make her food the way she likes it but me, nobody knows how to give her the perfect back rub but me, nobody..."

I cut her off. "Out of the question, my good robot! On Earth unscrupulous technicians would kidnap and dismantle you to learn about our technology. You wouldn't last a day."

It shivered. "Miss Veeba didn't say nothin' about that."

"No, I imagine she didn't." I glared at Veeba who'd just entered the saucer and was busily pretending not to overhear our conversation, a physical impossibility in a space of that size.

"I will attend to the take-off," declared Runchka dispassionately as s/he disappeared behind the door leading to the tiny cockpit. There was a flash of white light as the trism reversed the gravity surrounding the ship. Then, with a whir and a boom and whoosh, we were off. I held Veeba's hand as we watched the green and pink ball that is Zeeron fade into the distance through the porthole. For some reason I felt little more excited than had we been going to planet Quijmoor for a picnic. It's always amazed me how the most momentous occasions in one's life aren't necessarily the most dramatic.

The trip lasted only three weeks since Runchka knew a shortcut through the extremely dull 27th hyperspace dimension where time and width change places every forty-seven minutes and the color spectrum consists entirely of different shades of mauve. During our voyage I gave my compatriots daily lectures on Earth, discussing its history, customs, and culture.

"The last century has seen a challenge to the classical European bourgeois sensibility from an innovative global pop consciousness. The foremost exemplar of the latter is... Runchka?"

S/he looked uncertain. "Rock and roll?"

"Correct! The various world wars and genocides of the recent past were so severe that Earthlings lost faith in many of their barbaric ideologies. First in the fine arts, then in literature, music, fashion, and drama, a new spirit of playful iconoclasm replaced the reverence for convention, tradition, and religion which have been steadily losing power to...Veeba?"

"Oh, Norvex, I don't know," she said peevishly.

"You do, too," I insisted.

"No, I don't."

"Losing power to pop culture made ubiquitous by mass media!"

Veeba changed the subject. "Say, let's skip Earth and go sightseeing in the M16 nebula. I hear they have some columns of cool interstellar molecular hydrogen dust with evaporating gaseous globules that are absolutely enchanting."

I had to remind myself that Veeba wasn't really a student of mine and it wasn't especially important that she remember all this. She planned to spend most of her time collecting beauty products.

I also had to perform brain surgery, fitting each of us with a computerized micro-implant to translate our speech into English, the language of most television and moving pictures. As the prototype for my voice implant I used the actor Rex Harrison whose charming formality and flawless diction had always impressed me. Disney child-actress Hayley Mills' proper, but relentlessly perky intonations seemed appropriate for Veeba, while Runchka got the flat, tinny, mechanical sound of primitive Earth computers, and Gropvak received the spunky nasal Brooklynese voice of Thelma Ritter who was forever playing terrestrial maids with hearts of gold.

When not attending my lectures Runchka took it upon him/ herself to bone up on local customs by watching educational broadcasts, while Veeba immersed herself in Earthly pornography, claiming that the best way to understand a people is to understand their sexual fantasies, a dubious proposition at best in my opinion. For my part, although I tried to work, I'm afraid I wasted most of my time fretting unproductively.

By the third week we were all sick of each other. Veeba ignored my lectures entirely (while even the studious Runchka paid only scant attention) to spend ever more time pacing back and forth, and when gravity permitted, up and down, complaining bitterly about the tedium, lamenting the tastelessness of the ship's decor, and berating me for inviting her. "You know I hate traveling!" she would shriek, giving me an accusing glare. Runchka spent an inordinate amount of time in the ship's sensory-deprivation tank either conserving energy for the adventure ahead, or perhaps, as Veeba suggested, carrying on a torrid love affair with him/herself. The day before we were to make contact with Earth I insisted we all watch *The Wizard of Oz*. Veeba, who'd never warmed to Runchka, mellowed a bit when the latter discovered s/he could reduce her to tears of laughter by imitating the high-pitched voice of Glinda the Good Witch. It delighted me that the crew was finally, if belatedly, developing some camaraderie.

Once in Earth's orbit I used one of the ship's gadgets to perform what must have seemed like a miracle to the primitives on the surface. I simultaneously interrupted all Earth transmissions: radio, television, telephone, and internet. Then, dressed by Veeba in a shimmering pink frock with a diaphanous lavender cape and a white wig in a backswept hairstyle giving a feeling of breezy motion (aided by an off-camera wind machine), I delivered the following speech.

"Greetings, people of Earth! I am Norvex 7 of the planet Zeeron. As you have been speculating for quite some time, there is indeed life on other worlds." (pause to give them time to gasp in unison) "We have been monitoring your development since you began using radiowaves and are well acquainted with your civilization. In fact, I myself am a professor of Earth Studies at the prestigious Institute for the Study of Quaint and Primitive Cultures in Braxo City. I and my two colleagues, Her Excellency Veeba 22, also of Zeeron, and Runchka Bezoo of planet Felkus" (the two of them came up behind me to give the camera a solemn nod, then retreated) "happened to be in the galaxy and decided to pay you a visit. We would like to spend a few weeks visiting points of interest, collecting artifacts, and observing your way of life. Given that this is your first contact with alien life, you are doubtless worried that we intend to destroy or dominate your world. Rest assured we have no interest in such things. Invading, enslaving, or exploiting planets is quite out of fashion and our sole intent is to establish peaceable relations. Do not, I repeat, *do not* make any attempt to shoot at, bomb, or in any way harm us, or this vessel. Although we are a friendly and compassionate race, any hostility on your part would result in your immediate disintegration. We will be leaving our robo-maid Gropvak" (as evidence for the skeptical it came up behind me and waved to the camera) "on board while we visit your world. Should you harm us in any way, it will destroy several selected population centers with death rays and contact the defensive forces of Zeeron who would arrive in a trice and finish you off entirely. By the way, we noticed you have a space shuttle - would you be so kind as to give us an escort down to the surface of your planet?" (I was not about to land our saucer lest the Earthlings disassemble it to discover the principles of long distance space flight) "You might also want to ready us some rooms at the Plaza Hotel in New York City, which is where I think we'd like to start our vacation, or expedition rather." (I switched to an ominous tone) "You have four hours to respond."

The Earthlings mobilized their military forces and sent their primitive space shuttle to have a look at us while the Security Council of the United Nations, a global authority, debated the two options of granting us permission to land or blowing us up to forestall alien invasion. The general public alternately quaked with fear and scoffed with disbelief. A huge debate raged in the Senate of the United States (the nation where we intended to stay) as to whether we should be allowed in their territory. A powerful southern senator adamantly opposed our visit and was close to convincing his paranoid and malevolent cohorts to blast us out of the sky. I felt obliged to again interrupt Earthly broadcasts, this time using a voice modulator to make myself sound angry, mean, and scary. "We grow weary of this waiting. Are we to visit with your permission, or without?" By a vote of 51 to 49, we were granted special extraterrestrial visas, created just for the occasion, by the United States. Now it was up to the United Nations.

That deliberative body however, moved more slowly, and by the time the Secretary General finally contacted us we were halfway into a particularly engrossing motion picture and missed the call. The Earthling spoke with Gropvak, who I found out later told him, "Norvex can't speak with you now, Earth creature, he's busy watching *Auntie Mame*. Leave your number and he'll ring you back when he finds it convenient." Later I contacted the United Nations and learned that we were welcome to land, provided we agreed to be searched for weapons and deadly diseases - precisely the things we wouldn't *dream* of carrying, but which are rampant on Earth!

Veeba, wanting us to reflect the best and latest in Zeeronian fashion, put us in matching pink plastic body-stockings with yellow translucent platform thigh boots and belts. To my already stirring ensemble I added a blue metallic pendant sporting three ruby buttons which Klajo had given me. One button sent out an S.O.S. to Zeeron, not that anyone was likely to rescue me should they receive such a thing. The second could briefly shift the wearer into the 5th dimension, momentarily taking one out of harm's way. The third turned the pendant into a transmitter with a direct line to our ship. Veeba, jealous of my gorgeous jewelry, gave Runchka a white floppy, wide-brimmed hat and herself a zingy gold headdress to compensate.

After an interminable wait, the Earthlings managed to rig up a tunnel between their shuttle and our craft through which we were forced to crawl on all fours. We were met by two astronauts in unmercifully ugly protective suits, gazing at us with fear and wonder. One of them operated a video camera into which Veeba shamelessly mugged and blew kisses. Gropvak (gaily humming "We're Off to See the Wizard") obligingly made several trips back and forth bringing over our wardrobe which took up every available inch of space in the tiny cabin. In fact, the whole shuttle was a shabby little affair. Since the Earthlings don't have antigravity devices, their ships have to hurtle themselves about by burning explosive fuel which is entirely unsafe. We were advised to strap ourselves down and avoid small talk. As the shuttle entered the planet's atmosphere I saw Veeba's knuckles turn white from nervously clutching her armrest, and even the normally intrepid Runchka closed his/her eyes in terror. We all breathed an enormous sigh of relief once we landed.

It was a dark night on the planet's surface as we disembarked. "In a few days my colleagues will be seeing me on Earth television, a true scientific pioneer at work," I thought to myself, perhaps a tad pompously, as the Earthling's camera recorded me setting foot on the planet's surface.

Finished at last with the unpleasantness of traveling I stretched and inhaled deeply. The air smelled peculiar, weirdly acrid and harsh, a fact I thought it better not to mention. The astronauts gestured for us to accompany them onto a mechanical transport machine which took us to a low, flat, gray building at the end of a field. "The physicians will examine you now," announced the one who'd operated the video camera. He ushered us through a door, down a hallway, and into a sterile white room with all manner of what I assumed was primitive medical equipment. The three doctors, wearing protective suits and masks, awaited our arrival. After introducing themselves they asked us to remove our clothes and wash off our makeup for the examination. This put Veeba into a foul mood which only got worse when the actual examination got under way and her doctor demanded to look inside her orifices.

"I'm sorry about this, ma'am," he apologized.

"I can't *imagine* what you expect to find in there," snipped Veeba.

"Looks all right," he informed his compatriots.

"Now can I look up yours?" she asked.

"You'll have to ask the general," he answered uncomfortably.

This hideousness all took place under an unnerving invention called florescent light, which is unflattering to a degree unimaginable to residents of a glamour-world like Zeeron. After dressing ourselves, a soldier wearing an ill-fitting green uniform led us to an office where three older, stouter men, also poorly dressed, were seated behind a table. As we entered Veeba said "Hello" to one of the handsome young men stationed at the doorway. He neither answered nor in any way acknowledged her presence.

"I don't think he likes me," she whispered to me sadly.

"Not at all," I assured her. "It's a custom on Earth to station surplus young men with weapons at potentially dangerous locations and have them just stand there without moving or making any expression." It occurred to me that our worlds were so different that there must be thousands of things I hadn't thought to tell Veeba and Runchka. Was this all a big mistake?

The men behind the table stood up. "Welcome to Earth," said the one in the middle, wearing a slightly belligerent look on his face.

"Thanks, it's great to be here," declared Veeba emphatically as she collapsed into a waiting chair.

The man introduced himself and his colleagues although I promptly forgot all their names. "Your preliminary examination didn't reveal any discernible diseases, but we would like to keep you under observation to make sure that..."

Tired, and with my nerves on edge, I interrupted him - rudely, I fear. "No, no, no. I'm sorry but we'd really like to get to our hotel and have a rest. We've just come from the Andromeda galaxy and we don't intend to go through any more pinching, poking, or lying under silly machines. Out of the question. And this concept of removing blood with needles, well, you've just got to find a better way."

"I have been authorized to inform you that the United Nations Security Council has unanimously declared that you must meet with the strictest standards of..."

"Pish and tush on your United Nations!" I scolded, quickly adding, "And for the record, your planet harbors all manner of slimy, crawling, little microbey, moldy things which we wouldn't *dream* of tolerating on Zeeron."

"Be that as it may..."

I interrupted again, a highly effective way to throw Earthlings off balance. "Your Warriorships," I began, while holding aloft my necklace, "do you see this? Lovely, don't you think? Such pretty jewels! But this necklace is functional as well as stylish. Allow me to demonstrate." I pushed the Zerk button which, by shifting me to the 5th dimension, rendered me invisible to them for a few seconds. "While I was gone I could have killed any of you. Snuffed out your life like that," I snapped. "These other buttons signal Zeeron's intergalactic fleet to come to my aid, which as I may have mentioned, would lead to your total and complete annihilation. Now I suggest you call the Plaza Hotel and make sure our rooms are ready!"

Thereafter we were met with a bit more deference. In fact, our hosts almost immediately herded us into a flying airplane machine. As we settled down into our seats, Veeba became cranky. "There should have been a reception, not those awful doctors," she wailed. Once the airplane left the ground sheer terror overtook us and the complaining stopped. Flying is fairly new on Earth and planes crash all the time. Even when they aren't crashing they jiggle about in an alarming fashion. If a mechanical disorder develops all one can do is jump to the ground with a parachute and hope one doesn't land on anything. By the time we arrived at Newark airport we were all nervous wrecks.

It was early morning when we left the airplane and boarded a waiting limousine. Nervous, hungry, and now extremely fatigued, it was the worst imaginable moment for us to encounter an Earthly city for the first time. Veeba became almost hysterical as we drove along the highway. "Oh, Norvex, it's dirty and ugly!" She opened the window for some fresh air. "And it smells! The buildings are drab, and the people all look sick, and it's all positively horrible!"

She wasn't overstating matters in the least. The buildings and roads were quite seedy. The plants and animals did looked diseased, and the Earthlings themselves seemed to be on death's doorstep – defeat, despair, and misery etched into every line and wrinkle of their blotchy, blemished faces. An enormous percentage of them suffered from the Earthly ailment known as "fatness," which I'd always assumed was a rather rare malady. As for the air, I literally had to hold my nose to keep out the reek of pollution and decay. Television had emphatically *not* prepared me for this ugly reality. As we rolled along in the automobile machine my heart was sinking, but I tried to put on a brave face for Veeba and Runchka.

"Think of yourselves as archeological historians. You're seeing how people lived on Zeeron and Felkus thousands and thousands of years ago." Neither of my companions responded. I then noticed a camera pointing at us from the front of the vehicle, which was separated from us by a window, reminding me that the Earthly authorities were surely observing us. Surveillance of this sort, such bad form as to never be practiced on Zeeron, is rampant on Earth. I decided to turn the situation to my own advantage and put on a performance for the locals. "Why, I think this is fascinating! Perhaps we should come back and bring wondrous technologically advanced gifts for the Earth people, for which they shall be most grateful." Veeba shot me a funny look with an arched eyebrow.

As we approached the Hudson river, the towers of Manhattan became visible over the horizon. "That's New York City where we'll be staying!" I told my companions in an artificially chipper tone.

"It doesn't look terribly inviting," said Veeba. "Let's stay in the Emerald City instead."

"I believe that locale is fictional," I replied, staring with disbelief at the grime caked on the side of the George Washington bridge.

"Oh." She looked downcast.

"Cheer up, Veeba. You can't judge a whole planet by one small patch. What if a visitor to Zeeron only saw Zigrid City? He or she wouldn't think much of us, I'd imagine." I gave her a little peck on the cheek and squeezed her hand affectionately. She continued to grumble, but I could see the fascination in her eyes growing as we drove down the city streets which had been thoughtfully closed off so we wouldn't get stuck in traffic like the other vehicles. On the sidewalk passersby pointed and stared at us. Although they couldn't see inside our vehicle's tinted glass, many must have guessed who we were. In fact, we were hardly inconspicuous since armed soldiers on motorcycles surrounded us.

Runchka, too, gaped out the window in amazement. "There is plant life here which has adapted to the foul-smelling air substitute known as smog," he observed happily. "It is imperative that I bring home samples of these resilient and hardy species to my home planet of Felkus."

At that moment I saw a woman teetering down the street in a truly gigantic red wig, so big it actually *dwarfed* her. When I pointed out the hair piece to Veeba she pronounced it "Smashing" and I knew we'd turned a corner. Soon we were driven into an underground parking garage, and the guard from the front seat and several awaiting cohorts took us up in an elevator to a suite of rooms. A frightened-looking bellboy showed us the rooms, then a bespectacled little man in a dark suit came in. His mousy brown hair was in the short, neutral, parted-on-the-side style mandatory for most Earth men involved in power structures. As his eyes shifted around the room furtively he extended his hand for us to grasp and shake up and down as is the local custom.

"Allow me to introduce myself. I am Adrian P. Finley, Ambassador-at-Large to Other Planets from the United Nations. I am pleased to make your acquaintance." He spoke in the overly modulated tones of a career diplomat, which I suppose he was. "I've been privileged by the Secretary General to act as your guide for the duration of your visit. I am staying down the hall, and will always be on hand should you need anything."

"At the moment all I want is to rest," declared Veeba as she opened a door adjoining our sitting room. Inside was a large bed on which she immediately threw herself. Then, yawning, she kicked the door shut without so much as a "Goodnight."

"Please forgive her. I know it's only early afternoon here, but we have space lag and need to sleep as soon as possible," I explained.

"The hairdressers of Zeeron are known to be 62.6 percent more erratic in their behavior than the typical resident of that atypically erratic world," added Runchka.

"This isn't the Plaza, is it?" I asked, glancing around the charmlessly functional room.

"For security purposes we felt it would be better for you to stay here," explained Mr. Finley

Miffed though I was, I let it pass. "Well, what's done is done," I said, trying not to sound disappointed. "I'm too tired to care anyway."

"Yes, well, I'll leave you now," said Mr. Finley with an almost overly pleasant smile. "If you want anything just pick up the telephone and ask for me. We can speak later, and then, if it's not too much trouble, it has been suggested that you could address the United Nations tomorrow."

"Nothing would give me greater pleasure," I said as Mr. Finley bowed and left.

Dear Diary,                                            Tuesday, Sept. 24

Mrs. Van Vechten didn't have to go to work today so she made Daphne and me a delicious pancake breakfast. The really exceptional thing about her pancakes is that she uses Jägermeister and cherry brandy and all these totally sweet liqueurs instead of syrup. It's her specialty. Daphne thinks her mom does it to loosen her tongue, so she'll blab about her sex life and all the stuff teenage girls are afraid to talk to their moms about. I find that hard to believe since when it comes to drinking, Daphne will pass out singing *Sesame Street* songs before she'll spill a secret. She'd make a good spy.

Mrs. Van Vechten is so fun it's hard to believe she's a mom. She always wears heels, gobs of makeup, and super-tight dress suits to show off her figure. She looks sort of like a "lady executive" from one of the *Perry Masons* she's always insisting Daphne and I watch with her (her other favorites are anything by Hitchcock and this demented '50s psychological horror movie, *The Bad Seed*). I've hardly ever seen her nag or yell, and she lets Daphne stay out as late as she wants. The funniest thing about Mrs. V. is that she's always flirting with me in a cutesy way, like she'll ask, "Could you possibly open this jar of peanut butter, honey? Ooh, thanks. You're so strong!" She's what I think they call "a real camp."

From what Daphne tells me, her mom never planned on having a family and was an actual groupie when she was young. She used to call herself Kathy Quaalude, which is apparently the name of some drug that used to be popular. One day a handsome English guitarist came through town and when Kathy found herself pregnant by him she couldn't bear to waste his chromosomes. Apparently he had high cheekbones, good skin, big lips, and could play like Johnny Thunders, whoever that was. So, figuring one child wouldn't kill her, she produced Daphne. The rock star went away (which Mrs.V. says they always do) and baby Daphne was raised by Kathy's mom, Granny Meadmore, while Kathy concentrated on being a drug mess.

Finally a much older man, Dr. Van Vechten, married Kathy and got her cleaned up. She settled down to a life of rehab, career training, and suburbia. Daphne was brought home to live with her mom, and Granny Meadmore ran away to Florida before anyone could pawn off more unwanted children on her. Once Mrs.V. was employed and settled she divorced Dr. Van Vechten, winning a huge alimony, and they all lived happily ever after.

In addition to the pancakes, we were treated to eggs, bacon, toast, and pop tarts. I didn't eat the egg yolks (fatty), spent ten minutes picking the gristly part out of the bacon, didn't butter the toast, and scraped some of the frosting off the pop tarts. Still the meal was too weighty for me, and after I'd finished I felt like a pregnant woman, like a small animal was living in my stomach. It's a mystery how Daphne and her mom can eat such high-calorie foods without ballooning up. While we were eating, Daphne read us something she wrote for her psychology class.

"'Finally, Help for the Non-Abused' by Daphne Van Vechten," she began as Mrs.V. and I listened attentively. "For years I snickered at the wide array of self-help groups. They all seemed to be whiny, overly earnest, and have ludicrous names like "The Crystal Healing Circle for Pagan Bulimics" or "Stressbusters Incorporated." My attitude changed when I ran across some literature from Adult Children of Non-Abusive Parents (ACONAP, for short). The child within me who didn't need to be healed cried out.

"For years I'd lived a lie. My happy childhood was a secret I hid, fearing the resentment of the less fortunate. When my friends would tell me about parents who beat or disinherited them, put their pets to sleep, or shamelessly favored siblings, I would invent some exaggerated tale of family injustice so I could fit in. In reality my mother, though nowhere near perfect, managed to raise me without using bizarre punishments, violence, or verbal abuse. As the world now knows, thanks to Jerry, Geraldo, and Zhandra, this is freakishly rare.

"At ACONAP rap groups, I met others like myself and lost my sense of isolation. At my first meeting I told a room full of strangers how, as a child, I'd always thought *The Brady Bunch* gave a totally realistic portrayal of a typical American family and admitted my fears of being 'out of it' when a friend from a normal abusive family told me they were an absurd shallow caricature of Philistine, petit-bourgeois ideals. My admission was met with warm hearty laughter as my new friends assured me this was common. I heard many other heartwarming stories from ACONAPs and now look forward to 'Letting it all hang out' at my weekly meetings.

"Not surprisingly, relationships between normal abused people and ACONAPs are often strained. They often find each other's behavior mysterious, if not outright incomprehensible. One ACONAP told me how his girlfriend would come down with mysterious stomach pains on holidays. Eventually he realized it was a psychosomatic illness caused by her association of holidays with family get-togethers, which in her home always included arguments and indigestion. His girlfriend still won't get out of bed on Thanksgiving or Christmas, but at least he understands. Another ACONAP told how she always wanted to skydive, attend nude cocktail parties, tour Hindu temples, and seek adventure, while her partner preferred to snuggle at home, endlessly watching his extensive collection of animated Disney videos. From speaking with ACONAP counselors she realized that he was engaged in a doomed attempt to live out the fantasy of a happy childhood and was able to get him into therapy. The difficulties gay and lesbian ACONAPs have with normal partners are legendary. One faces violence, rejection, or at least a lot of stupid questions, while the other gets love, support, and maybe even some home-baked brownies for the domestic partner. Resentment is natural and a constant sort of friction.

"A typical response of the non-abused is to provoke hostility from parents so they can fit in, what ACONAPs call "antagonizing." Fortunately, most ACONAPs are content to rebel harmlessly with funny haircuts or body-piercings. Our permissive, casual society, however, makes it harder and harder for the pseudo-rebellious to play outlaw without harming themselves or others. Soon, loved children may have to turn to crime and crack to get the parental disapproval they seek. Needless to say, I never even considered such matters until I started attending ACONAP meetings. My understanding of the world has grown in leaps and bounds!"

"Oh, Lordy!" cried Mrs. V. while dousing a pancake with some peach schnapps. "I knew I was too permissive!"

"Well, I'm no ACONAP, so what's my excuse for antagonizing?" I asked.

"Actually, I hardly think either of you qualifies as an *adult* anything," observed the former Kathy Quaalude.

Daphne shot us a "keep quiet" look and continued. "The ACONAP support group I attend has members who've dealt with virtually every problem imaginable. One woman had joined the Catholic church because of assurances from misguided (and needless to say, abused) friends that when sex is forbidden and dirty it's more satisfying. She's since learned this to be a myth and embraced the open sexuality she learned from her parents and their fellow commune members. Another ACONAP with a famous parent was bitter because he missed the financial opportunities of writing a tell-all memoir about his terrible childhood. After counseling, he's recalled not only a spiteful uncle but a particularly unsympathetic piano teacher, and his book will be out this fall. Whatever problems you have from enjoying a happy childhood, I suggest you stop not suffering in silence and do as I did. Look up your local ACONAP chapter today."

"Fab!" I said when she'd finished. I truly do admire Daphne's writing even though she has stolen her tone and style from yours truly. "But the bit about the resentment from less fortunate peers..."

"Oh, I didn't mean you," she smiled.

"I thought it was very clever," said Mrs. Van Vechten, beaming with pride. "I hope your teacher finds it as amusing as you do," she added.

"It's not likely," admitted Daphne.

"But you don't care?"

"Not really," she shrugged.

"And you didn't read that in front of me to butter me up?" Her mom gave me an exaggerated wink.

"Of course I did." Suddenly Daphne was all sunshine and light. "Mother dearest, what will you give me for a basketful of kisses?"

"Oh darling, a bucketful of hugs!" responded Mrs. V. as they air-kissed like movie stars. "Well, I'm off to get my hair done. Would you two mind putting the dishes in the washer?"

"It might make us late," said Daphne, suddenly sounding very concerned and responsible.

"Late! The horror. Just leave them out, the roaches and mice will lick them clean. See you tonight, sweetness. Have a good day, Chester."

"I'll try."

"By the way, my hairdresser is unattached. He looks a little like Steve Buscemi. Interested?"

"Thanks, but no thanks."

"Chester likes boys his own age. One in particular, huh?" Daphne looked at me coyly.

"Who me?" I hate discussing my private miseries in front of people, even nice people like Mrs. V.

"Why don't you admit you're hot for Ted?" Daphne wheedled.

"I'm not 'hot' for anyone." Naturally I'd told her all about the note.

"This boy likes him but he's too afraid to talk to him," said Daphne. "He's really handsome."

"Why don't you just ask this Ted to the movies, or invite him over to do homework?" asked Mrs. V. naively.

"Because he couldn't be seen talking to a freak like me, not to mention I'm out of the closet and all his friends would call him a fag."

"It's true all his friends are jerks," agreed Daphne.

"Any boy who doesn't want to date you because you're out of the closet isn't worth dating," Mrs. Van Vechten announced. "Ciao!" She waved as she went out the door.

"She sounds eerily like a mother sometimes," observed Daphne.

"Can we just drop the whole subject?" I pleaded.

"You can't let fear rule your life, Chester. Ted's in a couple of your classes, isn't he? Just ask him about the homework or something."

"Are you *insane?* I can't do that."

"I know what you're thinking, Chester, but you're not ugly."

"I look like a chubby, teenage Morticia Addams."

"What are you complaining about? Morticia Addams is *beyond* gorgeous."

Though I hadn't had all that much, the liquor was making me maudlin. "You'll *never* understand what I have to put up with! You're beautiful, and you're a total ACONAP, your mom is totally cool. You've got it all."

"Chester, self-pity doesn't become you." Daphne scolded, "I don't think you can handle your pancakes."

"Hey, maybe your mom could adopt me!"

"That's actually not a bad idea. I'll see what I can do. Now, shall we be off to school?"

"What about the dishes?" I eyed the kitchen mess warily.

"Mom doesn't really want me to do them, she wants me to get to school on time. Knowing the only thing I hate more than education is housework she offered me the choice in the hope that..."

"Okay, okay, I get it. The reverse psychology bit. If she really wanted us to want to go to school she should try and get us to drop out, move to a haunted castle in Scotland and form a rock band."

**8**

Waking up the next morning – *my first morning on Earth!* – I was instantly exhilarated and eager to begin my adventure. I picked up the telephone and, before I could even ask for room service, was met with a cheery, "Hello." The voice on the line informed me someone would be in presently, and the second I hung up I heard a knock at the bedroom door. I opened it to find Mr. Finley gesturing for me to accompany him into the sitting room where we could speak without disturbing Veeba and Runchka who were still asleep.

"You know you each have your own bedroom," he began.

"Thank you, I know. On our world it's considered antisocial to sleep alone."

"I trust you were able to sleep soundly?" asked Mr. Finley as he sat gingerly on a sofa and gestured for me to join him.

"Yes. But you know, I *am* famished."

"I'll summon breakfast. Do you have any requests?"

"Belgian waffles and the stimulant bean drink known to your people as 'coffee' for starters."

"Certainly!" He took a small transmitter out of his pocket and muttered something inaudible. "They won't be a minute. Before I say anything else I must discuss a matter of the utmost importance. I am referring to the issue of your safety." He nervously twitched his nose. "There are multitudes of Earthlings advocating your immediate extermination on the grounds that you may be the vanguard party of an interplanetary invasion. For this reason I must request that all your

**79**

plans be cleared by me so that I can arrange for security precautions."

"No problem," I said as I heard Veeba yawn and stretch in the other room.

"Naturally I deplore the suspicious nature of such mistrust, but as we are forced to live with it, I think it would be most advantageous to our mutual purposes if I also accompany you everywhere to help assuage my fellow Earthlings' fears." The depths of such fears became evident just then as I went to the window to see if I could discern the source of a low rumbling sound.

The street in front of our hotel had been blocked off, but behind a row of barricades a block away was a throng of people angrily chanting and waving placards. There were doubtless some curiosity seekers, but most were quite obviously protesters calling for our expulsion or murder. I could make out one banner reading Zero Tolerance for Zeeronians!

"Pray let me assure you that we have the situation well in hand," smiled Mr. Finley, joining me at the window and closing the drapes.

"Let's hope so," I said, remembering many Earth dramas where such crowds break into palaces or embassies and wreak havoc. I was grateful we were on the 40th floor where the miserable mob would have a hard time getting at us.

He must have read my thoughts. "Please, don't worry."

"I'm not worried. I could destroy this whole city if I felt like it. *They're* the ones who should be worried," I lied, as Veeba stumbled into the room, followed by Runchka.

"I must say, you all look wonderfully composed this morning!" flattered Mr. Finley, doubtless amazed that our makeup and clothing were none the worse for wear after having been slept in.

"Glamour technology on Zeeron is the most advanced in the galaxy," explained Veeba.

Breakfast arrived, and after my first bite the Terraphile in me sparkled with delight. The crunchy waffles were perfectly complemented by the smooth, sweet whipped cream, and brilliantly offset by the succulent strawberries. The coffee, although bitter at first, grew on me once its renowned psychotropic effect took hold. I felt energetic and optimistic, in a nice, subtle way. Runchka became involved in dissecting one of the flowers which had been set in a vase to decorate our table and spoke not a word, while Veeba chattered away about how she admired Earth's many hairstyles. "The beehive, the Farrah, the mop top: all of them delightful!" Although she was the soul of politeness to Mr. Finley in person, the moment his back was turned (arranging for another order of waffles and coffee) she stage-whispered, "Norvex! He doesn't seem like any fun at all! And he smells funny. Let's lose him."

"His odor is no doubt due to the Earth custom of masking body scents with perfumes resembling the odors of local flora," explained Runchka.

"Veeba my love, we frighten them. Let them send who they will to keep an eye on us. And as I mentioned on the ship, I strongly suspect every word we say is overheard by Earthly ears, so do keep that in mind, won't you?" She put on a resigned face, but then quickly stuck her tongue out at our host's back. "They're more than likely watching too," I added.

As Mr. Finley rejoined us at the table I tried to set him at ease. "I must say your planet's food is every bit as delicious as television advertisements have led us to believe it would be. The whipped cream on the waffles has exceeded my wildest anticipation by bounds and leaps. It's cool, sweet, creamy goodness is most pleasing. Now I'm in a terrific mood and looking forward to speaking at your United Nations."

"We didn't know when you'd be getting up so we scheduled your talk for this afternoon. Still, with traffic and security precautions and all, we'd better leave right after breakfast," said Mr. Finley, smiling away. "I'm most eager to hear your speech."

"Oh good," said Veeba. "He loves to talk."

The ride to the U.N. wasn't long, but we were all horrified anew at the condition of the Earth city. Ill clad, unwashed, and rude pedestrians competed with primitive vehicles spewing toxic fumes to gain dominance on the narrow, dilapidated streets. Bodies of dead or unconscious Earthlings sprawled on the sidewalks like garbage. The noise was deafening, the smells putrid. Runchka turned to me with a look of horror on his/her face. "Norvex, it is indeed fortunate that I have had the opportunity to receive your excellent instruction regarding the extremely fascinating local culture. All the same, I think I would prefer to spend the remainder of this journey in the study of the indigenous vegetation of this vital and interesting planet."

"Certainly," I replied absentmindedly as I stared out the window at a store displaying sweatshirts on which someone had sewn sequins in the shapes of cats and palm trees.

Inside the U.N. building I felt somewhat buoyed by the calm, clean, hopeful atmosphere. Surely nothing too horribly wrong could occur in this environment! We were seated on a stage in a vast auditorium facing legions of drab-looking Earth creatures who eyed us gravely and suspiciously. Speaking extemporaneously I opted for a brief, trite, cheery talk conveying exactly nothing, during which I remembered to smile a lot and use forceful hand gestures. Runchka sat to my right looking impossibly earnest, Veeba to my left looking undiplomatically bored. I was relieved when after my closing remark, "May our peoples ever find friendship and peace the shortest route to prosperity and security," or some such prattle, I was wildly applauded. The Earthlings had apparently decided it was best to act as if they trusted us, although more than likely they did not.

At the reception immediately afterwards, Mr. Finley assured me I'd said exactly what was called for. As the guests swirled around us he became highly animated, dragging various indistinguishable heads of state over to exchange boring pleasantries.

"They all dress alike here!" whispered Veeba while he was off rounding up some new figurehead to introduce.

"Nobody will expect you to remember their names, I'm sure. Just smile and in a few hours we'll never see these people again," I consoled.

"And they try not to stare, but they *stare*," she added, helping herself to some tasty canapés.

"You could plead space-lag and ask to lie down till it's over. No, on second thought, don't. They'll be afraid you imported some exotic disease."

"I really don't feel too well. Are you sure this food is safe to eat?"

I was saved from having to answer in the negative by the arrival of Mr. Finley, for once without a president or king in tow.

"I hope you are finding the reception enjoyable, Your Excellency?" he asked Veeba.

"Absolutely lovely!" she replied. Veeba quite enjoys social lying when there's someone present to appreciate how well she does it.

"Wonderful, wonderful. You know everyone has so many questions. Perhaps you might allow me the privilege of inviting some of the more eminent journalists of our world to a press conference where you could..."

"Explain ourselves? Answer questions? We'd be delighted!" I said.

"Good, good." Mr. Finley actually smiled. "When would be convenient?"

"Let's get this out of the way, shall we?"

"Tomorrow then?" he asked.

"Splendid," I agreed.

"I'll arrange it immediately." He sauntered off.

"For some reason he makes me positively ill," gasped Veeba as soon as Mr. Finley was out of earshot. "He has a disingenuous air about him."

"He's probably on an extremely short leash," I speculated.

Veeba gazed pensively across the room. "I wonder who his master is?"

"Doubtless a committee of thoroughly objectionable potentates," I answered, just as a small dark man in a tuxedo who'd been about to introduce himself to us suddenly thought better of it and pretended to attack the hors d'oeuvre table instead.

"Your planet may be a wreck, but your blintzes are quite tasty," said Veeba with a friendly wink as she grabbed one and took a hearty bite. "I must get the recipe for my robo-maid. We Zeeronians just *love* the exotic!" He smiled and fled. Setting the natives at ease, I could see, would be no easy task.

We were then rejoined by Runchka, who'd been waylaid by an ambassador with an interest in ecology. "Norvex, the purpose of this social interaction remains arcane to me."

"It's a signifier of amicability," I explained.

"Try one of these," suggested Veeba, waiving a blintz in his/her face. "The Earthlings can really cook. Just don't try and talk to them, they're not allowed to say anything."

"Not all Earthlings are this guarded and dull," I informed her. "These are politicians. They don't create or discover, they just boss people around. Everyone hates and resents them so they become resentful, duplicitous, fearful, and arrogant. The poor things even have to perform their few legitimate administrative duties without imagination or compassion because of the planet's limited resources and primitive technology."

"Sad," muttered Veeba. The three of us spent the remainder of the reception close together, interacting with the natives only when decorum made it absolutely necessary.

On the ride back to the hotel Mr. Finley tried to discuss further plans but was silenced by Veeba's loud proclamation, "Don't anybody speak! I need absolute quiet to preserve the equanimity which is the source of my flawless and icy beauty."

Unexpectedly, the limousine ground to a sudden halt. "So much for your flawless and icy beauty, my darling," I remarked as a mob of Earthlings broke through the barricades and surrounded a building I recognized as our hotel. The soldiers of our motorcycle escort quickly dismounted and took up defensive positions with their weapons as a throng spotted our car and encircled it. Despite the soldiers' best efforts, a woman holding a crucifix in a position I was familiar with from many a vampire film made her way to the window of our car and violently shook her talisman in our direction, hoping, I suppose, to exorcise us. Her hate-filled face with its blazing eyes, flared nostrils, and angry red complexion was a mortifying sight. Runchka hid his/ her eyes, Veeba turned away, and I flinched. After a moment which seemed like an hour, a soldier got her in a chokehold and dragged her off. Then hundreds of uniformed police in riot gear, some riding on the backs of huge quadrupedal beasts, charged at the protesters from hidden positions a block or two away, dispersing the rabble. The barricades were quickly replaced and we were driven into the hotel garage unmolested. The whole scene only took a few minutes but we were all quite dismayed.

"Oh dear. I hope you will understand it's fear rather than malice which motivates them," apologized Mr. Finley.

"Whatever you say," said Veeba, looking unconvinced. "But please see to it that those unkempt hooligans never return." I noticed that she was shaking with fear and took her hand in mine reassuringly. "What was wrong with poor crazy woman at the window?" she asked me quietly.

"I don't know but I'm sure she's being taken care of now," I lied. Crossing the authorities is never a safe proposition on Earth.

We spent the afternoon relocating our clothes into the dressers, cabinets, armoires, and closets of our respective bedrooms. When we'd finished I requested a dinner of lasagna, garlic bread, and wine, all of which proved delicious although absolutely nothing like what I'd produced back on Zeeron so many years before. The wine contained alcohol, a toxic by-product of rotting fruit with a pleasant psychoactive effect a bit like rapture gas, a bit like the melancholy feeling one gets looking at old vids on a rainy day, and a bit like the giddiness one gets from being overtired.

After dinner we watched *Female Trouble*, a John Waters film which I'd asked Mr. Finley to get for us. It had never been broadcast by the Earthlings due to archaic taboos concerning various bodily functions and excessive irony, so we'd never seen it on Zeeron. Its brilliance surpassed my wildest expectations. The sight of the lead character, Dawn Davenport, bouncing on a trampoline in a negligee with a mohawk hairdo, her face a mass of scars, brandishing a gun, and screaming, "Who wants to die for art?" provided conclusive evidence that some Earthlings possess thoroughly civilized sensibilities.

"I so admire her assertion of an individual style in the face of suffocating conformity, absurd child-rearing practices, and tediously narrow standards of beauty," I said, clicking my tongue in approval.

Runchka expressed bafflement. "But, Norvex, 94.9% of Dawn Davenport's behavior is classifiable as criminally insane, and her individuality is only expressed through wanton cruelty."

"I haven't paid attention to what's going on, but I like the outfits," remarked Veeba.

"If she's cruel, it is because life on an uncivilized planet is cruel," I explained. "And insanity is sometimes the sanest response to a world gone mad."

Mr. Finley, who'd been squirming throughout the entire film stood up. "I think I should take my leave now. I'll see you all in the morning." After he left I scolded myself for the remark about Earth being a cruel, uncivilized planet, promising myself I'd be more diplomatic in the future.

Dear Diary,                                          Tuesday, Oct. 1

Man, dig those crazy space aliens! It's the funniest thing – they couldn't look less like the little gray creatures with almond-shaped eyes from *X-Files* and *Close Encounters* that everyone wears on tee shirts and stuff. They look more like some insane club kids or a cheezy New Wave band like you'd see on some VH1 '80s retrospective. Frankly, I have serious doubts they're for real, though Daphne is totally convinced, probably because she thinks the head alien, Norvex, is cute. Once you get past the fact that he's older (maybe almost forty even), and wearing a heck of a lot of makeup, you can see that he really does have a beautiful face: super-high cheekbones; aquiline nose; big, sensual lips. Kind of Italian and aristocratic. Daphne, Mrs.V., and I were watching the news, which kept showing the clip of his address to the United Nations over and over, when Mr. Jenkins from next door came by. He and his friends are forming an anti-alien vigilante patrol. If Zeeron tries to invade Maple Street, they'd better be ready to fight a dozen frumpy middle-aged guys with collectable guns!

Dear Diary,                                       Wednesday, Oct. 2

Maybe I'll get to spend the rest of my senior year here. I haven't discussed anything with Mrs.Van Vechten yet, but I don't miss home at all. Daphne says her mom doesn't mind me and it appears my own loving family is actually quite content to do without me, though Dad occasionally calls Mrs.Van Vechten and pretends to want me back. The only downside is that the basement carpet, which is always damp for some reason (I can't find the leak anywhere), is starting to smell thanks to the Indian summer heat. It's a toss-up whether I'll be killed first by school bullies or the fungi and bacteria in my underworld petri-dish hideaway.

The amazing thing regarding the former threat though, dear Diary, is that a hero approacheth. Ted actually stopped Erik from picking on me in the hallway today. I was at my locker putting my books away when someone kicked me from behind. I turned around and saw Erik preparing another kick, now aimed directly at my privates. Before he could deliver it though, Ted got him in a chokehold and said, "Leave him alone, Doofus." Erik went off cursing under his breath and Ted told me to scram. The way he said "scram" though, you could tell he really likes me. On the way home I saw my knight in shining sportswear playing basketball. He nodded to me again in that way jocks have of acknowledging people, just a teeny little lifting of the head. I almost fainted. Back at Daphne's I tried to practice the jock nod in the mirror, but it just looked like I had a crick in my neck. Needless to say, a certain someone has been headlining in my erotic fantasies!

I found this album, *Switched on Bacharach*, at Thriftmart that is simply not to be believed. The cover's got this woman with Christmas lights in her hair and the music is all moog synthesizer versions of all the cheezy songs like "Do You Know the Way to San Jose?" and "What's New, Pussycat?" I was playing it for Daphne when she let this little bomb drop. She is now seeing a married optometrist! Not her optometrist, but one from the same building. I don't see how she can let old guys do it with her. She claims she's tried younger men but they don't know what they're doing, they go too fast, and have no erotic technique. In spite of my ignorance on the subject of sex, I think I'd stay with Ted over Dr. Abromowitz, although I have to admit that for someone in his thirties he is pretty well preserved.


Dear Diary,                                            Thursday, Oct. 3

Today I was humiliated in Phys Ed by the President's Council on

Physical Fitness tests. I could only do one chin up and everybody laughed. After class Marvin Theadoracopolis and Linwood Del Vecchio grabbed my notebook and lunchbag and tossed them into the dumpster behind the science building. When I climbed in to get my stuff, they shut the lid and sat on it. Even though there wasn't any trash inside, the dumpster smelled just terrible. Imagine gangrenous wounds and rotting egg salad sandwiches with lots of mayo.

"I'm suffocating, let me out!" I screamed.

"Hey, we saw you and Daphne on T.V. last night. It was a documentary on the freaks of planet Zeeron!" They laughed loudly at this incredibly feeble joke.

I sat there trying to hold my breath and for some reason I had a vision of Kyle telling me, as he enjoys doing every few days, it's my own fault I get picked on because I deliberately dress like a freak, which is stupid because I've been picked on since I was nine and I only started dressing up a couple of years ago, and my hair didn't really get big and Robert Smith-like until last year. Then it struck me - *my hair*! I always keep a mini-can of Hyper-Hold Hair Spritz in my backpack in case it loses volume. It was totally dark inside but I found the can by touch and began to bang it on the side of the metal dumpster. The noise was much louder than my screams and the bullies jumped off the lid immediately, no doubt scared of being caught by a passing educator.

Marvin and Linwood watched me as I climbed out and onto the sidewalk, making wisecracks and references to the sort of bodily functions that amuse small children. As I tried to walk away Linwood tripped me and I fell, cutting my hand on the concrete. Then the pair of them ran away screaming about not wanting to get infected by my AIDS blood. I'd take Dad up on his offer to send me to private school except that I don't particularly want to go to *any* school right now (my nerves are wrecked!) and I'm not speaking to him anyway.

Daphne tells me Marvin is *always* bothering her. Once he rubbed his finger across her face then rubbed the same finger across a windowpane, and pointed to the smear. "Too much makeup!" he said all smug-like and walked off. Like *he's* supposed to be the one to decide how much foundation you're allowed to wear at Hubert Humphrey high. I really wish he wasn't so incredibly cute. He looks like a teenage Brad Pitt.

After school I went to the Snaque Shaque and, with a will of iron, forced myself to pass up a low-fat quadruple-fudge eclair for a totally fat-free coconut macaroon. I'm mystified how they got the fat out of the coconut though, which according to Mrs.Van Vechten, is extremely fatty, even though natural.

Dear Diary,                                                    Thursday, Oct. 10

What could I have done to deserve this treacherous fate? Was I a Nazi gym instructor in a concentration camp in a past life? Monday I arrived at school during lunch period - alone - because Daphne'd gone in early for art class which she never misses. The lawn by the science building is strictly for popular kids; by rights I shouldn't have cut through there on the way to the class, but I did. Before I knew what was happening, Erik Federico and his henchmen (and even one henchwoman) came out of nowhere and went at me like attack dogs. One of them, I think it was the rodentlike Preston Heath, even peed on my books which I'd dropped while covering my face from various fists that were trying to rearrange my features. Suddenly Ted raced into the fracas and pushed everyone away. My assailants retreated to the opposite side of the lawn and stared. Ted was acting all concerned.

Ted brushed some to the hair off my face so he could see the bruises. "Did they hurt you? Are you okay?" His face looked strange and tense in a way I couldn't figure out.

"Sort of, but I think we'd better go," I said. "I mean, I can't count on you to protect me all the time. Uh, thanks though." I started to walk off but was stopped by Ted's hand on my shoulder.

"I *wish* I could be there to protect you, all the time," he said.

"Thanks."

"Really."

"If there's anything I can ever do for you..." I said.

"Kiss me."

Unable to believe my ears I asked, "What did you say?"

"Kiss me," he repeated.

I'd always imagined the first time I kissed a boy would be in some romantic, secluded place like a forest glen, or a dark garbage-strewn alleyway in some big city, not on the lawn at school, surrounded by my mortal enemies. All the same, there was a certain pleasing nuts-to-youishness to getting my first kiss in front of Erik Federico that appealed to me. I stood on my tiptoes, closed my eyes, and puckered my lips. The next thing I knew I was flat on my back and my entire face was in great pain. After a moment of complete disorientation I became opened my eyes and saw Erik, his arm around Ted all dudely-like, and half a dozen other creeps standing over me, laughing their heads off.

"He almost kissed you, man!" said Linwood.

"He really thought you liked him! Ugly motherfucker," added Preston.

Ted addressed me directly. "You're a stupid, ugly, fat, zit-faced faggot and nobody wants to kiss you and nobody ever will." Maybe I'm deluded, but somehow he didn't look like he meant it.

Erik, who I'm sure planned the attack, had to have the last word. "How could you think anyone liked you? Haven't you ever looked in the mirror? If you or that dyke-whore Daphne ever show your faces again we'll kill you, so why don't you put an end to yourselves now and save us the trouble. Go home and die."

"Well, maybe I just will," I said. I read somewhere that you're supposed to humor insane people so they don't go berserk, though in retrospect I guess they'd *already* gone berserk. The bullies, unable to come up with an encore, watched as I got up, threw away my now broken sunglasses, brushed myself off, and (using a school newspaper) picked up my urinated-on school books. Though my heart was beating a million miles a minute I calmly walked to the nurse's office. I wasn't seriously injured, but Nurse Wojnarowicz put a band-aid on my head, took my blood pressure (why do they *always* do that?) and called Principal Osterberg. To make a long story short, Erik, Ted, Linwood, and Preston got suspended. The rest got away free because I didn't know their names. The principal called my Dad. I said I was fine and not to worry. Then I went to my dungeon hideaway and burned Ted's note, wishing it would work like a voodoo doll and he'd burst into flame himself. It's lucky for him I don't have telekinesis or a psychotic streak.

The next day at school everyone, but everyone, knew all about the incident and felt the need to swear their allegiance to the bullies and laugh at me for thinking anyone could like me. Even mild-mannered Lester Mott who has worse skin than I do called me a "fudge-packer" and a "rump ranger," and Krystal Bannings had the nerve to tell me I was selfish for putting a black mark on her boyfriend Linwood's academic record by getting him in trouble. If I were a normal, red-blooded American male I would've come to school with a gun and pumped lead into anything that moved, but instead I just started trying to spray people with Hyper-Hold Hair Spritz to keep them away. They just laughed and held their noses. I guess I was starting to lose it. Can anyone blame me though? It's been nonstop persecution for me since third grade when Jose Epstein-McAndrews called me a sissy and shoved my head into the toilet.

In the middle of American Government, Krystal's sister Jewel handed me a note with an *extremely* unflattering drawing of me on it. I got up and left the room, ignoring Mrs. McGillicudy's demand to "Please tell me just where it is exactly you think that you're going, Mr. Julian!" I walked home, or to Daphne's home, to be exact.

That evening Daphne tried to console me. "Rachel Cosgrove told Mary Lou Bedermeyer that Ted didn't want to hit you, but Erik sort of blackmailed him into it."

"What exactly does being 'sort of blackmailed' mean?"

"You know, Ted felt sorry for you and tried to get everyone to lay off you, but his idiot jock buddies teased him and called him a queer, so he had to go along with Erik's set-up to show he was a regular homophobic pig."

"Why am I not comforted by this knowledge?" I sighed. "Daphne, could you do me a favor? Forge a note from my Dad saying I have advanced neurasthenia and won't be able to go to school for a few days."

I haven't left the room since. I just hide down here like Anne

Frank, albeit with cable television. Daphne has been sweet, bringing me sympathy and meals, though never the petit-fours and watercress finger sandwiches I ask for.

Dear Diary,                                                          Friday, Oct. 11

This morning Ms. Van Vechten discovered why I'd become a hermit from Daphne, whom I strongly suspect she plied with pancakes.

"Chester, why didn't you tell me what happened at school?" She seemed agitated, if not angry, which is totally unfair since I'm an innocent victim.

It was awfully early and I was half asleep, but managed to pull myself out of my fetal position on the sofa and sit up. "I dunno."

"You can't just hide down here the rest of your life. For one thing it smells awful, and for another, you're supposed to be in school. I really don't see any option but to call your parents." She started up the stairs, Daphne and I followed. "Maybe they could find you a progressive private school," she suggested. "I can't see you having to go back and face all those horrible kids." She picked up the phone to dial. "Who's this?" After a moment's confusion I figured out someone else was already on the line. "Mr. Julian? I just picked up the phone to call *you*, I didn't even hear a ring. I assume this is about what happened to Chester." Daphne then hit the intercom button so she and I could share in the conversation.

My father's voice boomed out scratchily through the phone's speaker. "Nobody even told me he'd gotten it. Did you take him to a doctor? What did he say?"

"No, he seems fine, just a little depressed."

"He's always depressed," said Dad, spreading vicious rumors about me behind my back. How dare he? And actually, considering that I'm an outcast teenage Gothic homosexual, I think I have an *extremely* cheery disposition. Dad continued, "But do you have any idea how he got the TB?"

"TB?" she repeated. "As in tuberculosis? I thought you were talking about those awful boys who beat him up the other day."

"Beat him up? I heard it was just a scratch. No, I'm calling because

Kyle just told me all the kids at school are being tested for tuberculosis because Chester has it."

"Are you sure? He doesn't look any paler than usual, and he's not coughing." Mrs. Van Vechten put her hand on my forehead. "And he doesn't have a fever. You do get a fever with TB, don't you?"

In a flash it became clear to me what had happened. "Daphne," I whispered, "what did you write on that note?"

"That you had consumption, just like you asked."

"I said to say 'advanced neurasthenia', not consumption!" I hissed.

"Neurasthenia, consumption, what's the difference?"

"Consumption is tuberculosis, and it's totally contagious."

Mrs. Van Vechten overheard us. "Just one moment, Mr. Julian," she said, putting my father on hold.

"I just thought consumption sounded more romantic," explained Daphne. "Neurasthenia sounds like brain cancer or something yucky."

"Darling, neurasthenia was what women in the nineteenth century used to get from wearing their corsets too tight," said Mrs. Van Vechten. "...Or was it a psychosomatic response to the Victorian repression of female sexuality?"

Daphne looked sheepish. "Well, it doesn't matter now. Sorry, Chester."

Mrs. Van Vechten patted her on the back. "Don't be sorry, honey. He shouldn't have lied. Look, Chester, I know I shouldn't be saying this, but lots and lots of people just don't go to high school and the sky doesn't fall on them. Why not get a General Equivalency Diploma and go off to college? You're smart enough, and your family's loaded thanks to little what's-his-face, and there's just no reason for you to suffer this way. My God, this is the twenty-first century!"

I picked up the phone. "Dad? I don't have tuberculosis, it's all a big misunderstanding."

"Good. You know we do worry about you. Mrs. Van Vechten has a bit of an unsavory reputation, or so your mother tells me."

"I have less than no interest in the gossip your current wife brings home from the beauty parlor. Actually, I wanted to make a tiny suggestion about my future."

"Why not?" he replied. "I can't think what to do with you."

"Why don't I drop out of high school and take a general equivalency exam?"

"That's not the best way to get into a good college, Chester."

"Let me put this to you gently, Dad. The kids at school kind of want to kill me."

"If a boy bothers you, just punch him in the nose, he'll respect you for it. You'd be surprised."

"I'd be surprised if I lived another day. This isn't like the olden days when you were a kid, they only attack me in packs."

"Well, what about private schools or boarding schools?" he asked.

"What about *no* schools?" I suggested. "I think the best thing for me would be to get away to where it's peaceful and there are no teenagers."

"Sometimes I feel that way myself," said Mrs. Van Vechten. Daphne scowled at her.

Dad sighed heavily. "Listen, I haven't mentioned this before, but Dora once said that if you ever needed a place to stay..."

Alright! "I love you, Dad! Yes, yes, tell her *yes!*"

We agreed I'd stay with Dora (Dad's second wife, or maybe just the second since I was born, I forget), study for my G.E.D. which I'll take in the spring, then go off to college and have a fabulous life. The frosting on the fudge is that she lives in San Francisco. Things are really looking up!

The next morning Mr. Finley suggested we try a different breakfast, including such novelties as bird eggs, toasted bread, and a fried tuber known as hash browns. All were passable, though no substitute for Belgian waffles. Our hosts also put several slices of burnt dead animal flesh on our plates which we tactfully asked them to remove, explaining that Zeeronians don't char and consume carcasses. Mr. Finley, on the other hand, ate his "bacon" with terrifying gusto. I almost lost my appetite, while Veeba tactfully excused herself to the ladies room where I strongly suspect she vomited.

After the meal we discussed our plans. Veeba expressed an interest in seeing as many hairdressing salons as possible, while Runchka requested a tour of the planet's botanical gardens. I had a more extensive agenda.

"I'd like to see stage productions of *Bye, Bye, Birdie, Angels In America*, and *Cats*. And I simply must visit Hollywood, Tokyo, the Eiffel Tower, the Taj Mahal, Las Vegas, and Old Navy. Nor do I want to leave before seeing the Grand Canyon, the Louvre, Carnaby Street, Tomorrowland, and Transylvania."

"I'll see what I can do, but please remember travel may be somewhat difficult because of the security precautions," said Mr. Finley, jotting down my wishes in a small notepad.

"And I want to visit Auschwitz, Universal Studios, Africa, and Mayberry," I added, forcing him to write even faster.

"Exactly how long do you intend to stay?" he asked.

"Not more than a couple of weeks. I left in the middle of term and I don't want my students to get too far behind."

"Well, I'll see which of these spots can be most quickly prepared for you. We might not be able to fit them all in." There was a knock at the door. "Ah, that will be Signora Fratellini," he said, as if I should know who that might be. He opened the door and a comely, elegant, and efficient looking woman in an appealing light blue skirt-suit strode purposefully into the room. Her large eyes were framed by thick black glasses, and her light blonde hair was pulled in a tight bun, producing a sort of Tippi Hedren-as-librarian effect I thought most attractive. "Runchka, Signora Fratellini will be your personal guide." Introductions ensued.

"When would you like to leave, Runchka?" she asked him/her.

"Immediately, if possible. I am most eager to undertake the cataloging of this world's fascinating botanical life." S/he turned to us. "I am certain that you, Norvex 7, and you, Your Flawlessness Veeba 22, will be able to adequately meet the challenge of responding to the Earthlings' questions in the upcoming press conference without me."

"Certainly," I replied, without even thinking. "We'll be fine." Runchka threw a few clothes in a bag and unceremoniously left. I started wondering if I'd made a mistake in letting him/her get separated from us when a Mr. Irving Metzenbaum arrived and announced he was to be Veeba's personal guide. He was practically the mirror image of Mr. Finley, even speaking in the same suave manner.

"Your Excellency, it is indeed a great honor to meet you. I understand you desire to see our planet's hair salons. May I suggest we begin in Paris, France? There are a multitude of truly wonderful stylists there. I have taken the liberty of arranging for a plane to be at our disposal."

"I'm not getting in one of those airborne deathtraps again," Veeba declared firmly. "Why don't you stay here with us at the hotel and show me around New York? This city looks to be of a fair size. I'm sure you have plenty of salons here, don't you?"

"My only desire is to accommodate your wishes," he said with a slight bow.

"Oh, we'd better not even start on my wishes or we'll all be in a lot of trouble!" she responded, laughing gaily. Mr. Metzenbaum and Mr. Finley smiled at her little joke without mirth. "Seriously though, I do have a request. I can't seem to open the windows, and I'd like to get some fresh air in here."

"I'm afraid they've been sealed shut with bulletproof, shatter-resistant glass," revealed Mr. Metzenbaum, "for your safety."

"Never mind then. You're both dismissed," she said waiving our hosts away as if they were robo-maids.

Although I knew we were being eavesdropped on, I vented to Veeba. "Could you believe how transparent they were about trying to separate us three? I wonder if it was all right to let Runchka go off like that?"

Veeba put on a sad face. "We'll just have to struggle along without Runchka's sparkling personality." As we giggled she jumped on my back, playfully wrestled me to the ground. Soon we found ourselves making love for the first time in days.

"Where do you suppose the hidden cameras are?" asked Veeba while straddling me. She's a terrible show-off.

"Don't worry, I'm sure they can see us just fine," I assured her. Afterwards, as we lay on the bed, I rested my head on her shoulder and we went channel-surfing on the television machine. It was quite a pleasant snuggle save for the disturbing fact that we could always hear the faint rumble of the hostile crowd only a few blocks away. After a while we roused ourselves to prepare for the conference.

A ballroom in the hotel's basement was rigged up to serve as our auditorium, obviating the necessity of traversing the dangerous city streets. Veeba put us in yellow transparent jumpsuits with sleek, chic lines, and matching pink thigh boots, gloves, and goggles. Our outfits were topped off with short pink wigs set in masses of ringlets. Ever the show-stealer, Veeba gave herself a huge jeweled diadem.

Misters Finley and Metzenbaum arrived to escort us to the ballroom. "So you're wearing that, are you?" asked Mr. Finley.

"Don't you like it, Mr. Metzenbaum?" asked Veeba who had great fun pretending to be unable to tell our guides apart and calling them by each other's names.

"They'll be seated behind a table," whispered Mr. Metzenbaum into Mr. Finley's ear.

"It's fine," Mr. Finley assured Veeba.

It suddenly hit me. "Oh, our transparent suits..." *The genitals!* I almost forgot, nudity is forbidden except in remote tribal villages and Off, Off Broadway. "We'll remember from now on," I promised.

Once inside the auditorium our hosts led us onto a stage and gave us cushy chairs to sit in and the coffee drink, which both Veeba and I were rapidly falling in love with. We were lit for the television cameras by bright spotlights that Veeba insisted be dimmed with some rosy gels, the obtaining of which delayed our conference by half an hour. We utilized the time by drinking more coffee and applying extra makeup. Finally several dozen reporters were admitted to the room where they sat in the sea of chairs before us in their dull, dark suits with serious looks on their pinched, nervous faces. Earthlings don't really have the knack of making everything a party as we do on Zeeron.

The first question was remarkably easy. "Why do Zeeronians and Earthlings look identical? Are we of the same species?"

"I'm glad you asked that! Approximately seventy thousand years ago a mysterious race known as the Fraznaks sent radiation signals throughout the universe which caused indigenous life forms on planets capable of sustaining humanoids to evolve into replicas of themselves. As a result, humanoids from any of the 231 populated planets are so similar they can interbreed, even the parthenogenetic Felkusians, or the Tygonians who have three sexes. The Fraznaks were actually contacted at one point a few dozen millennia ago. Unfortunately they'd lost interest in their science project, by which I mean us, and were busy bringing rocks to life. They barely gave the joint Felkusian/ Mithribian expedition the time of day. I think we've all been feeling a bit snubbed on that account since then."

"Do you know where the Fraznaks came from? Did they give any clues as to our purpose? Do they worship God?" asked the next reporter, unfairly cramming three questions in at once.

"I'm afraid they didn't say where they came from. As for our purpose, it would seem that we're simply a by-product of an abandoned science experiment, entirely purposeless. As for God, I'm afraid we didn't ask." At this point two reporters (from religious newspapers, I was later told) walked out, loudly declaring that we were obviously phonies since our account of human origin contradicted their primitive superstitions.

"Could you tell us about your economy and technology?" asked one serious-looking chap in the front row.

"We enjoy universal material opulence and machines perform all labor that is tedious or distressing to us. People spend their time doing as they choose, the most popular careers being those of hairdresser, actor, musician, fine artist, fashion designer, gossip columnist, go-go dancer, and party-thrower."

"We don't work hard, we don't work long, and we don't do windows," said Veeba in an assay at levity.

I continued. "And we don't use money. Everyone does everything for free. Even bartering is considered to be in bad taste, although some unsavory elements do stoop to it."

Veeba piped in. "You see, we do things only to be *fabulous*. To do something delightfully well makes you fabulous, and to do something absolutely original and enchanting makes you *really* fabulous. It would be un-fabulous to expect something in return for being fabulous. To refuse to do something for someone else, provided they asked nicely, would be most un-fabulous. Somehow it all works out and everything gets done that really needs to get done. And then some!"

"Do you have pollution?" asked a young man squinting at us from the side of the hall.

"No. It is considered the height of rudeness to inflict one's filth on others. It's simply not done."

The next query involved sports. "We have no competitive sports at all. No teams, scores, points, winners, losers, or rules. For recreation we have orgies, nightclubbing, and performance art. Nor do we need exercise as we implant microcomputers in our brains that order our bodies to stay fit regardless of how little we move about."

"What of government?" asked a prim gentleman with

distinguished, graying temples.

"We prefer to do without it. Nor do we have any police force, planning committee, or authorities of any kind. You see, after the first few thousand years of cultural development, war becomes unprofitable and people become too mature to want to impose their taste on others. Soon after that prosperity, generosity, and good manners combine to eliminate commerce and private property. On Zeeron what happened was that everything got borrowed and borrowed and everybody sort of lost track of who anything belonged to. Without war or property there was no compelling reason to keep a government around."

"How do you settle disputes?" asked the same man. Veeba fielded the question.

"The involved parties' hairdressers settle things since they know all the dirt. Hairdressers also take charge in an emergency like a natural disaster, or when someone goes mad. We're not compensated for taking on all that extra responsibility and work like your Earth leaders are though," she sniveled bitterly.

"Actually, *Your Excellency*," I felt compelled to remind her, "I do think hairdressers get better seats in food galleries, are invited to more parties, and have better looking lovers."

"Oh, there are a few compensating perks," Veeba conceded.

Next, I anticipated a question. "Now, if I know my Earthlings, I bet someone will ask about family life. Baby Zeeronians come from hatcheries which produce infants who're adopted by people needing apprentices or wanting someone around for company. The average Zeeronian achieves maturity and leaves the hatchery at the age of thirty-seven and has a life expectancy of two hundred and fifty-five. As for mating habits, people marry whomever or whatever strikes their fancy, and stay together as long as it amuses them to do so. We have no sexually transmitted diseases, economic incentives for marriage, or moral objections to sex, so everybody is free to decide what pleases them the most."

A matronly woman asked, "Don't any women give birth biologically?"

Veeba set her straight. "Not since we learned how to hatch babies.

Who wants to get fat and have a living creature eat your insides? Oh, certainly not. Never." Many of the Earthlings were looking a bit put out at this point. "Of course, I'm sure your barbarian customs are quite nice, too!" she added in a truly pathetic attempt at diplomacy.

"You obviously have the capacity for space travel, what other technological marvels have been developed on ⟶on?" asked a large man in the front.

"The basis for most of our technology is the trism, an antigravity device we use to create perpetual motion machines which can generate unlimited energy. Turn a trism up all the way and *whoosh!* you've got a spacecraft-worthy propulsion system. Travel between planets is as frequent for us as travel between cities is for you here on Earth. We've also wiped out most diseases, developed the home skin rejuvenator, and we grow our protein in petri-dishes so we never have to eat dead animals. And the protein isn't all fatty and gristly, either," I said, thinking of that morning's disgusting bacon.

"And we have robots to act as maids," added Veeba. "No household drudgery."

"Do you have prejudice, hostility between ethnic groups, or social unrest?" asked a man in a fez.

"No," I responded.

"What of relations between the sexes?" asked a voice from the back.

"Although male domination is normal on many primitive worlds, absolute equality is the rule on all civilized planets."

A woman stood up and fixed me with a steely glare. "What about your weaponry? What armaments do you have at your disposal?"

Veeba responded. "You see we have these gun things big as houses that can destroy whole planets in the blink of an eye. And don't think we don't use them, we do, just *all* the time! Whenever a planet gets out of line, it's kerplooey!" She clapped her hands to demonstrate. Veeba's flip delivery seemed to undermine the seriousness of the threats she was making, which were nonsensical anyway, given what we'd revealed about the peaceful nature of our advanced society. As the audience didn't seem to know what to make of her assertion I quickly asked for another question, hoping to avoid the need for further deception.

A slim man with an intelligent face spoke up. "You have," he began hesitantly, "achieved a technologically advanced and enlightened society free of coercion, violence, and superstition. You live in harmony with each other, nature, and your own instincts. What would you consider to be your problems?"

"Our civilization is not the product of any intellectual superiority on our part," I began as Veeba shot me a look that said, "Oh please!" I ignored her and continued, "We are mentally and physically your identical cousins, as it were. We've simply enjoyed the benefit of some several thousand years more cultural evolution. Although we've managed to achieve much, as individuals we still suffer the same difficulties as you, albeit not exacerbated by as many social problems. We must endure vanity, jealousy, unprincipled ambition, unrequited love, boredom, stupidity, and occasionally even bad manners." The reporters seemed happy with my little speech.

"Why are you here? Why now?" requested a calm middle-aged woman in a print dress.

"As you know, I'm a professor of Earth Studies at Zeeron's prestigious Institute for the Study of Quaint and Primitive Cultures. I've spent decades examining broadcasts from your world and I'm extremely fond of your popular culture. Nor am I alone in my tastes. You might be surprised that many Earthlings, including Burt Bacharach, Pizzicato 5, Nina Hagen, The Archies, Devo, Beck, Deeelite, Lesley Gore, Marvin Gaye, The Fantastic Plastic Machine, Abba, The Isley Brothers, Blondie, and the B-52s, just to mention those who come to mind, have had hits on our world. There's also a cinema in Braxo City devoted entirely to Earthly cinema. I've seen films there such as *Casino Royale, The 5000 Fingers of Dr. T, Bell Book and Candle, How to Succeed in Business Without Really Trying, Breakfast at Tiffany's, What a Way to Go, Vegas in Space, My Fair Lady, The Trouble with Angels, Hustler White, A Hard Day's Night, Polyester, Skidoo,* and *Georgie Girl* again, just to mention those which come to mind, receive unanimous tongue clickings, our version of your standing ovation. We like you! We really like you! Unfortunately we can't pay royalties having no money and no exchange system. You understand, I'm sure." During this last response I was aware that many of the journalists looked perplexed and some seemed to be smirking.

"You've mentioned your affection for our television, movies, and popular music. Do your people feel similarly about our more serious cultural achievements?" asked a tweedy man with a carefully clipped salt and pepper beard.

"Since Zeeronians don't suffer much, I'm afraid our general public doesn't particularly relate to your more serious output. Knowing how difficult life is on your planet, though, I myself am a great fan of many works with graver themes. Movies like *Lady in a Cage*, *West Side Story*, *Carrie*, *Logan's Run*, *Sunset Boulevard*, *The Red Balloon*, *Boys in the Band*, *All About Eve*, and *Heathers* come to mind, as well as anything from Tennessee Williams, and the music of Dusty Springfield, Soft Cell, Roxy Music, The Sex Pistols, The Supremes, The New York Dolls, The Smiths, and early David Bowie."

The same tweedy man, looking put out, questioned me yet again. "What of Beethoven, Brahms, and Bach? What of Shakespeare? What of our operas and ballets? What of our more elevated cinema?"

I cut him off before he could question me about more tedious drivel. "On Zeeron we consider all art without prejudice, and our extremely advanced and objective opinion is that most of your popular culture is far more vibrant and interesting than the so-called highbrow works your planetary elites hold in such great reverence. Many programs which you dismiss as meaningless entertainment actually contain important insights and ideas. A colleague of mine, Elagjop 44, for instance, wrote his thesis on the archetypes of identity found in *Gilligan's Island*. His theory is that amongst all humanoids there are 343 personality types, each comprised of differing combinations of three of the show's seven characters. Everyone has one character they most resemble, their Type, another character with whom they share a few traits, their Latent Type, and a third character, their Permeating Type, whose personality ineffably suffuses their behavior. I, for example, am a Professor Type, with a Latent Mary Ann, and a Thurston Howell III Permeating. While, as I recall, Her Magnificence here, was a..." I'd forgotten but she helped me out.

"He said I was a Ginger Grant, with a Latent Mrs. Howell, and a Gilligan Permeating, though I think he must be all wrong about the last part." The audience, to my annoyance, seemed to find all this funny. Mr. Finley handed me a small note suggesting we adjourn the conference immediately, which I did.

Dear Diary,                                    Saturday, Oct. 12

Mom #2, or Dora, as she prefers me to call her, was only married to Dad for a couple of years. They had irreconcilable differences; he's an emotionally barren careerist striver and she's a crusading New Age loon. They started arguing as soon as they got home from their honeymoon. This was before Kyle was famous, so we didn't have a maid, and Dad was always harping on Dora to do more housework. She'd pretend not to be, but you could tell she was totally angry. Like Dad would come home and ask, "Why is this house such a sty?" and she'd say, "Howard, I feel this is the right time for me to explore my untapped potential, but I'm hearing that you feel my pursuit of enlightenment is inappropriate, that somehow it's interfering with my wife role." And he'd say, "No, Dora, I'm just wondering why this place is such a dump. I can appreciate your need for spiritual growth, but I feel you could choose to appreciate *my* needs for clean shirts and socks, or a nice home." And she'd say, "I'd like to explore why your agendas are dependent on my actions. Perhaps we should try integrating our value systems a little more, and stop playing 'the blame game.' "

And so on. When I think of Dora, I always remember this one day when Kyle and I were being little brats and refused to eat some dry and not very sweet carrot cake she made, demanding some Hostess chocolate something-or-other instead. She got us into the car and drove us to a farm owned by some friends of hers about an hour north of town. When we arrived she led us to this big field and pulled this carrot out of the ground and held it up to us. We were giggling out of nervousness because we thought she was going to hit us with it, adding physical to culinary abuse. Instead she began this sermon, "Behold the mighty carrot!" She really wanted us to understand the marvel of the carrot, to appreciate the miracle that we could even have the chance of ever eating carrots.

As Dad drove me to San Francisco, Drusilla in the back seat cooing at the "breathtaking" California coastline, he tried to impart his accumulated worldly wisdom to me. "You set the limits in life, Chester. You can have *anything* you want if you're willing to pay the price." I nodded, hoping he'd shut up or change the subject. No such luck. "I'm not sure you understand that yet, the part about paying the price. People *will* respect you, but you have to earn it, and sometimes you have to compromise. And I'm not talking just about what you want, but what you believe in too. Often as not, you realize later on that the people you thought were full of B.S. knew what they're talking about and you were in the wrong. Do you hear what I'm saying? Sometimes it doesn't hurt to bite your tongue."

"If you can have anything so long as you pay the price, then what's the price for being respected without having to compromise?" I asked.

"I'm afraid that might just be pointless martyrdom," suggested my brave father.

"What's the price for being respected without having to compromise *or* be a martyr?" I asked, not really trying to be difficult, but wanting him to see the flaws in his philosophy of sniveling conformity.

"Um," he looked back at Drusilla as if she'd have an answer, but she was busy gazing at the majesty of nature. "That might be working hard in the field of your choice so that people have no alternative but to respect you."

"And what's the price for being respected without martyrdom, hard work, or compromise?" I angled.

He narrowed his eyes. "Now you're being silly."

"Anyway, I'm *not* unwilling to compromise," I protested. "If my peers offered to make me a punching bag every other week, or the teachers insulted my intelligence and mocked my opinions only every other day..." I was stopped in mid-sentence by the sight of San Francisco's highrises poking through the fog. "Wow. Home."

"Your home is back in Saint Dymphna with me and your father," said Drusilla from the back seat. She's a big local booster and can't bear the thought of anyone finding happiness anywhere other than the ugly little town where she sits on the Chamber of Commerce. "Tell him, Howard." She poked Dad's back.

"Of course, your home is with us. But as long as you do stay with Dora I expect you to treat her with respect. She may have a lot of, well... ideas, but she's a responsible adult and you're to abide by her wishes as long as you're her guest."

"I will be obedient," I assured him in a monotone that was just this side of sarcasm. "And I'll be real careful about *ideas*."

"And if you change your mind about wanting to see a psychiatrist..."

"Daaaaad." I hope I don't inherit his tendency to be incredibly annoying. We exited the freeway and passed by several spooky old Victorian houses. "Those are really neat looking, sort of haunted," I observed.

"They're just charming," said Drusilla in her real estate agent voice. Then we both caught sight of a gingerbread-style house painted electric purple and lime green with a huge stained glass window with a scene of some dolphins playing in front of a pyramid. A flag with a unicorn on it flew from a second floor window. "People should respect the character of old buildings," she sniffed disapprovingly. What sort of person would do that to a house? Religious cultists? Colorblind hippies?

"And remember what I told you about, um, sex," whispered Dad.

"Don't worry, I'll wait till I meet Mr. Right. Then you can spring for a big wedding with lots of presents." Dad parked the car in front of a dirty white stucco apartment building which I could see by the address was Dora's. I leaned over the back seat to grab my suitcase and saw Drusilla looking weirded out.

"Usually the bride's parents pay for the wedding, but who pays if there's no bride?" She really looked shaken. "Do the grooms' parents split it fifty-fifty, or what?"

"I'll check Miss Manners,"I promised her, lugging my suitcase up the walk. I rang buzzer #3. Moments later Dora opened the door looking totally retro, though probably not on purpose, in a colorful Mexican peasant blouse and a maroon velvet maxi-skirt. I'd forgotten how Dora always has this radiant smile, like she's way too happy.

"Chester, look how you've grown. I haven't seen you in ages!" I let her hug me, though I dislike unnecessary physical contact.

"Howard, Beverly," Dora nodded cordially at my soon-to-be ex-parents, who'd heaved themselves out of the car and stood behind me looking ill at ease. As the geezers talked on the porch I went in to examine my new home. The living room was comfortably messy, full of dying houseplants, mismatched antique furniture, and old magazines. There was a dysfunctional fireplace and a mantel on which sat a bunch of huge, spectacular crystals. As I looked at a Georgia O'Keefe print on the wall a small dog ran up to me and began yapping. I leaned over to pet the little beast, but it retreated in terror. The adults came in, and after copious goodbyes, a manly handshake from Dad, and a kiss on the cheek from Drusilla, seventeen years of captivity ended. I'm free!

Sort of.

Dora gestured for me to sit down on the couch as she sunk into a wicker chair and folded herself into the lotus position. With her slightly unkempt mane of white hair haloing around her head she looked like some ancient sage. "Now, Chester, your father has told me all about the things you've been through, and I want to say from the start I think your parents, Howard in particular, are not behaving in an enlightened manner at all. Many of my friends and neighbors are gay, and I have great sympathy for what your people have suffered."

"Uhm, that's good, I mean, thanks," I said, wondering if that was the right thing to say.

"Now, a few things about the apartment. I'm afraid the walls in this building are really thin, so we've got to be pretty quiet or the neighbors complain."

"I'll use my headphones when I listen to music," I promised.

"And try to be quiet coming and going out. I'm driven half crazy by the man in number two slamming his door all the time. Now, as for me, I'm not here much. I get up at seven so I can open my shop, Crystal Blue Persuasion, by nine. I have yoga class on Monday night, tai chi Tuesdays and Thursdays, Japanese cooking on Wednesday, and "The Interplanetary Friendship Committee" on Fridays. Sometimes we meet here. I'll try to give you advance notice. It can get pretty crowded, though of course you have your room." She stood up and beckoned me to follow her down the hall where she opened the door to a small, little, tiny closet-like space.

"This was my meditation room. I've moved the shrine into the corner; feel free to use it whenever you need to get your head together."

"Sure thing," I said trying to sound perky, like someone who would never ever need to get his head together.

Despite the size of my room, the new setup is a pretty sweet deal. Minimal adult supervision, no school. The only drawback is that between work and the exploration of her human potential Dora never has enough time to walk Gwendolyn, the venomous little purebred Scottish terrier who nipped at my heels when I came in. To earn my way (above and beyond the cash Daddums is sending her to keep me out of sight and out of mind), I am to take the precious pooch for walkies every morning and evening. Dora seems like she's really glad I'm here, though of course it's only till I get my G.E.D., a matter of months not years, so she can afford to be gracious.

Sitting here in my room (which measures in at five feet by eight feet) it occurs to me that Dora is way, and I mean *way*, more downscale than Dad. Until I become a famous and successful whatever-it-is I'm going to be, I'll have to get used to gritty urban poverty. Besides a futon (and the shrine: a small table with a creepy statuette of some Hindu goddess, a few seashells, a dried-up orange, a little box of pebbles, four candles, and an incense holder), the only furniture is a dresser. I set my suitcase on top of it (unpacking seems silly, I'll be gone in less than a year) and put up a few posters to make the place a little more *me*. Then I called Daphne to let her know I'd arrived in one piece. She's insanely jealous that I get to live in San Francisco while she has to languish in a suburban cultural vacuum, and managed to invite herself to come up and visit tomorrow. It's a four hour bus ride each way, but she doesn't seem to care. I guess she can do her homework while she rides.

Dear Diary, Tuesday, Oct. 15

Daphne arrived Sunday shortly after noon. She must have gotten up at the crack of dawn, poor thing. We took BART (the local subway) downtown to do some shopping. The funny thing was that everybody but us fell asleep on the train. I thought it might be that there's not enough oxygen in the cars, but later on Dora, who did her thesis on Native American religion, told me BART runs over sacred Indian burial grounds and as a result the system is cursed, which used to make the doors open while the trains were running, but now only causes commuter fatigue and excessive fare hikes. I couldn't tell if she actually believes that or what.

Downtown San Francisco was crowded full of yuppie shoppers, tourists, bums, and more than a few cute boys. After checking out a few dull stores (cinnamon-guyabana shampoo, who needs it?) Daphne insisted we go to Haight Street where there're some hipper retail outlets. The bus ride was the exact opposite of BART - filthy, noisy, smelly, and, thanks to some thuggish adolescent gangs, scary. Nobody slept.

Almost every corner on Haight was crowded with drugged-out dirty kids in a confusing collage of youth culture styles. Punk rock Deadheads. Modern primitive Ravers. When we spotted some hippie kids, Daphne tried taking their pictures to let them know how quaint they were and this one totally cute boy with dirty blond dreadlocks kept insisting we give him a dollar. Even wearing a tie-dye shirt and torn army fatigues with big ugly brown boots, he was so gorgeous he *still* looked good. Life is incredibly unfair. Then we went to a head shop and Daphne bought a bong in the shape of a garbage can for some low-life she's dating (it seems the optometrist is long gone). After that I insisted we go into this clothing store, DMZ, where everything was displayed on jagged industrial-looking metal bars which stuck out of concrete blocks at strange angles. It looked as if a bomb had gone off destroying the building and scattering clothes everywhere.

I found a baby-blue nylon jacket with a safety-orange stripe that made me look positively human, maybe even chic. Daphne hated it.

"Chester, why are you purchasing that thing?" she groaned.

"This is what all the cute boys are wearing. And the vertical stripe makes me look thinner."

"If all the cute boys jumped off a cliff I suppose you'd jump off, too," she replied.

"Of course, naturally," I shot back.

"You look like some rave person." Daphne really hated this jacket.

"Does everything I wear have to be black?" I couldn't believe I had to defend my fashion decisions to Daphne. "Marilyn Manson doesn't even wear black anymore."

"Remember, black is slimming."

"Oh, Daphne, it's just a jacket."

She let it drop but I could tell she was put out. Back at Dora's we just hung around and managed to stay awake all night talking courtesy of an economy size jar of instant coffee. After a few hours I started feeling nauseous, and in the morning Dora found me hunched over at the kitchen table with Daphne combing the cabinets for some Alka Seltzer or Pepto Bismol.

"What are you two doing up?" she asked, looking confused and bleary-eyed.

"Nothing," explained Daphne.

"Have you got anything for a stomachache?" I asked.

"There's some peppermint tea in the cupboard by the sink. What're these?" Dora pointed at the Maxwell House and non-dairy creamer as if they were roaches.

"We were trying to stay awake till eight to see the rerun of *Hangin' In There* on channel twenty-two," explained Daphne. "But now Chester isn't feeling well."

"I'll never drink coffee again," I pledged.

"Your problem is the non-dairy creamer," said Dora authoritatively, as she examined the container. "It's not organic."

"Neither is the coffee," said Daphne. Suddenly the syrupy opening theme to *Hangin' In There* sounded from Dora's minuscule portable black and white television.

"Will my agony never cease?" I beseeched the heavens. After fixing me the tea, which did help a little, Dora sat with Daphne and me as we watched the show in mute horror. The episode was all about Kyle accidentally eating garlic and onions before a date. In televisionland even a tiny bit of either turns you into a human stinkbomb.

"People don't smell badly after eating onions and garlic!" insisted Dora. "The media are in cahoots with the A.M.A. to keep the public in the dark about the medicinal powers of herbs and vegetables. You know why? They're cheaper and safer than all the synthetic medicines that all the doctors and drug manufacturers are pushing and making money from." I was glad she realized how awful Kyle's show was, but somehow I can't imagine the scriptwriters getting a call from some doctor telling them to scare the public away from vegetables. That's just insane. Maybe Dora is paranoid. On the other hand, maybe she's right. I mean, who knows?

This evening, after Daphne had gone back to Saint Dymphna, Dora asked me if she and I were shacking up. Why doesn't anyone believe I'm a homosexual? I guess it would help if I got a boyfriend. From now on I'm going to try dressing more like a contemporary sexy gay boy and less like Edward Scissorhands. I don't care *what* Daphne thinks. Give me a date or give me death!

Dear Diary,                                        Wednesday, Oct. 16

I spent the day exploring the neighborhood which has a lot of craft and novelty shops full of hokey stuff to clutter up all the yuppie homes around here: handmade Guatemalan spice racks, imitation early American butter churns turned into flower pots, two thousand dollar imported German waffle irons. There's one really cool bookstore with all these magazines which I was skimming through, despite the crotchety old coot behind the counter glaring at me and then pointedly staring at a "No Reading" sign.

I found a magazine there called *Ganymede*, especially for young homosexuals. I didn't know such a thing existed since somehow the bookstore in downtown St. Dymphna (surprise, surprise) doesn't carry it. It's mostly articles about gay rights (nice, but no big whoop) and some profiles of well-adjusted, attractive, talented young guys, several of whom I'd marry in an instant. There's also a photo spread of what I guess is supposed to be a typical gay teen picnic in which totally posed-looking, half-naked stud-boys with no body fat lie around on a lawn, get in a water fight, play football, and eat sandwiches while smiling seductively into the camera. To read *Ganymede* you'd think the world consists entirely of gymnasts with capped teeth. Skin blemishes, the greatest challenge facing today's youth, gay *or* straight, go entirely unmentioned. Totally depressing. All the homophobia in the world could disappear tomorrow and I bet I'd still never get laid because of my skanky skin.

I was about to leave the store when I saw Kyle's face beaming at me from the cover of a nearby *Celebriteen* magazine. Out of curiosity I flipped to his interview. Next to a photo of him grinning toothily and holding a surfboard (he doesn't surf), is a pack of lies calculated to make him seem lovable. His "fave food" is *not* hamburgers, it's ChocoBuff shakes. He does not like girls with career goals and self-respect, he likes pretty, popular girls who giggle at his stupid jokes. He was quoted as saying, "I think it's important to put education first!" which makes me doubt the person who made up the interview has even met Kyle. Just when I thought I was as nauseous as humanly possible, I read Kyle's advice to his peers: "Be yourself, think your own thoughts, don't give in to peer pressure." It's enough to make you scream. Actually, I did scream and the man behind the counter asked me to leave the store, which I was all too happy to do.

Dora made this super healthy lentil loaf for dinner which she said was practically fat-free, and it was actually good. Why do people always make fun of health food and say it tastes like cardboard? After dinner I looked at this book Dad gave me on how to pass your G.E.D. test. It was written for morons.

Dear Diary,                                          Friday, Oct. 18
I really should write more often, but now that I'm a human being instead of a high school student I have other things to do. Getting into

a bar and standing near, and sort of even speaking with, actual male homosexuals being one. This miracle was made possible by Daphne's current love interest, Klaus, the one she bought the bong for. Apparently he's a cocaine dealer which is kind of tired if you ask me. Why couldn't he deal morphine, absinthe, or opium - something a little less Hollywood? Oh well, I should be grateful because all I had to do was give Daphne a small picture of myself when she was up here last weekend and he got me a passport to adulthood, i.e., a California Drivers License clearly stating I'm twenty-one years of age. It arrived by FedEx yesterday, so last night I looked through this gay weekly free paper, *Orpheus*, that has a newsrack on 24th Street, right out in the open. It was full of ads for local bars and clubs which mostly showed half-naked muscle men and promised techno or house music. Ugh. There was one though, The Barn, whose ad showed a bunch of cute young guys laughing and dancing with all these farm animals. I decided to go there.

The I.D. worked like a charm. I went in and ordered a beer, which smelled gross, tasted bad, and made me nauseous. I've never really liked drinking, except maybe for Mrs. Van Vechten's pancakes. One of the worst experiences I ever had was when Daphne decided we should live on champagne and flowers like some decadent author she'd read about and showed up at my place with two bottles of André pink and a bouquet of edible nasturtiums. In forty-five minutes I got a splitting headache and my stomach started doing the Macarena. Vomiting followed. Daphne didn't do much better and as soon as we recovered we went off to the Snaque Shaque and started scarfing solid food like there was no tomorrow.

The Barn really does look like a barn except there's all these antique children's toys from the '70s on the walls and Ms. Pac Man machines. It was crowded with cute guys, mostly in their twenties, who did seem to all be dancing, laughing and having fun, just like in the ad. The music (something called Hypno-House by DJ Mergatroid) was okay, but so loud I had a hard time eavesdropping. After roaming around for half an hour I finally sat down in a corner near the pool table and tried to look approachable. Nobody came up to talk to me so I started thinking about how pretty the sky had looked earlier that night as I walked from Dora's to the bar. There were several different kinds of clouds reflecting the bright moonlight and you could see the craters on the moon, which was orange and enormous like The Great Pumpkin. All that was set against a velvety black sky with a few bright stars twinkling away. Totally Maxfield Parrish.

I imagined myself standing on a hill holding hands with a boy, staring at the cosmos. It would be the 19th century, no compulsory high school education, no T.V., no *Hangin' In There*. I'd be a poet and my lover would be a freedom fighter from the Paris commune. In between writing and fighting the powers that be, we'd make mad, passionate love in our garret or while strolling through the golden fields of the nearby countryside. I was just envisioning his cloak and the lovable way a lock of thick black hair would curl over his forehead when my daydream was interrupted by the arrival of a reasonably attractive guy in baggy blue jeans, a tank top that said "Fayetteville Women's Basketball League," and a blonde buzzcut which complemented his Aryan good looks in an übermenschy sort of way.

"Anyone sitting here?" he asked, gesturing at the seven inches of bare bench between me and a young man who looked a lot like my interrogator except that his tank top had the number sixty-nine on it and he was sporting a knit hat.

"No," I said, mushing myself against the wall to make more room for the new guy I hoped was planning to seduce me.

"Nice sky out tonight," I said.

"Uh, I guess," was his reply. I waited what seemed like an eternity, then tried again.

"Don't you think the moon looked romantic?" I asked, tilting my head in what I hoped was a coquettish (or whatever the male equivalent is) way.

"I dunno," he said, turning away from me in a manner that could easily have been mistaken for rudeness. Just then a friend of his came up and engaged him in a long conversation about an art gallery opening they'd both attended earlier that night. They went over who'd been there, who'd slept with the painter, what parties were going on afterwards, and who was cute. Neither one mentioned the art, even in passing. I decided I could never marry such a vulgar Philistine, even if he was sort of cute, and retreated to the back of the bar to stand against the wall. Everyone around me seemed to be in cliques who already knew each other and I couldn't figure out how to meet anyone so I decided to leave. While I was walking home the fog came in, giving me a chill and hiding the beautiful sky. I want to meet to an eligible bachelor as soon as possible so I can start going on dates to exotic restaurants and theaters. If I never have stand around alone in a noisy, crowded bar again it'll be too soon for me.

Dear Diary,                                        Saturday, Oct. 19

I was channel-surfing this morning when I saw my hateful and carefully groomed brother walking along a beach in a dressy-yet-casual black tee shirt and sportscoat combination that made him look like a miniature Mafia hit man. I came in after the show had started, but I figured out that he was narrating a documentary about a T.V. special, "Young Hollywood Cares," done to benefit a children's clinic. Essentially it was an *American Gladiator*-style battle between the veejays from PopTV and the cast of *Muscle Beach Patrol,* a show about scantily-clad police. The contest took place during what Kyle called "a killer heat wave," and the two over-coiffed, over-tanned, and over-muscled teams seemed wilted in their body-revealing spandex athletic wear. During the first contest they fought with what looked like giant foamrubber toothbrushes while waterskiing. Next they had a tug of war arranged so that the losers would fall down an artificial cliff and be suspended by bungee cords. Finally there was a race to the top of a miniature Matterhorn built specially for the occasion on Venice Beach. As the rich, famous, and beautiful competed they were watched by a crowd of poor, obscure, and sickly children. Now and then the kids would be shown cowering in the shade and clapping , it was never exactly clear for whom or what. The documentary also focused heavily on the difficult working conditions of the techies, who all seemed to be overweight men with beards and baseball caps. They drank a lot of diet sodas and one of them actually keeled over from heat prostration.

The only person who didn't seem to mind the heat was celebrity judge Brick Roemer, the retired basketball star who'd declared for Christ shortly after his drug conviction. He was wearing a three-piece suit and not even sweating. He kept telling the other judges, supermodel/anorexia survivor Kristé and Jedediah Cooper Bradshaw (I don't think *anyone* remembers why he's famous), that the really incredible thing was not the amazing physical prowess of the stars, but the bravery of the kids. After the *Muscle Beach Patrol* team won, they ran around giving each other high-fives and screaming "Yesss!" while the veejays goodnaturedly shook their hands and vowed to get even next year. As a parting shot we were treated to the sight of a deeply tanned Beach Patroller with rippling muscles and frizzy David Hasselfhoff-style hair holding up a little girl with head gear, crutches, and a terrified look on her face so she could kiss Kyle, who is inexplicably her idol. I almost threw up my fat-free bacon'n'cheese croissantwich.

After watching that nightmare I went out exploring. Cities are much prettier than suburbs, even if they are dirty decrepit concrete jungles full of lunatics and bums. Saint Dymphna may be clean and safe, but it has no history and no surprises. That line has a nice ring to it, I'll have to remember to spring it on Dad next time he calls. No history and no surprises. Anyway, rode BART from 24th Street to Powell, then took a northbound cable car, getting off before reaching Fisherman's Wharf and all that tourist garbage. I don't know what neighborhood I was in, but walking around was fun because there were all these cool Art Deco apartment buildings, weird Asian knick-knack shops, and bizarre people to look at.

Heading in the direction I thought was towards Market Street I ended up getting really lost and was about to ask someone for directions when I saw a small hair salon called Mr. Larry's Beauty Boutique. It had a huge window in which a statue of Michelangelo's David stood in a fountain surrounded by fake ivy and plants. The inside was done entirely in peach, white, and gold, and was lit by an enormous crystal chandelier. There was a Models Wanted for Free Haircuts sign on the door, so I went in.

"Well, hello to yooouuu!" sang out a portly man in white sansabelt slacks, a mauve dress shirt with an enormous collar, and a gold silk scarf knotted around his neck.

"You're looking for hair models?" I inquired.

"Yes, indeedy. Here, let me get a better look at you." He sat me down in a chair and turned me toward the mirror. "Hmmm," he said, not looking very pleased. He tried to run his fingers through my hair which was impossible due to all the tangles and hairspray. "My... your hair... Is it this way on purpose? You certainly have a lot of hair, which is good. It's just that... Well, no matter, I can fix it. I'm Mr. Larry, the proprietor of this establishment, and I've been styling hair in this location since you were probably about knee-high to a grasshopper. I've seen all the styles come and go, and this one has to go. Ha, ha. Seriously though, I think you should go much, much shorter. Don't you agree?"

I looked at my gigantic, snarled mass of hair in the mirror. Excessive crimping and Clairol blue-black dye had damaged it pretty badly. It felt like straw and the ends were frizzy. "Yeah," I agreed, "short would be good."

"Perhaps you'd like something like this?" He handed me a magazine.

"Young Sun Worshippers 1965," I read.

"Nothing more than photographs of perfectly natural young men enjoying perfectly natural outdoor sports in the perfectly natural nude," he said defensively. "Just look at the hair." The handsome guys playing volleyball on the cover were sporting pompadours or DAs or whatever you call them. Like Elvis, sort of.

"Well, maybe something a little less greasy looking."

He found another picture inside. "What about something like this?" he asked pointing to a youth romping in a forest au natural. His hair had a sort of Mod/Brit Pop look to it, like that incredibly gorgeous Damon from Blur.

"How about like that but a little longer?" I suggested.

"You got it, Mister!" Mr. Larry replied.

I settled into the barber chair, feeling a little like a man putting his head on the guillotine.

"So, do you go to high school?" he asked in a voice so nelly I couldn't believe he wasn't lisping. The guys back in Saint Dymphna would hate him.

"No, I'm a free agent." I saw a six-inch strand of my hair hit the gold-flecked white linoleum floor. Scary.

"Oh, that's fine! I myself don't personally approve of high schools. Young people shouldn't be all cooped up together. No offense, but when teenage boys get together they act a lot like packs of animals. Disrespectful, violent, uncouth..."

"I've noticed the same thing!" I agreed.

"They're good at heart, it's just that they need a firm hand to guide them. And the young ladies aren't much better. Chewing gum, wearing lipstick, trying to seduce all those innocent young boys. I like the way the aliens do it."

"The aliens? Like on Zeeron, with hatcheries and all that?"

"Not so much the hatcheries, but the apprenticeships. Young people should stop school at age twelve or so and be apprenticed out to responsible adults. Instead of ignoring their education while trying to amuse their chums with bathroom humor and petty vandalism they could enjoy the uplifting company of adults."

"People would never learn anything," I objected.

"Well, we don't have to do it exactly like the Zeeronians," Mr. Larry said, as he snipped and combed. "Earthlings could go back to school when their hormones simmer down, say around twenty-one or twenty-two. By then they'd be mature enough to appreciate Shakespeare and remember how many senators there are and all that."

"It could work," I said to be polite. It makes sense a hairdresser would fall for all that alien nonsense since the they allegedly run the show on planet Zeeron.

"Everyone takes for granted that adolescence is supposed to be miserable, but I say why shouldn't everyone be happy?" He smiled at me, revealing a gold tooth and dimples.

"Not too short," I reminded him as I watched more and more of my hair cascade to the floor.

"I feel sorry for you teens really. At least other minorities are pitied and occasionally given some sort of symbolic retribution: Martin Luther King Day, Cesar Chavez Boulevard, Susan B. Anthony dollars, what have you. You poor darling adolescents get about as much sympathy as a plague of locusts. Something really ought to be done about it, especially since all that adolescent agony so often leads to mass murder and bad poetry."

"Did you go to high school, Mr. Larry?"

"Moi? Oh, heavens no. Mother took me out of school at a young age so I could help her around the house. She was a great entertainer and I prepared literally *thousands* of club sandwiches for her and her lady friends, as well as polishing the silver, setting up countless bridge tables, addressing thank you notes, and I don't know *what* all. Real work. Useful work. Not like flipping burgers in one of those disgusting fast food franchises. I'm convinced that much of the violence and brutality so common amongst today's youth is a result of the substitution of fast food for nourishing home-cooked meals. It's no wonder today's teens are obese and mentally slow." He looked at me and smiled, "Not you, dear, you're just fine."

"Don't you think it's hard enough just being a teen without having to work, too?"

"Nonsense. Think of the adventures you'd have: one year being a gofer at a museum, the next apprenticing with a theater company, the next peeling potatoes at a shelter. Why, a teen could even help me out around here!" He looked at me hopefully but I kept my mouth shut. Frankly, I don't care how they do it on Zeeron, I'm not about to work for free. Actually, the whole idea struck me as being full of holes.

"Wouldn't you be exposing teens to all sorts of exploitation?" I pointed out. "I mean, we could be turned into virtual serfs by unscrupulous managers trying to cut the payroll with free labor. All sorts of people could be put out of work by teen apprentices."

"Well, there would naturally have to be some sort of supervision. Anyway, if people are so worried about teens being exploited and abused they should might think about doing away with compulsory *families* rather than my absolutely terrific idea of compulsory labor," he said huffily.

"Are you done yet?" There was a ton of hair all over the floor. "You've cut an awful lot off."

"I'm just evening it all up now." He continued to clip and comb without slowing down.

"You know what I hate, Mr. Larry? Compulsory physical education. Nothing's worse than gym class. The other kids used to make fun of me and they'd keep knocking my soap on the floor of the shower and when I bent over to pick it up they'd scream all sorts of things I don't think I could repeat. It got so bad I stopped taking showers. It's not like I ever worked up a sweat anyway, except maybe by running away from all the jocks who wanted to kill me."

"That doesn't sound terribly nice, but still, I like a healthy young person. Surely you agree it's necessary for the young to get plenty of exercise?"

"Well, maybe. But don't you remember stuff like popular kids get to choose who's on their team, and they pick all the other jocks? Anyone who's fat or smart is picked last and gets beaten up and made fun of, and the coach never stops anything. Plus my friend Daphne says the competition and team spirit are psychological preparation for war."

"You're supposed to learn teamwork from sports," Mr. Larry corrected.

"I don't see how getting hit in the face with a dodge ball teaches good sportsmanship," I replied.

"Well, you're not in school now. I suggest you join the Y.M.C.A. and start swimming, or better yet weightlifting. There now, your hair is done." He smiled triumphantly. "And my, don't you look handsome!"

I looked in the mirror but had trouble recognizing the boy staring back at me. I guess it's true what Mrs. V. once told me, 80 percent of your personality comes from your hair. "It's great, thanks," I said quickly, probably without much conviction. With so little hair my face looked enormous and you could see all the zits on my forehead. On the other hand, I definitely looked a little butcher. "Come over here so I can get some pictures," suggested Mr. Larry.

"Pictures?" I repeated.

"You're a hair model, darling. I need a picture of you for my portfolio. Don't worry, you'll get copies." I followed him into the back of the shop where there was spotlight and a stool. "Sit down there and take your shirt off."

"Why should I take my shirt off?"

"People want to see your hair, not your shirt, silly."

"I'd rather not," I said, thinking of the acne on my back.

"Oh very well, suit yourself." He took a few pictures. "Now your profile." It was done. "Here's my card. Give me a call next week and we'll arrange for you to pick up your shots. Ta for now!"

I'm still not sure I really like my new look, but on the positive side I'll save a fortune on hairspray. It kinda looks glam, kinda *Velvet Goldmine*, kinda sexy! I wonder if I should go blond?

"Nobody mentioned our outfits!" whined Veeba as we took the elevator back up to our hotel suite with Mr. Finley.

"Your appearance probably startled them. Earthlings aren't used to such amazing glamour," he cooed diplomatically.

"But we looked terrific, simply smashing!" she wailed. "Startled or not, they should have said something."

"You could have paid them a compliment too, Veeba," I pointed out.

"But they looked awful, each and every one of them. Press corps? Press *corpse* would be more like it. Who outlawed flair and élan on your planet?"

"Allow me to apologize on their behalf," said Mr. Finley, his affable demeanor showing no signs of wearying.

"Their hair was invariably either too oily or dry and brittle, and the styles!" she shivered with disgust, unable to continue.

"Why were some of them snickering at me towards the end there?" I asked Mr. Finley, wondering why I even cared what the Earthlings thought. I was on the planet to impress my colleagues back on Zeeron, not my hosts.

"Nerves, I would suspect," he replied. "And please don't take any peculiar behavior you encounter personally. I'm sure they'd react just as oddly to any space aliens. Now I'm going to have to leave you for a while. There's some business at the U.N. I must attend to. The video you asked for, *Wild in the Streets*, is waiting for you in your suite."

"Thank you so much. I've seen it before, but I wanted Veeba to watch it. I find it fascinating, perhaps even eerie, how your media representations of American teenagers dating from the 1960s so closely resemble Zeeronians: the same flippant, happy-go-lucky, style-conscious amorality, with the destructive rage inherent in all humanoids cleverly sublimated into a competitive iconoclasm."

"Yes, fascinating," agreed Mr. Finley, looking at me with one eyebrow arched quizzically.

Back in the suite we ate a light meal by ourselves and settled down to watch the motion picture. Our snuggling in front of the television led us to the brink of amorous passion. When the film ended Veeba took out a canister of rapture gas and waved it at me playfully, her way of saying, "Let's make love."

"Must we? I dare say I like it better without the gas."

"Norvex, don't be such a fuddy duddy!" She slammed the can on the table.

"With that gas I could be anybody, even sex with a potted plant would be fun. I want you to want only me."

Veeba rolled her eyes at me. "You're sounding like an Earthling, and let me assure you it's not attractive in the least."

"Veeba, my precious, you have your preferences, I have mine. I don't see why you can't respect our differences. Talk about your typically Earthly failings!"

"Well, how about we compromise and just do a little?" She sat on my lap and nibbled my neck, just the way I like it.

"I think not," I replied firmly, stiffening to keep from enjoying the lovely tingles she was sending up my spine with her talented lips.

"You're not being very co-dependent." She stood up, glaring at me.

"The Earthlings think co-dependency is a mental disorder," I countered.

"The Earthlings think a lot of things. That doesn't mean *you* have to. Really, sometimes you go too far with your terraphilism. I just want to have a nice night of debauchery, and you have to get all... what's the term? Puritanical?"

"Yes, puritanical."

"And you have to get all puritanical on me." She collapsed into the chair facing me, now all set for a night of recreational rowing and recrimination. I made a mental note to ask Mr. Finley to get us a video of *Who's Afraid of Virginia Woolf?* for the following evening.

"If you need to find someone to make love to why not get yourself a native?" I asked.

"And risk catching some unspeakable disease? Ha, and I repeat, *ha!* If you like Earthlings so much, why don't you find yourself one?" she shot back at me.

"Don't think the thought hasn't crossed my mind," I replied peevishly, though actually it hadn't. Just then, our domestic discord was interrupted by a knock on the door.

It was Mr. Finley, who burst in and without so much as a "hello" related some startling news. "Your press conference has produced an unanticipated result. Telephone polls show that a majority of the world's people don't believe you're from another planet."

"Oh dear," said Veeba. "But we came in a spaceship!"

"I know that, but you must remember many Earthlings are rather suspicious," he consoled. "There are also some celebrities, including several prominent radio personalities, who're calling you frauds. I'm awfully sorry."

"Don't be sorry," I interrupted, an idea hatching in my mind. "This presents us with a golden opportunity. If we can convince everyone that we *are* in fact impostors, we might be able to get about unmolested by xenophobes, gawkers, and lunatics."

"You may have a point," said Mr. Finley. "Already the crowd outside the barricades has thinned considerably."

I went to the window for confirmation and discovered that he was quite correct. "If we could convince people we're practical jokers perchance they'd go away entirely."

Mr. Finley smiled. "I think it's a splendid idea. I can arrange for you to appear on a few disreputable talkshows over the next few days where you can just be yourselves and let the natural incredulity of the public take it from there. We could even invent a cover story for you, perhaps claim your ship is an old Soviet shuttle, and concoct fake terrestrial identities for you. We'll work out the details later. I know I shouldn't tell you this but protecting you has been an enormous challenge. Just this morning they discovered a religious fanatic with a pipebomb in the sewers a few blocks from here. You've offended quite a lot of people."

"What about looking foolish?" I asked. "Nobody likes being deceived."

"Don't worry, we'll live with it," said Mr. Finley elatedly. "In fact, even after you're exposed as a hoax we can have the U.N. insist you're on the level. Earthlings enjoy believing the authorities to be fools. Also, that way we can continue to foot your bills, guide you around, and protect you from the lunatic fringe."

"We really should have thought of this before we came," muttered Veeba, with an accusing glare.

"Next time someone invites herself to visit a barbarian world with me, I might decline the honor," I snapped back.

Mr. Finley made for the door. "I should be going. On behalf of all Earth, allow me to extend our sincerest wish that you sleep soundly." Seconds later a full scale argument erupted.

In the morning Veeba and I agreed overproximity was straining our relationship and decided to spend some time apart. For the next few days I toured museums while she visited important hair salons. In the evenings we watched television together, but slept in separate beds, maintaining a sort of armed truce, the arms being our sharp tongues.

In the mornings Mr. Finley breakfasted with us, and it was from a New York *Times* he brought with him that we learned of another unanticipated result of our press conference. Earth's entire critical establishment was united almost as one in lambasting Zeeronian taste in music and television, calling us boobs and lowbrows. It seems our aesthetics alone precluded our extraterrestrial origins in the popular imagination, which found us simultaneously effete and vulgar.

I ran into this attitude firsthand while leaving the Museum of Broadcast History where I'd just monitored some charming episodes of *Lost in Space*. Walking to my awaiting limousine I was assaulted by a barrage of sarcastic comments from passersby, who were fortunately kept several yards away by a cordon of police officers. "Go back to planet Pansy!" hollered a thickset man in an unbecoming yellow helmet, popular with manual laborers. "Read your Shakespeare! To eschew the immortal bard for the network's drivel is tantamount to heresy," offered a pale weedy man in a trenchcoat, angrily shaking his fist. It began to hurt my feelings that the Earthlings, whom I'd always imagined would be more sympathetic than my fellow Zeeronians, were in fact so often hostile and patronizing.

Veeba didn't seem to care though, possibly since she hadn't developed any fantasies about Earth. Also, spending the bulk of her time around beauticians she was exposed to a more sophisticated strata of society. She was, she assured me, routinely pronounced "Fabulous!" or "Simply too divine!" and showered with accolades. One stylist, Fabrice, befriended her and after a couple of lunches together, the two began speaking on the telephone daily. On his advice we watched an astounding motion picture called *Showgirls* which gleefully glamorized the behind the scenes travails of wage slave sex objects in Las Vegas, all of whom apparently hate each other and want nothing more than fame, money, and bloody red meat. "If this spectacle was produced entirely in earnest, then we Terraphiles are going to have a lot of explaining to do," I fretted.

"Perhaps it's meant ironically," Veeba suggested hopefully. "Fabrice did say it was a 'hoot.' "

"I'd like to think it's an example of double irony, saying one thing and meaning both it and its antithesis, but generally one doesn't find that level of sophistication in civilizations that have yet to fully integrate their conceptions of authenticity and artifice."

"What do you mean?" Veeba asked.

"Well, the Earthlings tend to believe that artifice is inauthentic."

"But that's absurd! The more *art* that goes into something, the more *artificial* it is, and the more it reflects the consciousness of the *author* of that art. It couldn't be more simple."

"You see, Veeba," I explained patiently, "the primitive mind believes in the 'natural' which is a mythological state of grace wherein something is untouched by consciousness, or at least self-consciousness. They believe authenticity is rooted in this natural state."

"Oh, but that's silly and horrid!" she exclaimed.

"Actually, such delusions are quite common on planets with less than nine or ten millennia of cultural development." I was thrilled that Veeba was finally taking an interest.

"Do planets really develop on such a regular schedule?"

"No, actually, things vary quite a bit. The Boxnogians didn't develop leisurewear until their seventh millennium."

"Fascinating. Maybe I should give up the hair game and go into academia."

"You don't mean that?" I really hoped she wasn't serious.

"No, I don't. But I am glad I know someone who keeps interested in things. Gives one something to talk about, doesn't it?" She put her arms around me and kissed the back of my neck. We started to make love for the first time in days. Just as I thought we were really clicking together and putting the arguments behind us, Veeba pulled out the rapture gas. I sighed loudly and shook my head no. She looked disappointed but joined me in sexual congress all the same. I couldn't tell if she was enjoying herself or not, which I found most disturbing.

Dear Diary,                                    Sunday, Oct. 20

While I was bleaching my hair today I called Daphne, who just about flipped her wig when I told her about Mr. Larry.

"He was wearing a small gold scarf around his neck," I began.

"You mean a *neckerchief*?" she shrieked with delight. "I like him already."

"And he has rings on practically every finger, which you really notice right off because his hands flutter around like mad when he talks, which is all the time. He doesn't lisp exactly... he sounds like a real nasal carnival barker."

"I'm having trouble imagining."

"You'll just have to get him to do your hair next time it needs doing."

"I will, definitely," she said with conviction. She will, too. Collecting and befriending strange old people is one of Daphne's passions. She loves antique ladies in leopardette coats, dapper old men in fedoras, anything from a long gone era. There's this one teetering dowager, Mrs. McGreggor, who runs a hat shop downtown in Saint Dymphna. She must have all of about a dozen customers, every one of them over eighty. Daphne visits her all the time and the two of them sit around and talk about who-knows-what for literally hours on end.

"Have you got a boyfriend yet?" Daphne asked, knowing full well if any halfway good-looking guy had so much as stepped on my foot I'd be on the phone to her within the hour.

"What do you think?" I replied.

"Chester, San Francisco is a gay Mecca. If you can't find someone there you're in serious trouble."

"I just haven't met Mr. Right yet."

"If I know you, I bet you haven't spoken to a member of the male sex since you got there. What about all those cute boys we saw hanging around in front of Random Records? Why don't you say hello to one of them?"

"I can't just go up to a complete stranger and say hello like some dork!"

"Why not?" she insisted.

I was horrified. "Are you *insane?!*"

"Chester Julian, did you know you're pathologically shy? I say hello to cute guys all the time."

"Like Brett?" This was a swipe at an old flame of Daphne's, a thirty-something biker wannabe. Daphne dumped him when a clerk at Spend'n'Save gave them an extra five dollars in their change and he totally blew his outlaw image by returning the money.

"Look, suit yourself, but just don't be whining to me about how you're wasting away as a celibate."

I'll show her, if it's the last thing I do on Earth!

Dear Diary,                                              Monday, Oct. 21

I found this incredible article on how to pick up guys in *Orpheus.* I think maybe it's supposed to be tongue-in-cheek, but maybe not. A lot of it has the ring of truth.

Bored? Lonely? Sick of Running Up Your Phone Bill with 976 Numbers? Fear Not! You Can Be Popular with Guys by Learning THE SECRETS OF SEXCESS!©
By Dudley Dallesandro

Are you always the best man and never the groom? Is love passing you by? Well, dry those tears and dust off that little black book, because soon every ring of the phone will bring you closer to a wonderful new world of fun and excitement. YOU can be the center of attention!

YOU can *acquire* and *keep* the love and admiration of desirable guys! Let's start by doing a quick reality check. What about yourself can you honestly say others would find attractive? Got it? Good. The first SECRET OF SEXCESS© is to FLAUNT IT. If you're funny—tell jokes. If you're rich—wear diamonds. If you're young—dress like a school child. If you're hunky—undress for success. If vindictive people call you vain or boastful—ignore them. In today's hurley-burley world nobody has time to discover the hidden treasures of good character. Mr. Hotstuff won't call up and ask you for a date on Saturday night because you're prudent, patient, or polite.

The second SECRET OF SEXCESS© is BE A ROMANTIC. A cynical worldview is fine for the world's fighters, but you are now a *lover*. Guard your beauty by thinking only beautiful thoughts. Be charitable in your assessment both of others and yourself. Put a flattering face on human foibles. He's not an alcoholic, he's wrestling with inner demons. You're not a failed painter, you're a struggling artist misunderstood by vulgar conformists. They're not ugly, they're challenging traditional western concepts of beauty. Studies show time and again that the most lovable people are the people who love others the most.

The third SECRET OF SEXCESS© is UNDERSTANDING THE HUMAN MALE. Men come in several varieties and each type must be approached differently. This is going to take some homestudy but here are three of the most common types:

1. The Sexhibitionist. This flirty, flaunty creature is a major tease. His secret is he wants you to want him, *badly*. He's obsessed with the thrill of conquest. The trick is to play it cool towards him but make sure he sees you flaunting it for someone else. If he thinks his charms aren't working on you, he'll make overtures - *to which you won't respond*. Then, when he least expects it, compliment him in public. After that, feign indifference. Repeat the process until he's completely unsure of himself Then *pounce!*

2. The Shrinking Violet. He's shy. Possibly he's bored by the banality of cruising and dating, perhaps he just doesn't want to get hurt. Whatever the reason, he ain't out there lookin' for love. This type is invariably

surrounded by a gaggle of friends (usually female). Your strategy is to befriend them, but *ignore* him. Eventually he'll get jealous and crumble into your open arms.

3. The Specialist. Most people find someone they like and then find something they like to do together. The specialist finds something he likes to do, then finds someone to do it with. If a guy hasn't responded to other approaches, he may be a specialist. Since the hanky code is out of fashion, the best way to deal with specialists is by being charmingly candid about one's own desires, then asking, "What are you into?"

The fourth SECRET OF SEXCESS© is DO YOUR SEXERCISES© EVERYDAY. A sexercise is any exercise that makes you sexier. The following is a short list of scientifically tested attractiveness enhancers. 1. Take mud baths. Wonderful for the skin. 2. Start weight training. Yes, even if you're a femme! Marilyn Monroe lifted weights, did you know that? 3. Do yoga and stretching - to prepare you for all the sexual acrobatics you'll be doing. 4. Find someone who was raised before the '60s or attended a Swiss finishing school to teach you poise and posture. Gracefulness is an absolute must, even if you're working a "rough trade" look. 5. Practice stripping seductively out of whatever you plan to be wearing when your intended enters your boudoir. 6. Facials. Do facials. 7. Listen to your voice on a tape recorder and practice sounding sexy. 8. Look at how you smile in the mirror and find a flattering way to do it. 9. Repeat one hundred times everyday, "I am a sexy guy!" 10. Learn to be at ease with your body by dancing naked until you drop from exhaustion. These are just a beginning. Try and come up with your own SEXERCISES!

The fifth SECRET OF SEXCESS© is to HAVE A GOOD COME-ON LINE. Sure it's hokey, but *it works!* Try a zany opener like, "Did you know baklava is actually made out of old yellow pages baked in honey?" and see what he says. If you're the more direct type, try, "You know, you've got beautiful eyes." Another route is the campy, "What's your sign?" Believe it or not, many desirable guys are actually shy, so it's important to make the first move and not sit around waiting for Mr. Hotstuff to move in on you.

The sixth SECRET OF SEXCESS© is WEAR A MACHO FANTASY OUTFIT. Funny femmes are tolerated by cruising boys as a passing amusement but are rarely taken home at the end of the night. Fortunately nobody expects you to actually BE butch, only to LOOK butch. If hyper-masculinity doesn't come naturally to you, dress like one of the Village People, but only until you find something more contemporary. Naturally, if you're a gender-bender you have to go in the opposite direction and wear a FEMME FATALE FANTASY OUTFIT, but be prepared to resign yourself to tranny-chasers and straight men.

The seventh and final SECRET OF SEXCESS© is BE GOOD IN BED. Word gets around and if you play the field for awhile everyone will know if you're a hot tamale or a cold vichyssoise. There's no way to fake this, you actually have to be considerate and imaginative. If you find yourself having trouble in this area there are more than enough books and manuals that will tell you how to drive a man wild in bed. Remember IT'S NOT HARD TO KEEP A MAN, IF YOU CAN KEEP A MAN HARD.

If you remember these secrets and develop a proper regimen of SEXERCISES© you'll be snaring guys in no time. Anyone who so much as intimates your erotic lifestyle is anything less than glamorous is just an old sourpuss. Now get out there and get laid!

I decided to try a few "Sexercises" and go in search of a boyfriend. I slathered my face with rejuvenating blue goop I found in Dora's medicine cabinet and practiced removing my clothes seductively. Repeating "I am a sexy guy" was just too stupid to go through with, but I did walk with a book on my head (the enormously heavy *Every Womyn's Guide to Midwifery* which I found in the living room bookcase) to improve my posture.

After my facial I dressed to go out, squeezing into tight black stretchpants and a silky red shirt which I left unbuttoned half the way up like all the models are doing now. I accessorized with a thick black studded belt, and for shoes decided on my patent-leather brothel-creepers with leopardette tops. I wore several studded leather cockrings for wrist bracelets as an added erotic touch, and topped it all off with a pair of silver wraparound sunglasses. Maybe not exactly a macho fantasy outfit, but more come-hithery than usual. I also slathered on not one, but two layers of foundation to hide the oozing inflamed mass of zits I sometimes call my face, which had received no visible benefit from the facial. Then I took Gwendolyn on a walk, ending up at Collinwood Park, which I'd read in *Orpheus* is a hot spot for cruising.

The park itself wasn't really a park, but the fenced-off playground for some grammar school. There were a fair number of people hanging around, walking this way and that, and a few old odd guys skulking behind trees leering seductively. The more handsome types walked around confidently and stared at passersby with choosy-shopper looks. I pulled Gwendolyn's leash tight so she couldn't run up to every passing stranger and started strolling. I hadn't been there a moment when I ran into Mr. Larry walking two yipping pomeranians not much larger than dust bunnies.

"Chester! Ooh, let me see your hair." His tiny pooches began jumping all over me but completely ignoring Gwendolyn, who looked sort of hurt in her doggy sort of way. "Did you bleach it yourself?"

"Yes."

"You did a good job, but you might want to use a toner. Makes it less brassy." He yanked on his dogs' leashes. "Down, Gimlet! Down, Cosmo!" The dogs ignored him and continued their friendly assault.

"A toner?" I asked.

"Like a blond dye. I'd do it, no charge. Your photos will be ready tomorrow, we could do it then." He smiled lecherously and began kneading my neck with his meaty fingers. "Or, if you like, you could come back to my place now and I'd do your hair *and* give you a backrub." The massage felt sort of nice and if he wasn't half a century older than me I might have considered his offer, but I didn't want to lead him on.

"No, I'd better get on with walking Gwendolyn here. She belongs to my new Mom and, you know how mothers can be. I'll pick up the photos tomorrow afternoon though."

"Well, then, I'll see you tomorrow," he said with a wink.

I waved and walked off. Fifteen minutes later I started to get discouraged because nobody was cruising me and I was thinking about going. Then a cute guy in his mid-twenties with freckles, short red hair, and a wrinkly forehead that made him look worried in a cute sort of way passed by. To my amazement he looked back at me and smiled. I smiled too.

"Hey," he said, walking over and leaning on the fence a few feet away from me.

"Hey," I said, trying to sound confident, carefree, and natural (and probably failing).

"You're just a wee bit of a thing, aren't you? What 'choo doin' out here all by your lonesome?" He was being friendly to me! The funny thing was, if I'd closed my eyes I almost would have thought he was a black woman instead of a white guy because of his vocal inflections.

"Walking my dog. What's your name?" I asked, leaning against the fence.

"Franklin. Yours?"

"Chester. So, Franklin, what's your sign?"

He laughed. "Virgo. Yours?"

"Aquarius."

"So what's it like being a Virgo, Franklin? Are you virginal?" I don't know where I got this from. It was like I was being fed lines from some internal teleprompter.

"A virgin! Me? I'm a full-on ho, child."

"Gee." I was at a loss. What type did that make him? Sexhibitionist? Specialist? I didn't have time to ponder the subject. He was on the make, his eyes roving up and down my body.

"It's kinda late. Don't you have to get up early for kinnergarten?"

"Too young, I don't start till next year." Again, where were these lines coming from? Could I be a reincarnation of some music hall floozie? "Actually I've just finished high school, and I'm engaging in some independent study. What do you do?"

"I'm a stripper."

I involuntarily gasped.

"At the Showboat," he continued.

I'd seen the theater's ad in *Orpheus*. The place showed dirty movies "round the clock" and its "dancers" not only bared everything, but if the ad was to be believed, masturbated publicly. "Is it true, that you, you know, wank-off on stage?"

"Yeah. It's like, I dance around to some music throwing my clothes off and gyratin' sexy-like. When I'm totally naked I get a hard-on..."

"Isn't that hard? I mean, difficult?"

"I got me a good imagination. I just think about boys at the beach, boys at the gym, boys at the baths, whatever. Then I go into the audience and lap dance all the mens for tips."

"Wow. That is *so* sordid! How does it pay?" It's important to find out how much money men have if you're going to become involved with them. As Daphne always says, "It's the difference between getting taken out for sushi and dutch treat at Schlocko Bell."

"I do all right. I got no complaints. Except maybe it gets kinda dull. Sometimes to keep innerested I try an' figure out which actors the guys in the audience look like. Like there'll be an Ernest Borgnine, maybe a Leslie Nielsen, a couple Jack Klugmans. The other day there was this guy who looked fully like Tom Arnold, coulda been his twin brother."

"Do you ever get women in there?" I wondered.

Franklin chuckled to himself. "Once we got an entire busload of Japanese tourist ladies who stood in back and tittered through my whole show, like, 'Hee, hee, hee!' with their hands over their mouths. Every time I went within three yards of 'em they cringed and ran away." He mimicked a timid Japanese woman giggling and running away, which got him some odd stares from passing cruisers.

"So these guys can't like, kiss you, or do anything to give you a disease?"

"Nah, sometimes they try, but I put 'em in their place. Lot of 'em are married. Tourists from Iowa or Biloxi or wherever, so they're kinda timid. Won't even touch themselves. They just sit there looking with these big hungry eyes. Some do jerk off, and the way they do it's like monkeys in the zoo. No technique, just this rapid..." He gestured with his hand.

"My friend Daphne was telling me about Herbert Marcuse's theory that sexuality concentrates in the phallus because industrialization desensualizes the rest of the body."

"Herbert who works at the Touch Me Lounge on Polk Street?"

"Maybe. Daphne's really into sex workers. She read some book about sacred temple whores and how prostitutes subvert the patriarchy. She's always going on about it. We even rented *Sweet Charity* and *Gypsy* from Schlockbuster. Normally I like horror movies."

Franklin changed the subject. "Seriously, how old are you?"

"Just turned sixteen," I lied.

"If you're sixteen, I'm Janet Jackson," he laughed.

"What's the matter, Janet? Sixteen too old for you?"

"Yeah, but just this once I'll make an exception."

We walked to Franklin's apartment which was just a few blocks away. Neither of us spoke which somehow was more nerve-wracking than romantic. The second we were through the door of his small room he turned on some Christmas lights and began French kissing me before I even had a chance to unleash Gwendolyn, who started barking and running around in circles, getting all tangled up in her leash. It's so weird to have a tongue in your mouth. Someone else's, I mean. It's like a live, warm, wriggling chicken liver. First it sort of wrestled with my tongue, then it slithered over my teeth. When had I last had them cleaned? Figuring it would only be polite to reciprocate, I pushed my tongue around in his mouth. "Now what should I do with it?" I wondered. When had he had his teeth cleaned? Did he brush regularly? Floss? I tried to overcome my squeamishness by commanding myself to stop thinking and go with the moment. "Just slither!" I ordered myself. "Slither your tongue around in his mouth."

After a few seconds I pulled away to catch my breath and quiet down Gwendolyn who was choking on her collar. Franklin excused himself and while he was gone I snooped around his room. It was pretty empty, just a milk crate full of CDs, a boombox, a mattress, and a half dozen Princess Leia action figures. Nothing much to go on; no books or photos. There weren't even any posters or decorations on the wall, which now that I think of it, is sort of weird. Franklin came back with a doggie-dish of water and a forty ouncer for us, then put on a CD which unfortunately turned out to be "You Gotta Get On Up and Keep Pushin'Yo Body" by Alisha K. and the Jay Bees. I totally hate house music. The wailing diva vocals, piano riffs, and dull thud of the bass-heavy metronomic beat are like fingernails on a chalkboard to me. If we get married, I decided, Franklin will have to burn all his Alisha K. CDs.

"Could you find something else to play?" I asked as nicely as I could. "I hate this."

"But it's Miss Alisha, she's the *tee!*"

"Anything else in the world would be just fine. Well, not anything, but..." Thankfully I spotted a Bjork CD, "What about this?"

"Okay, whatever." He was obviously disappointed that I didn't share his reverence for Miss Alisha, but eager to get back to business. First though, he took out a pipe and insisted I get high with him. Although I've always been in favor of drugs in principle, I'd never actually tried any. I think what they say about pot paranoia must be true, because no sooner had I inhaled than I had a vision of the ancient Users Are Losers and Just Say No! posters on the walls of my high school guidance counselor, and as I tried to keep the hot smoke in my formerly pristine lungs, visions of McGruff the Crime Dog danced in my head. It didn't take long before I felt confused and was struck dumb. After a few tokes, we returned to the business of love.

I don't want to make the reader of these pages blush... but what the heck, I will! After more kissing Franklin pulled away and stripped stark naked. Knowing what was expected of me, I followed his lead. I couldn't help but think that once he saw what a chubby, acne-ridden monster I am he'd scream or tell me to get lost, but nothing happened. The second I achieved full nudity Franklin leapt on top of me and began grinding his loins into me. "Dry humping," I think it's called. One of his hands found its way down to my posterior and began doing truly unmentionable things. I asked him what was up, in a casual sort of way. He was having fun and I didn't want to upset him. "I wanna nuts-to you," he said, for once sounding like a white boy instead of some sassy black chick.

"You have a condom?" I asked with great effort. The pot made speaking difficult.

"I wanna do it natural," he explained.

"Are you insane?" I asked, trying not to sound shocked, but rolling onto my back.

"Aw, c'mon, baby, lemme do it natural," he pleaded. (A man pleading for me!)

Survival instinct overcame my pot-induced dumbness. "There's a certain disease you may have heard of..." I began.

"But it feels so *good*," moaned Franklin.

"No. Non. Nyet. Nein. I'm planning on staying absolutely safe, and will never, ever have unprotected sex with anyone, under any circumstances, for any reason," I said, removing his hand from the vicinity of my love tunnel. "Anyway, I'm not in the mood."

We went back to making out, which was wonderful. Daphne is right, sex is the best thing ever; better than chocolate, money, and movies. I *tingled* for hours afterwards. Depriving teenagers of sex has to be the cruelest, most despicable form of child abuse there is. The one part I could do without is all the talking, which just sounds so incredibly corny. Though, as I mentioned, Franklin's voice had dropped several octaves into a sexier register, he was still saying such stupid stuff: "Young, so young," and "Ooh, baby," and "Smooth, smooth skin," and like that. Ugh.

After seven minutes and twenty-three seconds (in my drugged state I'd become somewhat obsessed with the digital clock next to the bed) Franklin climaxed all over me. He immediately became sort of mechanical, like his mind was elsewhere. I got nervous worrying about taking too long and wondering if I was doing the right things. After three more tortured minutes Franklin remembered he had to meet some friends at a nightclub and called it quits. Though I would have liked for him to stick it out just a little while (at least till I finished!) it was just as well since Gwendolyn was getting restless and kept trying to eat his shoes. We exchanged numbers and Franklin said to call him sometime! Do I hear wedding bells?

Over the next few days Mr. Finley took us around to various talkshows as part of the plan to erode our credibility with the Earthlings. The most memorable was *The Zhandra Phillips Show*. Getting out of our limousine in front of the studio we could see a few protesters a block away waving placards reading God hates Zeeron! and other such effronteries. Once again, my feelings were hurt. Living all of one's life on a planet where disdain is shown by nothing stronger than a withering glance can make confronting out-and-out hostility difficult.

We were first ushered into a brightly lit room and seated in plush orange chairs arranged around a low coffee table on which there was unfortunately no coffee. In front of us were some large cameras, and behind them, several rows of raised seats in which curious Earthlings sat quietly staring. After a few minutes during which an enchanting young man insisted on powdering our faces, to eliminate glare he said, despite our assurances that it was unnecessary since Zeeronians never leave the house without slathering on plenty of anti-glare foundation. After he left, Ms. Phillips, looking chic in a lavender satin pantsuit with a bow at the neck, her hair a helmet of short frosty curls, strode onto the set. As the audience hooted and applauded, I was immediately seduced by the supremely confidant but humble way she acknowledged their love and support with a slight bow and a warm smile. Masterful.

Veeba and I stood to shake her hand, although I'd explained to Veeba before that it was customary for biological females to remain seated. "Norvex 7, Your Magnificence Veeba 22, welcome to my show, welcome to Earth," she said, her voice radiating as much warmth and power as her physical presence, which is to say, a lot.

"Thank you, it's nice to be here," I replied with a large, bright smile.

"That is a stunning ensemble you've got on, Ms. Phillips," said Veeba.

"Why, thank you, Your Excellency."

"Just call me Veeba."

"Veeba, such a lovely name," said Zhandra warmly, while gesturing for us to sit down. "And I must say you look something spectacular yourself!" Veeba did look nice in her purple fake-fur body-stocking with gold suede go-go boots and turban. I had opted for the black and silver ensemble I'd worn leaving Zeeron. "And you look nice as well, Norvex. My audience is probably curious, does everyone on your planet dress up like this? Is this normal?"

"Oh, yes," Veeba replied. "We get a lot of our fashion inspiration from Earth actually. Or at least from your golden age."

"What we call the Terran Miracle," I explained. "The period roughly corresponding to... Oh no, Veeba!" A pink globe swelled from Veeba's face, like the symptom of some unknown alien virus.

"Norvex! Are you all right?" asked an alarmed Ms. Phillips.

Then the globe popped, and I realized Veeba was blowing a bubble with gum. "Veeba, you've gone native!" I cried without thinking.

"What? Oh, the bubble gum. Love the stuff. Fab. Really."

"Now, I'm going to presume all my viewers saw your press conference, but there were a lot of questions left unanswered." Zhandra was not one to be sidetracked by a mere bubble. Her composure was as awesome as her figure. "For example, do you attend schools on Zeeron?"

"Not exactly. We do have information galleries in which fact artists perform," I answered.

"In your interviews I hear you use the words 'gallery' and 'artist' a lot. Why is that?"

"You see, Ms. Phillips," I began.

"Please, call me Zhandra," she interrupted.

"With pleasure.You see, Zhandra, on Zeeron all occupations are considered arts. A food artist serves his art in a food gallery, sex artists practice their art in love galleries, and so on."

"Fascinating! And do you have talkshow artists?" asked Zhandra, mugging for the cameras as the audience laughed heartily.

"As a matter of fact ,we do have conversation artists, and a lot of Zeeronians watch them perform on our television, which is holographic, three dimensional, and even has smells. We also have plenty of documentaries and dramas, but mostly comedies. In fact, a few of our shows were even inspired by Earthly T.V., *The Graxdap Clan*, was a series about the cohorts from a hatchery who form a musical ensemble that resembled your *Partridge Family*. The star was Ushkapp 45 who bears more than a passing resemblance to Gary Coleman from *Diff'rent Strokes*, and it was successful for two seasons."

"Three!" corrected Veeba.

"Isn't that fascinating!" said Zhandra.

"What really fascinates *us* is the way your planet started developing civilized tendencies then pulled away.Whatever happened to Free Love, Ann-Margret, day-glo clothing, living in geodesic domes, and the elimination of wage slavery?" I asked, sincerely wanting to know.

"I'm afraid we'll have to get back to that after a word from our sponsors." Zhandra smiled and winked at the camera as the audience burst into applause on cue.

Unfortunately, Zhandra had no answers to my queries. The interview staggered on for a few minutes as we told of various extraterrestrial marvels, then Zhandra let her audience ask questions. A woman with a careworn face in a gray dress so ugly it would have caused convulsions in onlookers had she tried to wear it on Zeeron began, "I'm a mother of three, and I can't see how you can sit there and talk about Free Love. What about child molesters? Here we lock up sexual perverts.What about the rights of the child? And love galleries! I get all the love I need from my *husband.*" Here the audience applauded. "It's just not right. What about AIDS? Have you no shame?" Her disjointed syntax temporarily jarred me, but Veeba quickly responded.

"Zeeronians are by and large exceedingly attractive people, and we really can't help ourselves when it comes to having sex. Look at me. Could you resist?" The audience hooted, especially the male members.

An obese woman wearing a huge wooden crucifix asked the next question. "Since you have Earth television, you must have heard the word of the Lord, the Gospel."

"Yes," I said, nodding.

"And have you accepted Jesus Christ as your personal savior and washed yourself in the blood of the lamb?"

"No," I replied impatiently. "Next question."

A pale, earnest young man spoke up next. "With all your advanced technology could you help us to cure diseases like cancer?"

"The health artists on Zeeron all use extremely advanced instruments. If they brought them here you might disassemble them and learn more than would be safe for you to know about our technology. Even a simple Felkusian aurascope could potentially be rewired to create a dangerous weapon. But just as soon as you eliminate all war and conflict I'm sure someone would be happy to drop by and help you out."

"Poor creature," I thought as I looked at the disappointed face of my rather handsome questioner. "Doomed to die at an obscenely early age, probably from some easily curable ailment."

At the conclusion of the show Veeba and I demonstrated a Zeeronian dance, The Gyration, to a song by Ignord 44. This was an idea of Mr. Finley's which he assured us would help convince the Earthlings we were impostors, although why I'm not exactly certain. The overhead lights were dimmed and colored spots flashed rhythmically as we got up on pedestals (no Zeeronian dances on the ground) and began moving to the beat. Zhandra, who was keen to learn the moves, imitated us, chuckling at herself goodnaturedly all the while. The audience went wild with laughter and applause, egging her on, chanting, "Go, Zhandra! Go Zhandra! Go Zhandra!"

When we got back to the hotel Mr. Finley assured me we'd done a wonderful job. Some t.v. newscasters were already referring to us as the "so-called visitors from another planet."

Dear Diary,                                        Tuesday, Oct. 22

I called Franklin and he agreed to come to Mr. Larry's with me to pick up the photos. I figured he could act as a sort of chaperone and at the same time be extremely impressed that I'm modeling. I arrived first and not wanting to go in alone, waited for him on the corner. He showed up twenty minutes late looking pale and shifty-eyed with beard stubble, like some harried lowlife criminal from an old *Twilight Zone.* I wondered if he'd looked as seedy the other night and I just didn't notice because of the dim lighting. Still and all, he was sort of sexy.

"Sorry I'm late. DJ Keropi was at Substratum and he was hella fierce! I just got home right before you called an' I'm feelin' sketchy."

I wasn't sure what he meant by sketchy, but not wanting to sound naive I let it pass. "All right then, let's go get this over with, then maybe we can do something fun." Inside the shop we discovered Mr. Larry ogling the scantily clad teens on a rerun of PopTV's *Bodacious Beach House Summer Special.*

"Oh, Chester, I'm so glad you're here. Who's your little friend?" Mr. Larry stood and held out his hand.

Franklin stared at Mr. Larry's hand with confusion, then shook it. "Franklin," he muttered.

"Pleased to meet you, I'm sure. So Chester, I think the pictures came out marvelously. Here take a look." He handed me a manila envelope containing some three by five glossies of me looking just as ugly as I always have, maybe even more so. My lack of chin was especially noticeable in profile and the lighting was just harsh enough to make every pore visible, but not wash out the blemishes the way bright lights sometimes do. All in all, an incredibly bad job.

"Thanks, Mr. Larry," I said, tucking the envelope and photos under my arm to keep them away from Franklin who was rudely trying to grab them for a look.

"So why don't you two come in the back and I'll get you some soda pops."

"Got anything harder?" asked Franklin, looking around and coldly appraising the salon.

"Funny you should ask! I just happen to have a nice fresh pitcher of Long Island Iced Teas! Come with me." He grabbed us each by an arm and dragged us into the back of the salon where there was a lounging room furnished entirely in Art Deco. "Have a seat," he commanded, pulling a pitcher from a small refrigerator in the corner. We both sank down onto a mint green sofa with pointy armrests as he poured our drinks.

"So, Franklin, you look just the teensiest bit familiar. Have we met?"

"Probably," said Franklin surveying his new environs with the same cold, appraising look in his eyes.

"I've always said that San Francisco is really a small, small town. A mere village really," chuckled Mr. Larry.

"Ain't it the truth. No privacy in this burg," agreed Franklin bitterly as he absentmindedly picked up a novel from the coffee table. "Who's Desmond LaTouche?"

"Don't young people read anymore?" sighed Mr. Larry.

"I read," I countered, though I didn't mention I had no idea who Desmond LaTouche is.

"Well, thank goodness young people still drink," said Mr. Larry, handing Franklin his cocktail. Somehow, though, he managed to spill most of it all over Franklin's pants. I couldn't tell for sure, but I think he may have done it on purpose.

"Oops!" said Mr. Larry.

"Shit!" screamed Franklin.

"Terribly sorry, let me wipe you up." Mr. Larry found a towel in the drawer of a '30s vanity that looked like it should've had Jean Harlow sitting in front of it. "You know, Franklin, you have my sincerest apology, but there is really no call for foul language. I've never approved of profanity. When I was young we never swore. Everyone at least *tried* to be charming and civil. Then the hippies came along, and oh my - the language they used! You have no idea! Every other word!"

"I'll get the rest," said Franklin, grabbing the towel from Mr. Larry who'd been drying dangerously near his crotch.

Mr. Larry sat down with a sigh. "It always sounds like the person swearing is going to lose his temper. I want to be lighthearted and gay. Is that too much to ask?"

After a moment's pause Franklin found his voice. "Seems to me people can be just as nasty without four letter words as with. If you're upset it's more honest to let people know it."

Mr. Larry smiled condescendingly. "Oh, I know the argument. Decorum is a big phony facade covering up life's brutal passions which you young people find so terribly stimulating and authentic. Well, I don't see what's so wrong with sweeping a little anger and frustration under the carpet."

Franklin protested. "All I said was..."

"I know," Mr. Larry interrupted. "And believe me, I understand that there are situations that allow for varying degrees of impropriety. Muttering an inaudible synonym for defecation after dropping bus change into the sewer, though evidence of an unsettled mind, may reasonably be forgiven, provided neither children nor members of the fairer sex are within earshot, and one is a seasoned veteran of several foreign wars. In a similar vein, the sailor who lives up to his salty reputation with repeated references to intercourse may be forgiven on the grounds that he is quaint. But when young people, often as not from good families, imitate millionaire rap stars and sports 'personalities' " (he made little quotation marks in the air with his fingers) "by swearing at the drop of a hat, not that anyone wears hats any more..."

"What are you going on about?!" screamed Franklin in utter confusion.

"It's just that I don't see why you can't stick with darn, golly, and merciful heavens. My mother would have put me in stockades for any language stronger than that." Mr. Larry held out a second Long Island Iced Tea which Franklin grabbed and immediately took an enormous gulp of. I realized I'd been so mesmerized by Mr. Larry's bizarre performance I hadn't touched my own and tried a sip. It tasted delicious. More like cola than iced tea though.

"This may be slightly off the subject," I interjected. "But my friend Daphne says that 'Nuts-to you' is a short hand way of saying 'I nuts-to you' which is really a threat of rape. It's a holdover from an earlier stage of evolution when we were apes living in tribes and practiced anal intercourse to establish social hierarchy, the low status males ritualistically offering their rumps to higher status alpha males, who then ritualistically sodomize them."

"Sounds like a leather bar!" said Mr. Larry. "I do wish those people would seek help for their perversion and stop parading around in their shocking outfits. But enough of our monkey friends. Tell me, do you boys play that rollerblading game I've seen on television?"

Irritated that he was trying to change the subject right in the middle of a perfectly fascinating and scientific observation, I continued. "Low status males also try to appease higher status primates by grooming them. They become sort of like primate hairdressers."

Mr. Larry scowled. "How interesting. So, Franklin..."

At the mention of his name Franklin jerked like a marionette. "Okay, okay, I'm sorry! It's just I had a long night. Hey, thanks for the drink, I really gotta go." He drained his almost full glass with one swallow and stood up.

"Nice to have met you, Franklin. If you ever need your hair done, you know where to come!" chirped Mr. Larry, opening the door and all but pushing Franklin out of it.

"I should go, too," I said.

"Oh, but you jut got here!" protested Mr. Larry. "Sit down and finish your cocktail." He leaned towards me and leered. The spicy smell of his cologne was overpowering.

"Sorry, but it's almost dinner time. My current mother is expecting me."

"He has to go home to Mother," said Mr. Larry to no one in particular. "Well, let's set up an appointment, you still need a toner."

"I'll call you," I promised, running outside the shop to catch up with Franklin who wasn't waiting for me. "Hey, Franklin, what're you doing now?"

"I'm going home, child. Miss Thing in there just worked my last nerve. And you with your monkeys and your anal intercourse!" He rolled his eyes.

"Need any company?" I asked hopefully.

"My horoscope said I should seek inner wisdom and avoid socializing this week."

"Well, I'll call you."

"You do that," he said.

When I got home I felt vaguely depressed. Burning the photos didn't cheer me as much as I'd hoped so I called Daphne and told her about my affair with Franklin, not mentioning his wanting to "do it natural" so she wouldn't think he was a total creep and not realize what a conquest I'd made. Instead of being impressed though, she was all disappointed.

"You mean you didn't get off? With a man you picked up in a park? In San Francisco? You must have done something to turn him off."

"Daphne, he said he had to meet some friends! And anyway, it was my first time making out. You wouldn't expect me to be able to drive a car if I was just thrown on the road without any lessons? Why are perfectly normal boys like me expected to go off and have *intercourse* without ever having even kissed anyone before?"

"It should come naturally, Chester," she admonished.

"But mine is an unnatural love."

She just snorted at that. Maybe I won't call her. I swear, she thinks she's the queen of sex.

Dear Diary,                                     Wednesday, Oct. 23

Ouch! Got my eyebrow pierced. Once it heals I think it'll look pretty fierce. As I was riding the bus home trying not to think about the pain I saw a billboard that read, "Sex with a minor is a major offense!" with a picture of a man on a prison cot behind bars. Underneath it offered the helpful advice that a minor is anyone under eighteen. As if I didn't have enough problems getting laid without the government reminding everyone I'm jailbait! When I got home I called Franklin to tell him about my eyebrow, but got his machine and had to settle for leaving a message.

Dora closed her shop and came home to watch the so-called aliens on *Zhandra Phillips*. As usual their outfits were totally cool, and I guess Zeeron sounds like a pretty great place if it exists, which I sincerely doubt. Dora is totally convinced though. I don't know how she can take them seriously. That dance, The Gyration, was so ridiculous, I laughed out loud. It looked like a cross between a psychotic trying to do ballet and a mime pretending to hula-hoop. I have to admit though, the song they danced to sounded pretty cool.

Dear Diary, Thursday, Oct. 24

This afternoon I was leaving a CD store on Polk Street and this old geezer in a suit discreetly asked me if I was "working." He thought I was a callboy! A street hustler! A prostitute! Someone thought I was handsome enough to be *paid* for sex! I must look pretty hot. Could it be the piercing? Celebrated with two pints of sugar-free mango-chocolate frozen dessert snack. I tried to tell Daphne and Franklin but got their answering machines.

Dear Diary, Friday, Oct. 25

Today I astounded myself with my bravery by descending into the shadowy homosexual netherworld in search of Franklin - I visited the Showboat Theater. Talk about scary! First of all, it's in a terrible neighborhood, a total cesspool of depravity. Getting off the bus I was immediately asked for spare change by a man with one leg who was sitting on a filthy concrete block that was probably supposed to be a bench. His fake leg was just sitting there in front of him, unattached. The saddest thing was that he was black (or African-American or whatever) but his leg was white. I put a quarter in the dirty styrofoam cup he was holding and he barked, "Gimme a dollar!" I told him I didn't have anymore money, which was a lie, and felt guilty as I ran away.

It was only three blocks to the theater, but on the way I was offered mota, rock, codeine, xanex, wellebutrin, crank, horse, and works by a series of unsavory-looking deviants in dirty out-of-date clothing. Where are the police in this town? Doesn't anyone care that vice is festering like an open sore on the city's sidewalks? I walked quickly, afraid that at any moment some thug would club me, take my money, and sell my body to unscrupulous medical researchers. Luck was with me and I reached the Showboat unharmed. The theater is in a shabby old building with a cheezy looking marquee that openly advertises, Live Nude Boys! Every Hour, on the Hour! Any business that tried that in Saint Dymphna would be firebombed by the quaintness patrol. I was about to go in when two perky (and not unhandsome) Christians in ill-fitting suits walked up and handed me a particularly hateful anti-gay religious tract. I ripped it into tiny pieces which I threw in the air like confetti and shouted, "Hail Satan!" The Lord's messengers smiled nervously and moved away to preach at the assorted drug fiends.

At the ticket window I showed my fake I.D., paid ten bucks, and was admitted into a small lobby decorated with movie posters from various smutty films. One wall displayed naked pictures of the strippers. They were mostly boy-next-door types, cute, but not in a way you'd necessarily notice right off. I found Franklin's photo and felt kind of bad for him because of all the guys he was the scrawniest. Also his picture made him look kind of forlorn, like maybe his dog had just died or something. I asked the guy at the ticket booth when he'd be on and was told his show was at seven. It was only half-past five so I had a lot of time to kill.

Leaving the relative safety of the lobby I slunk into a seat in the back of the mostly empty theater to watch a cops-and-robbers-themed porn flick, *Car 69, Where Are You?* I got aroused even though the guys were all old oily bodybuilders (not exactly my type, but I'm only human). At a quarter-past, the movie stopped and a spotlight illuminated a small stage in front of the screen, while a voice came over the intercom. "Gentlemen, welcome to our six o'clock show with Colby Cummings. Touching the genitals or the buttocks of the performers is prohibited by the city and county of San Francisco, but we won't tell if you won't! As always, tipping is a great way to get the performer's undivided, up close and personal attention. Now, here's Colby for your enjoyment!"

Some fancy colored lights started flashing, loud dance music blared, and a guy with a blank look on his face came out and started bumping and grinding. After a minute he slipped out of his tank top and shorts, then, naked except for his motorcycle boots, jumped off the stage. He proceeded to stand over each of the seated lechers wanking on his enormous John Thomas while they shoved tips into his boots and groped his firm young body. It wasn't till Colby was displaying his love tunnel to a man two rows in front of me that I noticed a tattoo of Peter Rabbit having tea with Piglet and The Mad Hatter on the small of his back. I was so distracted by the bizarre image I didn't realize I was next in line for his attentions till it was too late. Part of me wanted to run out of the theater, but another part wanted to stay and get my money's worth. Lust and curiosity overcame my good sense and I stayed, which I hope doesn't indicate any weakness of character on my part, but which it probably does.

As Colby stood over me I dug out my wallet, removed a dollar, and put it in his boot. I was feeling shy but I screwed up my courage and put my hand on his chest. He felt really good to me, but I don't think I was doing much for him. From the look on his face he could have been balancing his checkbook. Humiliated that he had no interest in me while I had so much in him I withdrew my hand and he moved on. After me he visited a man in the back row with dark sunglasses and a cane who started this long conversation, like he was talking to a friend. "Ah, it's Colby, isn't it? Howya been? Still seeing that barback from the Purple Parakeet?" Colby just grunted yeahs and nahs, like he didn't want to talk, then went back up on stage. After a tense minute of onanism, he climaxed to some halfhearted applause. The movie came back on right in the middle of a scene where a prison warden was sexually harassing one of his inmates in a totally unethical manner.

I decided to get some air and went through a door marked exit and found myself going down a staircase into a dark basement. At the foot of the stairs were several doorways heading off into various dark, spooky corridors. Choosing one at random I ended up in a small room in which a television showing the video from upstairs blared away. The booming, sadistic voice of the warden demanded, "You like that, punk? You like gettin' that ass slapped?" There was also a ratty couch on which lurked who knows what microscopic bugs and infectious bacteria along with three men entranced by the riveting prison drama. Scoping them out I couldn't help but think of Franklin's game of trying to figure out which character actors they resembled. John Candy, Bill Moyers, and James Earl Jones, I decided after a moment's consideration. The Moyers-like man had crazy, glassy eyes, and he gave me a look which I presume was a cruise.

Not interested in meeting him I plunged through another doorway and found myself lost in a labyrinth. Trying to retrace my steps back to the television room I was shocked when a hand from out of nowhere grabbed in the general direction of my genitals. I inadvertently screamed in terror and the hand retreated to its owner who I could now see (my eyes were adjusting to the darkness) was a Dan Ackroyd-like man in a white shirt with either a blood or a ketchup stain on it. I hurried off blindly, ending up in a room with a pool table. There were two young guys in dirty denim in the middle of a game. One had a tattoo of Li'l Devil on his arm with the slogan Born to Raise Hell! The other had an unlit cigarette dangling from his mouth and an Ozzy tee shirt. I only mention these facts, dear diary, to let the reader know that I had indeed descended into the deepest layers of Hell. Amazing myself with my own courage I asked for and received directions to the lobby from the dangerous-looking duo.

Once in the comparative safety of the upstairs I breathed a sigh of relief and sat quietly in a corner, wishing I was invisible. Just after seven o'clock Franklin rushed in and, without seeing me, bounded up a flight of stairs and through the door at the top marked Dressing Room. I considered letting him know I was there, but since he was late anyway, decided to go into the theater and surprise him. His show was pretty much a repeat of Colby's, but when he got to me, Franklin got this real smarmy smile.

"Here I thought you were a innocent kinnergartner, and where do I find you? A nasty strip show. Busted!"

"I came here to see *you*. I was waiting in the lobby, but you were in such a hurry you didn't see me. I've never been here before."

"Whatever." He waved his John Thomas back and forth in front of my face teasingly. "I'd let you suck it, but then everyone else would want to suck it, too." How could he think I'd want to suck it right there in front of all those people? I mean, I sort of did, but I never would! "You come visit me after the show, child. All right?" I nodded and he moved on back to the man with the cane. The man grabbed Franklin's John Thomas and got this big smile.

"Ah, Franklin. How's tricks? You still up to no good?"

"Whatever," said Franklin, prying the man's hand.

"How'd you get so big?" asked the blind lecher, rubbing Franklin's stomach.

"That's my secret," said Franklin, putting his leg up on the armrest. The man put a dollar in his sock and Franklin bolted back onto the stage, stroked himself a few times without coming, waved to the audience, and left. As I walked into the lobby I was thinking, "Do I even want to know someone as sleazy as Franklin?" Admittedly I got turned on by his show, but then we teenagers are *always* getting excited. Since I don't exactly have a bevy of suitors pursuing me with flowers and marriage proposals I decided I was in no position to get judgmental and knocked on the dressing room door.

"That you, little one?" asked Franklin as he let me into the room, which was undecorated except for a gigantic mirror and what looked like a Patrick Nagel print of a scantily-clad muscle man. "Like my show?" he asked as I sat on a huge old sofa.

"Oh, uh yeah, it was really, really hot, Franklin." He was still stark naked, and his slightly freckled body was glistening attractively with sweat.

Franklin smiled cutely and took my hand in his, then placed it on his manhood. Not sure what to do I began masturbating him. He made no move to reciprocate, so I put my other hand to work on myself. "Yeah, baby, that feels good," he moaned, leaning back against a wall, shutting his eyes and thrusting his hips forward. After a minute, or maybe more like thirty seconds, I was ready to come, but where? At home I always use a handkerchief, but there was nothing handy. "Yeah, that's right, baby, do it," groaned Franklin in a deep, faraway voice. Then he spoojed all over my pants.

"Franklin!" I screamed in what I hope wasn't too prissy a voice. He just laughed and pulled some paper towels from under a table and halfheartedly wiped me up. No longer in the mood, I rezipped my pants.

"Thanks," said Franklin as he lazily began getting dressed.

"How did that blind guy know your name?" I asked out of real curiosity.

"Oh, he knows all us dancers by the feel of our dicks, it's like dick braille." He laughed stupidly.

"He's a freak, but really, so's everyone when you get down to it. I thought you weren't, but then I saw you in that audience, screamin' for dick like the rest of 'em."

"I was doing no such thing!" I protested angrily. "Maybe I'd better go."

Ignoring my threat, Franklin took out a pipe and a lighter. "Righteous bud," he said. "You wanna toke?"

"I most certainly do not," I said, realizing with irritation that I still had a hard on.

He shrugged and inhaled deeply. "You goin' out tonight?' he asked, the marijuana fumes still in his lungs.

"Maybe," I replied casually.

"Think I'll drop by the Manhole, maybe I'll see you there."

I took this as my cue to leave. "Yeah, maybe. Ciao." I turned and left as he started laughing that pot laugh. Maybe I should join a computer dating service.

I got home around nine and found Dora finishing the last of her Tofushimi (a meatless, soy-based sushi substitute) dinner. Despite my natural wariness (Tofushimi?) I tried a little and was pleasantly surprised.

"So what exactly is it you do all day?" asked Dora while pouring herself a glass of organic sake.

"I'm studying for my G.E.D. I should start looking at colleges soon."

"What about the rest of the time?" she asked.

"Not much," I replied, trying to imagine a plausible hobby for myself.

"I really want to *know* you, Chester, I don't *know* you." I realized Dora must have been drinking for awhile because she was being all emotional and sloppy. "You're not my son, but you could have been... my son. Why'd you get your eyebrow pierced? It's so unnatural." She stared at my face as if it was a crossword puzzle problem she could solve. "Though I suppose that's the point or something."

"I just like the way it looks. Daphne thought it was a good idea." I went to the kitchen and got dessert.

"What's that?" she asked.

"You never have enough desserts in the house so I picked up a chocolate chip cheesecake."

"It looks delicious, did you get it at Sappho's Savories?"

"No, they were closed. It's from the supermarket, but I made them give me a paper bag even though they tried to give me plastic."

"I'm glad you're environmentally aware. I didn't really know if Goths - that's what you are, right, a Goth?"

"I prefer to think I'm beyond definition."

"I didn't know if it was *hip* for Goths to care about the environment." She stared at me again in that way she has. "Tell me, have you met any boys here? I imagine that's one reason you wanted to come to San Francisco."

"That and wanting to get away from Saint Dymphna where the ignorant peasants were about to burn me at the stake. I did sort of meet one boy."

"You *are* practicing safe sex?" she pried.

"Actually, my virtue is intact," I informed her.

"Well, tell me about him," she asked, taking a bite of cheesecake. I wasn't about to tell her I made out with a pothead stripper, but was saved from having to make up a cover story by her distressed reaction to the dessert.

"Chester, are you sure this is still good? It tastes funny. What's the expiration date?"

"It's fine, I've eaten it before, it always tastes this way."

"This really doesn't taste right." She distorted her face hideously.

"It's fat-free. You can't expect it to taste as good as fatty cheesecake, but we're avoiding hundreds of fat calories with each slice," I said, helping myself to a second one. My lovelife momentarily forgotten, Dora went into the kitchen and started rummaging through the recycling. On finding the container she nearly had a coronary.

"Chester! This has hydrogenated oils! They're really bad. Carcinogenic. And it may claim to be fat-free but it's loaded with sugar."

"I didn't see any sugar on the label," I protested.

"There's evaporated cane juice, corn syrup, fructose, and about a half-dozen other sweeteners. And it has 320 calories a slice, and this one little pie allegedly has twelve slices!"

"*Everything* has calories," I countered weakly. 3,840 calories for something I normally eat at one sitting does seem like a lot though.

She shook her head. "Why not just get a regular cheesecake?"

"You know I have a weight problem," I replied.

"You do not, you're just at an awkward age." She poured another glass of sake. "Believe me, it'll pass. Here, Gwen!" she called out, putting her plate on the floor. Gwendolyn excitedly scampered into the room and began to attack the cheesecake, then stopped in mid-chew, let it fall out of her mouth and walked away with a dejected look on her face.

"I'm totally fat. You just haven't noticed because I dress to disguise my flab," I explained.

"Those Madison Avenue sharpies and the fashion industry have convinced everyone to hate their body," said Dora with a sigh. "Would you clean up tonight? I'm dead tired." She went to her room, the bottle of sake tucked under her arm. I hope she isn't developing a drinking problem.

Dear Diary,                                          Saturday, Oct. 25

Daphne was in town today to do some shopping. She couldn't stay the night because of a date she had with Klaus, so she actually spent eight hours on the bus to be here for one afternoon. That's dedication. Or is it desperation? Whatever, she's really gone on this Klaus guy and wants to look good for him.

I would have been happy to tell her all about going to the Showboat, but somehow the fact that I'd once more failed to get off made the whole story seem so lame I decided to keep my mouth shut. Of course my decision lasted all of three minutes and then I had to tell her everything. Fortunately she's so obsessed with her own wonderful sex life she didn't even bother to condescend. She just told me to forget all about Franklin because he was sexually selfish and then insisted we had to hurry off to this cool clothing store she discovered on the web called Skullduggery, located in the heart of the Castro, the gay neighborhood.

That sounds so inviting – *the gay neighborhood* – like you could go there and find a boyfriend waiting for you on the street corner. Actually it's pretty creepy. There are all these guys wearing skimpy tee shirts and shorts, even when it's cold and foggy. The stores are all cutesy upscale boutiques, often as not displaying smutty pictures (always muscle men, never seventeen-year-old Goths) in the windows. There are also some cute younger guys, a few of them even walking hand in hand, and kissing right out on the street and everything. Where do they find each other?

Skullduggery is way rad. They have not only Goth clothes, but tech-wear, neo-glam stuff, and cocktail/tiki/retro outfits. Daphne and I spent hours modeling outfits in the floorlength mirrors.

"What do you think?" asked Daphne, emerging from a dressing room (the walls of which were covered in astroturf) in a tummy-revealing slinky black blouse with little skeletons on it.

"Fantastic. Klaus is a lucky man."

"You should see him, Chester, he's really handsome. He looks a little like Matt Damon crossed with Trent Reznor."

"Wow." That was an impressive combination.

"Yeah, and really good cheekbones. And in bed... ooh la la!"

Just then I spotted a rack of shiny black skintight vinyl jumpsuits. "Hey, Daphne, what about *those*?!"

"Try one on."

"Me?"

"Of course you," she insisted. "Why not?"

I cringed. "They look more like something you would wear."

"You're dying to try one on." She was right. I went into a dressing room and just managed to squeeze into a medium. Not waiting for me to come out and model, Daphne joined me inside.

"Oh, Chester!" She was speechless. I stared in the mirror and witnessed a miracle. I was no longer a fat nerdy geek but a hot - you read me correctly, Diary, *hot* - number. Like, maybe somebody will want to take me home and keep me! Unfortunately I had only $18.43 to my name and the jumpsuit was on sale for $199.99, so I left the store empty-handed. These days my piddling allowance is barely enough to keep me in fat-free brownies and nail polish. Back in Saint Dymphna I used to get money not only from babysitting but by selling the baseballs, hockey pucks and such I received as presents from various relatives who refused to believe that I loathe all sports. Those were the days.

After shopping we walked home, marveling at all the sophisticated people rushing busily around us. Daphne loves San Francisco, and has even applied to U.C.S.F. so she can hopefully move here next fall. "Chester, this city is a veritable whirlpool of social happeningness! You are so lucky to live here. I bet you'll get a boyfriend in no time."

"I don't know, Daphne, it's pretty hard to meet people. And being a Goth could turn out to be a definite social drawback. Most of the gay guys I see around don't exactly look like they listen to Christian Death, Bauhaus, or the Virgin Prunes."

"We need to go out to some nightclubs. I'd go to The Ghastly Chambers again in a minute. I'll bet you'd meet a boy there." Daphne dated some guy who worked there as a dancer once and he managed to smuggle her in hiding inside a coffin he brought to use as a go-go platform. "Everybody dresses to the nines, the music's great, and there were these girls in manacles playing with live snakes."

"I dunno," I said, remembering the few times Daphne and I had gone to all-ages Goth events in L.A. "Sure, everyone in the Goth scene is vaguely bisexual, but nobody ever hits on me. Plus, I hate snakes."

"What's with you lately?" She eyed me suspiciously. "You seem awfully tentative about everything. Anyway, where else are you going to wear that vinyl jumpsuit?"

"Okay, okay, we'll go soon."

Back at Dora's, Daphne insisted on trying to prepare a wine granita with a bottle of cheap Merlot we found in the pantry. She said she couldn't face a four hour bus ride without "fortification." We didn't have a recipe but she claimed to remember how to make it from watching some Martha Stewart wannabe on T.V. When it was done she served me a bowl with great flourish. "How does it taste?" she asked, fully expecting me to tell her it was nectar of the gods.

"It's okay," I said to be polite.

She sniffed her dish. "Just okay?" She sampled some. "It tastes like licking the inside of an expensive Italian leather handbag."

"No, really, I like it," I lied.

"It probably would have been better if we'd had sugar instead of brown rice syrup for sweetener. I can't believe Dora doesn't keep any around. What if her guests want to sweeten their coffee?"

"Well, it's probably better for us. This is probably the healthiest wine granita ever."

Daphne changed the subject. "That suit looked really great on you. I'll bet your Dad would croak if he saw you in it."

"Not to mention my evil stepmom."

"Your parents should give you the money. It's no fair you have to construct your queer identity without any funds."

"Don't you worry. I'll get the money somehow," I vowed.

Over the next few days we so-called visitors from another planet roamed about New York with our security entourage, sightseeing and collecting artifacts to take back to Zeeron. Veeba filled our suite to capacity with brassieres, nail polishes, shampoos, eyeshadows, hair dyes, wigs, nylons, lipliners, pantyhose, frocks, petticoats, pumps, boas, garters, barrettes, wigs, blushes, and conditioners. One could barely move without knocking into, or stepping on top of, some sort of beauty enhancer. "The Museum of Glamour History is going to have a whole wing on loan from the collection of Her Splendiferousness Veeba 22!" she exulted.

We also received several samples of the local flora from Runchka which the hotel staff was kind enough to water for us. I myself had a delightful time collecting music, art, and literature I felt would enhance the Terraphile position. What wasn't delightful was waking up one morning to discover Veeba, frozen in fear before the mirror in the bathroom.

"Norvex, help me, I've contracted an alien skin disease!"

There was indeed a blemish on poor Veeba's right cheek. "I'll call Runchka," I assured her, trying to sound calm.

"Is it contagious?" she asked, hiding herself behind the door.

"I don't think so," I said as I picked up the phone. "Get Finley or Metzenbaum in here immediately."

Mr. Finley arrived at once and was most reassuring. "Don't worry, blemishes are extremely common on this planet and are seldom evidence of anything serious."

"I know," said Veeba. "I saw this television commercial for an acne remedy where this boy was attempting to initiate sexual intercourse with a girl and she recoiled in horror when she saw his hideously disfigured complexion."

Mr. Finley wrinkled his nose with distaste. "I *hardly* think he was trying to initiate interco... well, you really shouldn't believe everything you see on television. I'd be happy to call Runchka for you. S/He's in Pennsylvania, so I imagine s/he could be here in a couple of hours if necessary."

"Absolutely," I said firmly, turning on the television to distract Veeba. We watched ugly, greedy people play sickeningly simplistic games of chance till finally Runchka finally arrived, medical bag in hand.

"I am distressed by your ailment, Your Terrificness. Allow me to administer treatment." S/he sat down and removed a long, thin instrument from the bag, pointed it at the blemish, and pushed a button. "This will not produce discomfort," s/he said while the whatever-it-was shot Veeba's face with an energy beam.

"Ouch! That burns. Is it gone?" Veeba looked at me fearfully.

"You're all better," I said, kissing her cheek.

"What caused it?" she asked.

"I believe skin blemishes are a result of the local cuisine which contains amazingly high quantities of fat, sugar, and inedible chemical additives," opined Runchka.

"Perhaps we should have brought our own food supply," suggested Veeba in a slightly acid tone. "And just how much longer are we going to stay here anyway?"

"At least another ten days or so," I replied calmly. "The local food won't endanger us in so short a time. Right, Runchka?"

"The likelihood is minimal. I will leave a spare blemish eradicator with you if you wish."

"Please do," said Veeba. "And by all means, let's get ready to leave soon."

"Look, we've only just arrived," I pointed out. "I haven't even met any stars yet! I haven't seen Hollywood!" I understood her desire to flee, but to gain any sort of credibility within academic circles I'd really have to stick around a bit longer. After Runchka departed, Veeba went to meet Fabrice and I spent the remainder of the day in bed recuperating from the blemish ordeal.

The next morning I accompanied Veeba to a fashion museum where we delightedly discovered an array of lovely garments by André Courrèges, Rudy Gernreich, and Oleg Cassini. "Brilliantly colored, boldly patterned, and brazenly original, these have what it takes to make it in the intergalactic arena," said Veeba who really ought to know. "If they don't always measure up to the best of Zeeronian clothes it's doubtless only because the designers didn't have access to our advanced fabrics or the microcomputers that allow moving colors, and..." She was stopped in mid-sentence by the sight of a mannequin sporting a Paco Rabanne minidress made of phosphorescent plastic discs strung with fine wire. "Norvex, can it be?"

"Why, it's exactly like the Gralgar 3 frock you gave me on our tenth anniversary."

"The card here says 1967. What year would that have been on Zeeron?"

"Let's see... 33,408."

"Gralgar said she'd just made that dress when she gave it to me in 33,418." Veeba was shocked.

"She must have seen this dress on a broadcast from Earth, copied the design."

Veeba scowled. "Plagiarism. How *unfabulous*."

I looked on the bright side. "Actually, this is something of a win for us Terraphiles. Just think, Earth has designed fashions which can pass for Zeeronian."

"Norvex, something is bothering me. With all these lovely fashions here, why are the Earthlings so drab? When I was a girl, I was apprenticed to a fashion artist, Xichka 3. Once she took me to Krufdang to look at some fabrics. Even then, when I was too young to have strong tastes I disliked the styles there. Busy, intricate, dark, layered, ooh *awful*. I used to have nightmares of being clad in their native garb and wake up screaming. But Krufdang didn't have a Vivienne Westwood working right there on the planet. I mean, look at this Pucci, the pattern looks like how I feel on rapture gas. The Earthlings have no excuse for dressing so poorly with such fab designers right here."

"You must remember the Earthlings operate with an exchange economy. These are expensive garments and most Earthlings are poor..." I stopped as she wasn't listening to me.

"Why don't you wear some of these clothes, Mr. Metzenbaum?" she asked, gesturing to a particularly smart cocktail dress.

"I'm Mr. Finley, Your Excellency, and I don't think that silver lamé would flatter me," he replied.

**17**

Dear Diary,                                  Sunday, Oct. 26

I left two more messages for Franklin, but he never returned them. Despite the battering that gave my self-esteem (or maybe because of it) I decided to go out and meet a stranger in the night. I briefly considered Goth clubs listed in the papers, but ultimately decided I'd rather hit a gay spot so I can meet an eligible bachelor, fall in love, and live happily ever after.

I started out at the Man Hole, the bar Franklin had mentioned, which is located South of Market, home of much trendy nightlife. The place was really dark inside with walls covered in posters for bands I'd never heard of. Earsplittingly loud stoner-rock blasted from gigantic speakers which combined with the feisty roar of the crowd to create a real racket. Every now and then a big hairy bare-chested bartender would ring this giant cowbell and everyone would scream at the top of their lungs, then laugh like it was the funniest joke ever. Overall, the bawdy atmosphere reminded me of the audio-animatronic Pirates of the Caribbean ride at Disneyland crossed with a biker bar from a rerun of *CHiPs* or *Quincy*.

The clientele was mostly older guys dressed like lumberjacks, but there were a few handsome young hipsters, too. I went up to the bar and ordered a beer, more or less like a regular human being. I didn't even have to show my fake I.D. Sitting down on a bench against the wall I saw directly across from me a stunningly handsome guy of about twenty-five with wide cheekbones and piercing blue almond shaped eyes that suggested a Viking heritage. He was wearing faded blue jeans, a plaid shirt over a tank top, and a baseball cap; more or less what everyone else was wearing, except that it made him look more like a grunge-rock guitar god than a lumberjack. I imagined myself kissing his blood red lips, running my fingers through his long dirty blond hair, convincing him to shave off his scraggly, unattractive goatee. Strengthening my resolve with a swig of beer, I went up to him and said, "Hi!"

"Hi," he said without much enthusiasm.

"What's your name?"

"Scout." He didn't ask me mine so I volunteered it.

"Hi Scout, I'm Chester." I held out my hand to shake his, but he let it hang in mid-air. Desperate for an opening angle I used the classic come-on line. "What's your sign?"

"Huh?" he asked, not looking at me but staring fixedly ahead at a poster for a band called Satan Claws which showed a fat devil in a Santa suit flying through the sky in a sled that had fins like a '50s Cadillac pulled by eight demonic reindeer.

"Your astrological sign. You, know, like in horoscopes?"

"Leo," he replied without looking at me.

"I'm an Aquarius. Leos and Aquariuses are supposed to get along well together," I casually mentioned while trying to look seductive by licking my lips.

"Look, no offense, but I'm huntin' bears tonight."

"Pardon?"

"I like bears."

"Meaning exactly?"

"You're a cute little kid, but I'm not into chicken." He repeated, "I like bears."

I already knew I was a "chicken," having encountered the slang term for a young man in several novels I'd read while trying to educate myself about the seamy underbelly of the homosexual world which I hoped to join. From what I'd read, chicken are supposed to be highly desirable, and it seemed unfair to me that Scout wouldn't be interested in us. None of the books had ever mentioned bears though.

"So what exactly do you mean, 'bears'?" I asked in what I'm afraid might have been a snotty tone.

"You know. Big hairy men. Natural men," he explained, again not looking at me, but staring off into the middle distance.

"Lumberjack types?"

"Yeah." There were in fact plenty of bears around. Still, I felt I hadn't grasped all the nuances of the situation.

"If I'm a chicken, and you're looking for bears, what are you?" I asked.

"I'm a coyote," he replied.

"Ahhh, I see," I said, realizing I was in way over my head.

"You know, this is a punk leather bar," he said, looking at me in a withering way. I wondered if wearing my new nylon jacket was a mistake.

"My best friend's mom, Mrs. Van Vechten, was a punk rocker. I really like her."

"Your best friend's mom?" he echoed incredulously.

"She slept with someone from Bow Wow Wow."

"That's not punk," he said, putting on his black leather in what must have been a subconscious effort to reaffirm his identity.

"She did a lot of quaaludes, bleached her hair white, and tried to learn how to play the drums," I added. He just snorted. He reminded me of the punks in high school, straight boy skate-jocks who spent all their time deciding who was, and who wasn't, *really* a punk, and screening their little clique against the horrid threat of "poseurs." They were always throwing food at me and Daphne. "So dressing like Fonzie from *Happy Days* and standing around gay bars trying to look bad-assed while listening to Aerosmith, *that's* punk?" I asked.

"What*ever*, man," he said turning away from me in disgust. "And it's not Aerosmith, it's the Inbred Cornholers!"

"My mistake," I admitted, leaving Scout to his bear hunt and retreating to the back of the bar, which smelled heavily of pot. I was looking for a place to sit when I saw Franklin talking to the most amazingly, stunningly, handsome guy I've ever laid eyes on. He was in his early twenties and wearing a yellow nylon racing shirt (revealing a lean muscular physique), blue nylon jogging pants with red stripes down the sides, and baby blue Airwalk sneakers. His wavy unkempt black hair with pointy sideburns and gorgeous Italian features were those of a true love-god. Yowza!

The beauty said something to Franklin who looked unhappy and walked off in a huff, almost stepping on my foot, but not seeing me. I didn't mind. I decided that the beauty might well be a much better match for me than Franklin, who, by not returning my calls, had proved himself to be undependable.

As I approached the beauty I noticed a thin silver cross hanging from a chain around his neck and hoped he wouldn't mind that I had an upside down cross around mine. "Hi! My name's Chester, I'm a friend of Franklin's. I just saw you talking to him." I was fully prepared to get the brush-off, but instead the beauty started talking at me without looking at me which was unnerving.

"Hey, I'm Zack. Whussup? That's a cool jacket. Too light for me though. On account of I drive a motorcycle. Gets cold, 'specially in the fog. Gotta wear leather. Man, am I baked. Got any pot on you?" His eyes bounced from his shoes to the wall to my face, then back to his shoes.

"No," I said, wondering if his strange behavior and rapid-fire delivery could be the result of marijuana. Back in high school the kids who got stoned seemed to get more relaxed and giggly, while Zack seemed fidgety and tense. Suddenly a beeper pinned to his pants pocket went off. He checked the number.

"Shit. This dude's been buggin' me all week. I turned a trick with him last Friday and now he won't leave me alone. Wants to take me to Greece, some island. Skorpios, I think. Can't go though, I'm taking classes at the University of Massage. The guy's a freak is why I don't want to call him back. Into playing with food. Not that I don't like whipped cream and chocolate, but... what'd you say your name was? Lester?" I wondered if I should interrupt him and tell him my name was Chester not Lester, but decided against it. "Yeah, a cool jacket. Nah, I can't go buying jackets like that. Too fuckin' cold. No summer in San Francisco. I come from Indiana. Gets real hot. It's fall there now, but we get Indian summer. No Indians though." He laughed. "I love Indian food. Spicy. Makes me sweat. Gotta sweat out all the toxins."

As he kept rambling I stared and stared at his perfect, perfect face. He could easily have been someone from a T.V. show or even an underwear model. I was so happy to bask in his presence I didn't even mind that his conversation lacked depth and substance, which Mrs. Van Vechten once told me is a common character defect in the young.

"I left my wallet chain at this dude's house. Seems like nobody wears wallet chains anymore. I mean, not nobody, but less people. It's fashion. One minute it's in, the next minute it's out. Right? God, I've got to burp." He did as I turned away in embarrassment. "You wanna beer?" he asked me as he drained the last of his mug.

"Sure," I said, stunned at his generosity. He disappeared for what seemed like days, during which time I finished my beer and watched the ravings of a man dressed sort of like a confederate soldier who I think was having a "bad trip." Zack returned and started right back into his monologue. He was in the midst of noticing how orange juice tastes funny if you drink it right after brushing your teeth when I suddenly felt like I was going to throw up. I really don't like beer. Fortunately it was a false alarm, but I must have looked pretty sick because Zack noticed.

"You okay?" he asked.

"Yeah," I lied.

"Do you party?"

"I can't say I've been to many parties, but I'd certainly like to go to more."

"Come with me," he ordered. I followed him to the smelly bathroom and into a toilet stall that was separated from the rest of the unsanitary looking space by a chainmail curtain. He pulled out a small baggie of white powder. Using the cross around his neck he dug out a tiny bit of the substance and held it up to my nose.

"Is that cocaine? I've only just begun to experiment with narcotics. I've seen all the talkshows and T.V. movies though."

"Cocaine?" He was incredulous. "It's crystal," he explained as if I was supposed to already know. For a pusher he wasn't very understanding. I didn't mind though as he was leaning towards me and I could feel his warm breath on my neck and smell his body. I was ready to swoon, but instead I snorted. Instantly my nose burned, lightning flashed, and I felt like I'd just woken up, though of course I was already awake. My alcohol nausea disappeared, but I felt jittery and over-amped, like I'd drunk three hundred cups of coffee. I watched Zack do his drugs, then all of a sudden I was *sure* I was going to have a heart attack.

"I don't mean to alarm you, Zack, but I think I'm dying. Could you call an ambulance?" He just stood there looking alarmed, for once at a loss for words. "*Now!*" I shrieked, collapsing against the wall.

He came to life. "You're okay, man, you're okay! Just breathe." How did he know I was okay? I noticed that I was not, in fact, breathing, so I took his advice and tried inhaling and exhaling, which did make me feel slightly better, though not much.

"I guess I may live after all," I gasped. "You can cancel the ambulance."

"Whatever," he said, leading me out of the stall past the urinal where a man who looked like an exceedingly prissy and clean-cut auto mechanic was thirstily eyeing the urine of a bear.

Zack bought me another draft beer which I downed like water. The drugs had apparently altered my physiology and I could now swill booze like a salty old sailor. Zack must really like me I thought to myself, to be getting me drunk and deranged for free. He was rambling again, but I couldn't follow his every word. My mind raced to nowhere in particular, my heart beat so quickly it scared me, my skin felt hot, like I had a mild case of sunburn, and I started perspiring like the time I caught the flu and got nightsweats. Interrupting Zack's observations about the way every *Star Trek* movie is better than the last one, I asked if we could go outside for some air.

Once out the door I started feeling euphoric and confident in a way I'm completely unused to. I couldn't be sure if it was the drug or the attentions of a male homo sapien that was responsible though. Zack said we should go to Substratum which was, he claimed, a few blocks away, though we had to walk for about twenty minutes to get there. Zack kept up his monologue so I didn't have to come up with any conversation, which was actually a relief because my mind was going a million miles a minute; spinning wheels within wheels. Finally we arrived at a warehouse with all its windows painted black, like something super-dangerous and illegal and exciting was going on inside. At the door there was a short line of handsome, hunky gay boys and one or two pert-looking best-girlfriend types wearing sassy little black jackets. Fortunately it moved pretty quickly and in no time we reached the entrance where the bouncer looked at my I.D. funny, but didn't say anything. In a way it's disturbing that people are willing to believe I'm twenty-one. Has the stress of being a social outcast prematurely aged me?

After paying our outrageous twelve dollar cover charge we went through the door and walked down a long hallway lined with benches on which sat dazed-looking clubgoers drinking bottled water and whispering (sweet nothings?) in each other's ears. The darkened windows shook alarmingly with every bass heavy thud of the music coming through the walls, and I could easily imagine the whole building shaking into pieces and collapsing. At the end of the corridor was a padded door like you'd expect to see in a mental ward which opened to a cavernous room where everyone was dancing to techno-jungle-deep house-breakbeat-whatever music so loud it hurt my ears. It made me long for the Inbred Cornholers.

We made our way to the bar where we were waited on by a shirtless demigod. Since beer doesn't agree with me I asked for a Harvey Wallbanger, but he didn't know how to make one, and since I didn't either I had to settle for a martini. Not only was it served in a miniscule glass totally filled with ice, but with tip it came to eight dollars! At the coat check Zack French kissed the gorgeous guy behind the counter and didn't even have to pay the two dollar fee. Beauty certainly has its privileges. I kept my jacket on because there was a door in the coatcheck room open to the street and I was worried criminal types could sneak in and steal stuff. "That was Andy," explained Zack. "He and I did a few videos together. He used to have the world's biggest collection of poppers but he sold it to a disco museum in Germany to get money for his penis enlargement surgery." I made a mental note never to tell Zack any compromising secrets.

The drug was making me antsy so I was glad when we finally set our drinks down on an ice machine and shoved onto the dance floor. A lot of people were doing The Gyration though it was way too crowded for all that flailing around. Zack's dancing, on the other hand, was so casual it looked like he was only fidgeting to the music. He kind of just stood there and undulated. As usual I did the twist which Daphne and I learned from watching old movies and is so simple even I can do it. Zack seemed to have finally run out of things to say (a relief to me since my mind was whizzing too fast for words) but he did have to keep greeting all the sexy guys who passed by, each of whom greeted him with hugs, kisses, "Whussups?" and full body gropes. Whenever he got busy bonding with his buddies I moved into the center of the crowd to hide the embarrassment of dancing by myself.

After a while Zack said he'd be right back and ran off with a couple of handsome guys in the direction of the rest rooms. I went to lean against the wall near where we'd left our drinks only discover they'd disappeared. Eight hard-earned dollars up in smoke! Although I wasn't the person who'd earned them, I was outraged. Just then, who should I see but Franklin, bobbing and weaving around the dance floor like a drunken boxer, his eyes shut in what appeared to be blissful appreciation of the horrible music. I called out to him but he didn't hear me, so I waded into the mass of dancers and tapped his shoulder, startling him.

"Hey, the kinnergartner! How you doin'?"

"Okay, I was just hanging out over there by the ice machine." He took my hint and followed me off the dance floor, sneakily feeling up several buffed shirtless guys as he pushed through the crowd. Franklin himself had his tee shirt stuffed in his back pocket and his freckled torso was covered in a light sweat which smelled really good. I was overcome with the desire to lick him all over. Help, I think I'm becoming a pervert!

The moment Franklin slumped against the wall he looked totally exhausted. Suddenly he jerked his head oddly. "Hey, did you just see a cat?" The music was so loud and his voice was so weak and raspy I could barely hear him. "Or maybe a dog, a really small... whatchacallit... chihuahua?" He laughed. "I am so sketchy, child! I've been here since eleven."

I glanced at my watch. "It's only eleven-thirty now, that's not so long."

"Eleven this morning," he explained. "Only left once to go over to the Manhole an' meet some friends." I was momentarily struck dumb as I tried to figure out what could make a person to spend so much time in a disco. Crystal, I guessed. Have evil druglords conspired with immoral nightclub proprietors in a fiendish plot to turn America's youth into an army of pleasure-seeking zombies who spend every minute of every day buying overpriced drinks in warehouses to which they've been charged steep admission fees? More than likely I'd say.

"Franklin!" called out a petite voice. "It's me," said a tiny girl in ponytails tugging on his arm.

"Oh, hey," he said looking down without much enthusiasm at the elfin creature calling his name.

"I haven't seen you in hours. Have you seen Melissa? She went off with Kerry and Jason and I need to find her."

"Nah," said Franklin, his eyes searching the crowd for something.

"Hey," she said to me. "You a friend of Franklin's? I'm Mittens."

"Pleased to meet you," I said, holding up my hand to shake before realizing it was inappropriate in this hyper-casual environment and waving idiotically instead.

"Want some water?" she asked me, taking a plastic bottle out of her Pokémon backpack.

"Yeah!" said Franklin grabbing the bottle and taking a huge swig before handing it to me.

"Do you have Lionel's phone number?" Mittens asked him.

"Lionel?"

"You know, Harold and Rico and Jimmy's roommate?"

Franklin shrugged, took the bottle back from me and took another large swig before returning it to Mittens.

"You do know him!" Mittens insisted. "Big shoulders? Always

wears suspenders but calls them braces? He has my television set. I loaned it to him so he could watch porn videos with this date he had over last week and I haven't been able to get ahold of him since." Franklin couldn't have looked more bored.

Mittens scanned the crowd. "He usually comes here on Saturdays, I hope he's all right. I haven't seen *Teletubbies* in days." Her voice drifted off as if she was too overcome to continue.

"I gotta get outta here," Franklin mumbled. With what looked like a huge effort he pried himself from the wall and staggered off towards the exit.

"Bye! Call me!" screamed Mittens before turning to me. "So how do you know Franklin?" My mouth was dry, I could barely hear over the music, and I really didn't feel like talking, but I answered just to be polite.

"Met at a park."

Mittens smiled prettily. "I love going to the park. Hey, you want to do a bump?"

"I could never get into disco dancing," I admitted.

"No, silly," she laughed as if I was a wit, though we were far, far, far from the Algonquin roundtable. Maybe as far as it gets. "Not *the* Bump, *a* bump. Of crystal, silly!"

As I shook my head no (the thought of being any more awake than I already was struck me as indecent) I caught sight of Zack through the crowd.

"I gotta go. Nice meeting you, Mittens."

"Yeah, nice meeting you! Are you coming back? We'll be at the Wind Down later, meet us there, okay? See ya! Tell Franklin to meet me..." She kept talking till I was too far away to hear.

"Hey," I said to Zack, who looked at me like he was trying to remember who I was.

"Oh... Lester, hey."

"Chester," I corrected, though I couldn't be sure if he heard me.

"Let's get out of here," said Zack. Pushing our way towards the door through the crowd of drug and hormone crazed dancers we saw a muscular, shirtless man collapsed onto the floor. Someone, presumably a friend of his, began screaming and pushing away the nearby dancers to keep him from being trampled. Two security guards arrived and dragged the limp body through the crowd to the street. We followed them outside where the shock of breathing fresh air was physically jolting.

"I told him not to drink on GHB but he didn't listen," explained the collapsed man's friend to the guards.

"Whatever. Ambulance is on its way. Happens all the time," said one as they set the body down behind a nearby dumpster so the people going into the club couldn't see it.

"Let's get away from this drama," said Zack, walking up the street. "So what're you up to?"

"I don't have any plans. I feel really good and really bad at the same time right now," I replied, trying to forget the image of the handsome GHB victim.

"That's cool."

"What about you?"

"I dunno."

"Would you like to come to my place?" I asked. The chemicals coursing through my addled brain were making me bold.

"How you gettin' there?" he asked.

I didn't have any cab money and couldn't see waiting for a bus in my present condition. "I guess I'll hoof it," I decided.

"Hoof it? You know, you talk funny sometimes," he observed.

"I'm not from around here, I only moved to the city a couple weeks ago," I explained, not mentioning that the real reason was having spent my entire youth hiding in the public library to avoid getting beaten up instead of wholesomely socializing with other youngsters.

"Whatever. I'll walk you home," he offered. My heart would have missed a beat but the drug had made that physically impossible. In fact it was beating so fast I was afraid I was having a heart attack again.

Halfway back to Dora's, Zack suddenly realized he'd left his jacket at the coat check, (it was worth $900, or so he claimed) and we went back to get it. On the way we passed Wowee Burgers, an old '50s drive-in on South Van Ness. The place was closed but there was some sort of performance going on in the parking lot where a couple dozen people were watching three guys doing a dance routine and singing along to some ghastly distorted music from a boombox while being filmed by a video camera. One wore a suit made of, I think, ratty old wigs, making him look a little like the lion from *The Wizard of Oz*. Another was in a blue fun-fur bathrobe, and a third was nude except for a bejeweled posing strap and some daisies in his green hair.

"Hey, let's see what's going on over there," I suggested. "Maybe they're filming a music video or something."

Zack squinted as two identically dressed Japanese drag queens came out and started lip-synching to something in unison. "What is *that* drama? Just ignore it and maybe it'll go away."

"It might be something good."

"Mothra Stewart!" screamed the M.C. as a man in a papier-mâché moth costume and a blonde wig came out flapping his wings.

"Might be somethin' real bad." Zack didn't even slow down.

It struck me as unattractive that he could be so completely indifferent. "How do you know you won't find it interesting? Remember green eggs and ham!"

"Green eggs and ham? Whatever. They look like those stupid aliens."

"What's so stupid about the aliens?" I asked. He didn't answer. "I mean, they're kinda funny." He didn't say anything so I figured I better change the subject. "You know my brother's in showbiz. Ever hear of Kyle Julian?"

"Know him from L.A., cool dude."

"You know my brother?"

"I think so. He's the one on that show with the family."

"He's on *Hangin' In There*."

"I forget the name, there's this mom and this dad, and these kids... yeah, he's got a hot ass."

"He plays Devon."

"I don't remember the name of the guy he plays, but he's got this really hot ass. Boy, we had some fun! Man, I gotta get that jacket back, it was a gift from this record producer I know. A millionaire. Flies me to L.A., pays me to pose on a marble pillar like a Greek statue while he sits in the dark and whacks off. Easy money."

It seemed unlikely he really knew Kyle so I let the subject drop. In fact, I gave up on conversation altogether. The silence didn't seem to bother Zack, but as usual it made me nervous. When we finally got back to the club, it was closed.

"This sucks. Hey, you know, I gotta go home an' crash," said Zack. Apparently he was so preoccupied with his misfortune he forgot all about picking me up.

"So..." I didn't know how to make the next move, but he saved me.

"Here's my number," he said, scribbling on a match book. "Gimme a call sometime."

I didn't tell him that he was going to be my husband, I'll let him find *that* out later. I think my "in" is that Zack likes to brag, and I, being a lowly pathetic teenager, am the perfect person to brag to. It's nice to be perfect for something!

Dear Diary,                                                    Tuesday, Oct. 29

I will *never* do drugs again. They might have given me a brief vacation from my low self-esteem and nerdly inhibitions, but the crash is worse than math class, worse than the flu, worse than *Hangin' in There*. I spent what remained of Saturday night and all day Sunday walking around, reading, and doing the things I normally do, but in this altered state that made everything seem exciting and urgent, but in a scary way. Once I finished my diary entry Sunday night I started to feel really, really, really tired but just couldn't fall asleep, and lay in bed with the covers over my face, only getting up to change CDs (Sergio Mendes to Cocteau Twins and back again to soothe my jangled nerves). Hours and hours and hours went by and I finally konked out Sunday morning around eight, then slept straight through to this afternoon when I woke up feeling like all the life energy had been drained out of my body. I told her Dora I was sick and she made me some miso soup with hijiki seaweed (I actually hadn't eaten since Saturday!) which helped a little. Afterwards I tried to decide whether to rent a movie, read a book, or call Daphne, but decided instead to call Zack and see if steamy sex with a love-god would make me feel better.

I got ahold of him around seven and he said he'd be over around eight but showed up a little after nine carrying a bottle of Jack Daniels. This presented a problem since Dora was sitting in the living room eating soba noodles and discussing the aliens with a friend on the phone. I didn't want her to see us drinking since she restricts herself to pot and wine, and takes a dim view of strong spirits. Thinking quickly I put my finger to my lips to shush Zack and stuck the bottle down my pants. Leading him through the living room I introduced him to Dora who was too preoccupied to notice the huge bulge in my jeans and into the kitchen where I poured the liquor into glasses.

"So, did you get your jacket back?" I asked as Zack played with the amusing magnets on the refrigerator door.

"What jacket? Hey, you like staying here?" he asked, wrinkling his nose like a bunny rabbit to show his disapproval.

"Beats my real home." I hid the bottle in my pants again, handed Zack a glass of hooch, and led him to my room where we sat on my futon, mere inches apart.

"Bottoms up!" he said cheerily. The whiskey burned my throat and made me instantly feel like I was underwater, feverish, and horny. Zack started going through my CDs.

"Who's Mel Torme?" he asked with a wince.

"Just this guy."

"I have over two thousand CDs."

"Wow. What kind of music do you like?"

"Prodigy, Rage Against The Machine, Cypress Hill, you know, stuff with like, an *edge*."

"How interesting," I said, deciding not to mention that I hate those bands since I was hoping to set a romantic mood. Once he's mine I'll slowly educate him and improve his taste in music. I put on Fat Boy Slim, hoping it was aggro enough for him.

"Damn, this booze is making me warm," he said, lying down on my bed and casually removing his shirt to reveal his lean muscular physique. He has zero percent body fat and washboard abs like the people on T.V. infomercials. Nearly dying of lust I tried to stay calm and act nonchalant as I lay next to him.

"Yeah, it makes me warm too," I agreed, though I left my shirt on since I didn't want him to see my love handles and the acne on my back. Zack started in with his tales of working as a high-priced callboy. The running theme was that he didn't have to do anything but was so irresistible he got paid anyway. I tried to think of a conversational opening but the liquor was striking me dumb. After a while I lost enough inhibitions to casually drape my arm around his shoulder. He didn't seem to notice and continued his story about some sugardaddy who liked to have sex on his desk in a downtown highrise office. Frustration combined with alcohol made me bold. I sat up and straddled him, my legs on either side of his narrow torso. He looked up at me as if he didn't understand what was going on, so I kissed him on the lips.

"Sorry, dude, I did some crystal earlier, I'm not really into any scenes right now," he said as if he was used to having to turn guys down, which I bet he is. I lay back down.

As the hours dragged on I learned his opinion on every band that's ever appeared on PopTV, every bar in the city, and all about his dysfunctional fundamentalist family. His mom, Bobby Jo, is a guard at a woman's prison, and his dad, Buck, manages a Christian rock band called Kingdom Cum, the lead singer of which gave twelve-year-old Zack his first blowjob, simultaneously winning him over for Jesus and homosexuality.

"I mean," Zack turned to me with a serious look on his perfectly symmetrical face, "I believe in God, but like, some of the rules those churchy types come up with are totally whack."

Just then the CD ended and I put on Stereo Total and was saved from a further theological speculation because the songs were in French which reminded Zack of how he recently paid ninety-five dollars for some Parisian DJ's deep-progressive-house mix. Daphne has told me that the sight and feel of naked flesh can make men abandon their reserve, so as Zack droned on I got up and dimmed the lights while ever-so-casually removing my shirt (being careful not to turn my back

to him and expose my zits). Half naked and three-quarters drunk, I lay
back down next to him.

"Gee, am I ever tired," I said, faking a yawn.

Zack scooted over to make room for me, and incidentally keep
his body from touching mine. "Hey, you know, you oughta join a gym.
I go to the Y.M.C.A." I was too crushed to listen to the rest. Then I got
angry. Okay, so I'm not cute enough for him, but would it have been
too much trouble to use a little tact while rejecting me? I have my
body issues! As Zack described his grueling work-out routine I got a
major pain in my stomach, probably a psychosomatic manifestation of
festering sexual frustration. I almost screamed, but managed to hold
back. "This might just not be the right time," I thought. "There's always
tomorrow!" Then I laughed out loud because I reminded myself of
that terrible song from *Annie*.

"What's so funny?" asked Zack.

"I'm just tired, I always laugh when I'm tired. Maybe you'd better
go." Zack left without a fuss and I wasn't too sorry to see him go.
Naturally I know all about men being selfish pigs from my reading,
not to mention everything Daphne's told me, but Zack seems to be
exceptionally swinish. Of course I'm a man too, but nobody has given
me a chance to be a pig yet. When that day comes, however, I fully
intend to roll in the mud and oink with the rest of them.

Dear Diary,                                    Wednesday, Oct. 30

Dad called today. I was so busy painting my toenails and watching
*E.T.* on television that I forgot to be impertinent. He was going on
about the importance of a good education and I was saying "Yes" and
"Uh-huh" when a commercial came on and I remembered I desperately
needed a vinyl jumpsuit.

"Oh, Dad, by the way, I need some money for new clothes."

"What's wrong with the clothes you've got? Wait, don't answer
that, *I know* what's wrong with the clothes you've got. Ha, ha, ha." He
is such a comedian. "The question is, are you thinking about buying
some clothes that you can apply for work in, or are you wanting some
more of that, uh, gloom and doom stuff, what do you call it?"

"Goth, Dad. It's an expressive reaction against the culture of sun-drenched hedonism and conformist banality, heavily influenced by 19th century Romanticism, Surrealism, and Weimar German avant garde culture."

"Well, it makes you look like Alice Cooper."

"Who's she?"

"Or some kooky Victorian eccentric," he added. "It's all very cute when you play dress-up in high school, but you're in the real world now. I don't suppose you've thought about a suit?"

"Most of the jobs that hire seventeen-year-olds don't really require suits."

"When you're applying for a job though, you always wear a suit and a tie."

"All right. I need money for a suit."

"I'd like to go shopping for one with you. I can remember the day after my high school graduation your Grampa took me out to buy my first work suit..." The commercial ended so I have no idea what he said next but I'm sure it didn't involve sending me any much needed money.

## 18

The next day the U.N. launched its disinformation campaign. A rocket launch pad was "discovered" in Siberia and the head of the Russian space program "identified" our ship as a missing Soviet-era craft. Then in London a wealthy eccentric, Sir Monty Spaulding-Cox, held a press conference in which he "admitted" purchasing the ship for us as a publicity stunt to promote his new orbiting sanitarium. He was, the story went, planning on sending overwrought Earthlings into space where a brief zero-gravity vacation, he asserted, would rejuvenate their beleaguered bodies. "If you're feeling the weight of the world on your shoulders, that's *gravity!*" he was quoted as saying.

Using reverse psychology, we appeared on the television news insisting that we were in fact extraterrestrials, and to further discredit ourselves, accused our accusers of themselves being evil space aliens. The press wasted no time in deciding we were the liars, branding us the hoax of the century and demanding an apology. Polls showed the percentage of people believing us to be authentic aliens dropping into the single digits. One of the daily papers ran an article that well summed up public opinion, the most telling line of which read, "The only thing truly alien about these flagrant frauds is their spaced-out taste in music and television."

Freed from the media circus and public scrutiny which had dogged us before, it was much easier to get around. Fewer people stared, and when they did they were bemused or disapproving rather than frightened or angry. I proceeded to investigate offices, stores, and factories where Earthlings toiled like machines for literally hours on end. I visited parks and beaches strewn with garbage. I dropped in on prisons, schools, and other spirit-crushing institutions where the regimentation and drab interiors almost reduced me to tears. Theaters, galleries, churches, and other places of entertainment, although far from pleasant, seemed wonderful by comparison. Although I tried to render myself dispassionate I couldn't help becoming slightly overwhelmed and depressed. Perhaps, I theorized, it was the very hideousness of Earth which gave the planet's fantasy its flair. We on civilized worlds cannot imagine the urgency with which barbarous people need to find escape. The mystery then, is why other barbarous worlds don't produce great motion pictures like *Barbarella*, *Hairspray*, and *The King and I*, or artists like Kenny Scharf and Margaret Keane.

Through her hairdresser friend Fabrice, Veeba managed to befriend some vivacious young scenemakers who congregated at nightclubs and wore the best of Earthly fashion. To my surprise, these people were charmed by her. Although she is sort of my girlfriend, I confess I'm amazed when other people don't find her a tad obnoxious. She began to go out with them at night while I, ever the good academician, stayed home to order my notes.

Without Veeba I grew lonely, and was thus unusually interested when I came across an invitation for her, Runchka, and me to attend a reception to be held in our honor in San Francisco by a group calling itself the Interplanetary Friendship Committee. Thanks in part to Veeba's socializing we had become the darlings of the avant garde culturati who craved novelty and shared our enlightened opinions. This sounded like a grand opportunity to meet some of our admirers.

"Veeba, have you seen this invitation?" I asked.

"Yes, darling, Mr. Metzenbaum showed it to me this morning," she replied from her bedroom where she sat doing her makeup in front of her vanity.

"Shall we go?"

"Well, I called Fabrice and asked him about the group . He told me that these Interplanetary Friendship people are some tired old biddies who used to be called the Society for the Exploration of the

Supernatural and ExtraTerrestrial. Every year they glom onto something, the Loch Ness Monster, healing crystals, the Dalai Lama, Bigfoot, whatever, and throw it a reception. They're just thrillseekers. I really have no interest in them." She finished gluing on her two-inch metallic blue eyelashes and waltzed toward the door giving me a peck on the cheek. "Now I'm going out and I won't be back for *three days*, that's how many parties I have to go to."

"Three days?" asked Mr. Metzenbaum sounding dismayed. He and his assistants had to accompany her everywhere.

"That's not all that long, by Zeeronian standards," I informed him, sticking up for Veeba.

Veeba twirled around in front of a mirror. "Everyone's celebrating this quaint local festival called Halloween, it should be fascinating. They dress up in costumes and eat disgustingly sweet foods."

"Would you mind if I went?" I asked.

"To San Francisco?" she replied. "Why should I care what you do? Do I look all right?"

"Wonderful as always."

"You're just saying that, you don't mean it," Veeba pouted. "I can tell."

"Are you trying to start an argument?" I snapped.

"Not at all, I wouldn't dream of usurping your role." Veeba stalked out the door. Mr. Metzenbaum gave me a helpless shrug and followed her. I was only too happy that she wouldn't be accompanying me. A little (or perhaps even a big) break would do us good I decided. At once I called Dora Julian, the president of the Interplanetary Friendship Committee.

"Ms. Julian? This is Norvex 7. I just received your kind invitation."

"Mr. Norvex!" Her voice gushed through the receiver. "I'm so glad you called! Oh my, let me collect myself. This is such an honor!"

"No, no, the honor is entirely mine. I must say I'm extremely intrigued with the idea of visiting San Francisco. I just loved *What's Up Doc?* and all the *Thin Man* films."

"Yes, well, so you'd like to visit."

"Quite. It'll be just me actually. Veeba and Runchka are otherwise occupied. Oh, but there is some good news, you won't have to pay for my visit. The U.N. covers the cost of all my travel and hotel arrangements. I know that's a big problem for you - financing, taxation, and mortgages and all. I would like to make the visit soon though. We're not planning on staying on Earth much longer. How about this weekend?" I suggested.

"I'm afraid that's rather short notice. We have to rent a hall, and send out press releases, and get a caterer..."

"Well, how about next weekend?"

"I suppose that could be arranged," she replied enthusiastically.

"Would you prefer I make a speech, or were you thinking of something more informal?"

"Whatever your wisdom leads you to believe is best for us."

"My wisdom? Ah yes, well, I'm a bit speeched out right now. How about a nice party where I can meet all sorts of interesting people and just chat?"

"Fine. This is so exciting I can't believe it! All my life I've known somehow that there was *more*. I don't know how I knew, but I just *knew*. The everyday world is so predictable and mundane, but the universe is so big. It couldn't all be supermarket lines and late alimony checks, there would have to be something fantastic somewhere. And now something fantastic is here!"

"I'll take that as a compliment, if I may. Now, don't worry about a thing, I'll have the U.N. security people contact you to make arrangements. Thank you so much. Goodbye."

Veeba kept to her promise and didn't return for several days, during which time I toured the Natural History Museum, lunched with Yoko Ono (I'm sure I've seen her on planet Buxmort, but she insists she hasn't been), and, at Mr. Finley's invitation, saw a sporting event. The "game" was held in a stadium wherein athletes in ugly uniforms shamelessly competed with each other to do something, I'm not sure what, with a ball while "fans" screamed like savage animals and consumed vast quantities of food-like substances. It was horrific.

Finally the day arrived to depart for San Francisco. To get there I was forced to again trust myself to one of Earth's disagreeable flying airplane machines. Although we made it to our destination safely our journey was not without stomach-churning turbulence, which, disconcerting though it was, compared favorably with the agony of the in-flight film, a sentimental comedy about an intellectually retarded man who battles heartless bureaucrats to save a children's playground. The ability of primitives to endure smarm is almost inexhaustible, and the less said about their distrust of intellectual capacity the better. We arrived a day before the reception and checked into a hotel with a rotating restaurant on the roof.

San Francisco turned out to be a cute, toylike town nestled amidst hills and water, where bridges and ornate buildings combine to charming effect. I decided to stay for a few days after the reception and then nip down to Hollywood (where Veeba could perhaps join me) for a look at some television and motion picture studios. After that, I thought, we ought to conclude our visit to Earth. To linger longer would be to tempt fate. Mentioning my plans to Mr. Finley, he enthusiastically endorsed both Hollywood and a speedy return to Zeeron. I gathered the U.N. was nervous our ruse would be discovered and a public outcry ensue.

On the day of the reception I wore a simple yet elegant black suit by Jean Paul Gaultier, a talented Earth designer, adding the Zeeronian touch of matching my hair color to my day-glo chartreuse socks and shirt. Earthlings are not only lazy about changing hair color, but lazy about even matching their natural hair and their outfits. As I examined myself in the mirror I was happy to note a subtle but indisputable change from the sad countenance which had stared back at me in the faculty lounge of the Institute. I looked, if I may be so immodest as to suggest it, heroic, commanding, and adventurous. As I was admiring myself Mr. Finley entered my room wearing yet another charcoal gray business suit.

"So you're wearing that, are you?" I asked. Normally I don't think the clothing of one's companions are any of one's business, but there *are* limits. I could barely gaze at him, my disgust with his sartorial blandness had grown so severe.

"If my outfit in any way offends you I would be more than happy to change to whatever you deem appropriate," he said, his voice betraying not a hint of irritation at my rudeness. Such selflessness disgusted me and I was about to take him up on his offer when he smiled wryly. "Just don't ask me to wear anything *too* loud, okay?"

Pleased that he'd lightened up enough to joust with me I told him to forget it. Just then the phone rang, and it was announced that Dora Julian was waiting for us in the lobby.

Dear Diary,                              Thursday, Oct. 31 / Halloween

Last year Daphne and I spent All Hallows' Eve with her then-boyfriend Monty (who's got some major Goth damage going on) in this huge graveyard at the end of town full of fancy mausoleums and huge memorial statues. We tried to invoke the spirits of the dead using Monty's spellbook but nothing happened so we switched to summoning Caacrinolaas, the Grand President of Hell. He must have been busy visiting other bored teenagers because he didn't show either. After a few hours and a pint of vodka, Monty claimed he'd been possessed by Pharzuph, the demon of lust and fornication, and began making out with Daphne. I spent most of the night trying to read Byron by moonlight which was less romantic than it sounds, especially since I kept getting distracted by the heavy breathing and squeals of ecstasy coming from a certain nearby tomb. On the way home Monty promised that if he ever developed any homosexual inclinations I'd be the first person he'd call. That was nice, but despite a strong inclination towards cross-dressing (about which Daphne told me in graphic detail), he's remained rabidly heterosexual, which is too bad because Monty's way cute.

Hoping to find something fun to do I called Zack and Franklin, but couldn't reach them. In desperation I went to the Castro to see the festivities: fifty thousand beer-swilling yuppies in Dockers, Nikes, and Tommy Hilfiger (the same people who, the rest of the year, point at Daphne and me and say, "Hey! Halloween's over, you can take your costume off now! Hyuck, hyuck, hyuck") milling around and staring at five hundred drag queens. I left after fifteen dull minutes. It was a lucky thing I came home when I did because I caught this weird '60s stop-motion animation kids' T.V. special, *Mad Monster Party*. One of the puppet things was creepy old Boris Karloff and another was Phyllis Diller with marabou feathers, a cigarette holder and everything. Truly spooky.

After the show I noticed from the packaging that the organic Halloween candies I'd been scarfing down during the show weren't fat-free and in a panic I weighed myself. What a surprise! I've lost six pounds since I left home and now tip the scales at a mere 147. If this keeps up I'll be waif-like in no time!

The man known as my father called to check up on me, and torment me with the news that Kyle's been signed up for yet another season of *Hangin' In There*. The show should have been canceled, high ratings or no, on purely aesthetic grounds, but there is obviously no justice in the universe. Another thing noticeably absent in the universe is space aliens. It's come out that our extraterrestrial visitors are frauds, though the Interplanetary Friendship Committee believes otherwise. Dora and her friends are telling anyone who'll listen that the whole fraud story is a cover-up. I sort of feel sorry for her being made a fool of since she's been pretty nice. I think I can sort of say I honestly like her, I guess.

Dear Diary,                                         Friday, Nov. 1

Today Dora got a call from New York. She's going to host some big party for one of the phony aliens. Before the hoax was exposed she couldn't even get the time of day from their handlers. It's kind of pathetic that she and her friends are clinging so hard to their alien fantasy. Well, I guess life can get pretty boring, so why not? Anyway, I'm supposed to help her out at the reception as an hors d'oeuvre server. I tried to get out of it and she, for the first time, became sort of parent-like.

"I don't think I ask terribly much of you. Really, it should be an honor to help out during one of the most momentous occasions in human history. You might ask yourself why it is you don't want to expand your horizons and create new life-memories by encountering people from other worlds..." And so on. I wonder if being forced to meet a space alien counts as child abuse?

Her tone was irritating me, so I sassed her. "Since the space aliens don't believe in God and don't have any religion, will you be talking to them about the Goddess?" Dora's library is overflowing with books on paganism, Goddess worship, and paranormal mumbo jumbo.

Dora winced. "You may think you are being clever, but you're just closing yourself off from the unknown. There's more to the mystery of existence than we can comprehend. Where did time, and space, and matter, and energy, and the law of gravity all come from, eh, Mr. Know-it-all? Skepticism only says *No* but existence itself is a great big *Yes*." Feeling she'd scored a point she smiled without mirth. It occurred to me that sometimes she looks just like an apple doll.

"There could definitely be some sort of deity in charge of everything, but do you really think it's some ecologically conscious, pro-choice, nurturing *woman*? The universe sucks! What about death and pain and growing old? God as a sadistic junior high school Phys Ed teacher, or a vicious right-wing Army drill sergeant, I could believe. But would some nice Goddess create earthquakes, influenza, or high school? If there's an omnipotent being he, she, or it has a mean streak a mile wide."

"Suffering helps us learn," said Dora "And I don't think we understand the term Goddess in the same way. I conceive of the Goddess as divine energy within you."

"If you ask me, the creator is probably the mean nasty old man in the Old Testament. AIDS and herpes are exactly the sort of thing a sex-hating god like Jehovah would come up with to punish fornicators."

"Those diseases don't just affect fornicators," countered Dora.

"So what?" was my retort. "That's perfectly in keeping with His style. He's always punishing the innocent along with the guilty. Remember, we're talking about the deity who killed the first born of all of Egypt because he didn't like their Pharaoh's Jewish policy, the God who ordered Abraham to sacrifice his son to prove his loyalty, just for kicks! And let's not forget the incident where he had bears devour some children for making fun of Elisha's baldness." Daphne has this cool book from the Church of His Satanic Majesty that catalogues all these heinous things from the Bible.

"If it's any consolation to you," Dora shot back, "I argued till I was blue in the face to keep your father from sending you boys to Sunday school."

"But don't you see? Maybe they're right! Maybe the God of the Bible is real. Maybe the universe is run by some guy who gets off on watching people suffer!"

Dora sighed. "In my experience we bring a lot of pain on ourselves by choosing the path of selfishness. We have free will that allows us to create our own reality. In that way, the Christians really are onto something. We can be saved from suffering through our own free will."

"Oh, lucky us," I countered, "we're given a choice between salvation through self-denial and obeying God's inscrutable and unpleasant whims or damnation as a result of wickedness, insubordination, or partying too much. Why weren't we given an easier choice, say between sex, chocolate, and playing with kittens?"

"What I meant was, we can chose a path of enlightenment and growth, or..." Dora looked confused. "So what are you saying, you're going to become an Episcopalian like Howard?"

"No way! I'd never worship a cruel and arbitrary God, even if he was omnipotent. Anyway there could be other explanations for the state of the universe. We could inhabit a polytheistic cosmos with a bunch of almost omnipotent deities, some nice, some not, carrying on and feuding like the warring parties on Mount Olympus. Or there could be one deity with a split personality or a substance abuse problem."

"Chester, I'd like you to take a look at this book about accessing your inner divine energy, you don't have to think of it as a Goddess." She began looking through the bookcase. "Maybe you could think of it as a Diva. I've often thought that when gay men worship Barbra Streisand, Liza Minelli, Cher, or whomever, they aren't so different from those of us who venerate Kali, Athena, or Mother Nature. We must each find our own path."

"Siouxsie Sioux maybe...but Babs? Liza? Cher?" I rolled my eyes.

Dora launched into her typical lecture. "I'd suggest you start with meditation. It really clears your mind. Normally our consciousness is full of extraneous activity. Chanting or sitting quietly allows us to discipline our thought."

"If I want to clear my mind I watch television," I said truthfully, if not proudly.

"Clearing our mind quiets our desires, which are what bring us pain. Once we have severed our attachments to the material, we can attain enlightenment. Buddhism teaches that we're all reincarnated again and again so we can learn from each incarnation. Eventually we learn to eliminate all desires and attain nirvana, the end of the cycle of reincarnation." I'm paraphrasing here because Dora was using a lot of fancy Hindu words that I didn't quite catch.

"But I don't want to end the cycle of reincarnation! Why would anyone ever want to be nothing? I *like* being alive. I *want* to come back *again* and *again* and *again*. Life isn't all pain and misery. Sure, people die and there's disease and stuff, but there's also new clothing, and puppy dogs, and cute guys, and ice cream on a hot summer day. I want to have fun! *I want to live!* Even if I have to spend a lifetime as a toad, at least there'd be nice juicy flies, and boy toads! Maybe if you're some peasant who works fifteen hours a day for rice and beans it's rough, but this is America! We have amusement parks and shopping malls and fast cars and cheeses from around the world. Not only do I want to come back, I don't want to go away in the first place!"

"Here." She handed me a book, simplistically entitled, *Accessing Your Inner Divine Energy*, with the picture of a frighteningly calm woman in a turquoise-blue cowlneck sweater smiling blissfully on the cover.

"Gee, thanks," I said, sarcastically.

She yawned. "I got up at five today to make arrangements for Norvex's visit and I'm beat so I really need to go to bed now, but I hope we can talk about this again. Take a look at that book, it won't bite you." She gave me a wink and went to her room.

I called Daphne who was thrilled when she heard about the space alien reception and is angling to get an invitation. She thinks the extraterrestrials are the greatest thing since safe sex and finds their "liberated" attitudes inspiring. I guess I'll bring her along for company. What am I going to wear?

Dear Diary,                                    Saturday, Nov. 2

Life is so weird. Things that you want to happen never happen, then they happen all wrong. It began when, without calling first, Zack came by last night. Dora was holding a meeting in the living room with a bunch of noisy space-nuts, so we went out for a walk. I could tell right away he was high on something because his speech was even more disjointed than usual and his eyes were kind of glassy. We spent a couple hours wandering around, finally ending up on Polk Street. He was telling me, again, all about his amazing exploits as a callboy. I think he's going to have to give up "the life" when he becomes my boyfriend. Not that I'm jealous or anything, I just get bored hearing about it. He's worse than Daphne, although she's not a sex worker yet. Anyway, who should we run into but Mr. Larry, the nelly hairdresser! It seems he and Zack are acquainted from "business" and we stopped to talk.

Mr. Larry was extremely friendly and acted all put out that I didn't follow up on my "promise" to let him fix my hair. We'd only just said hello when Mr. Larry took Zack aside and they began whispering. I could tell from their glances in my direction that I was the subject of their little conference. Zack then came over to me and broke the news that Mr. Larry wanted to hire my services, *if you know what I mean*, for two hundred dollars! I immediately said yes. It did briefly occur to me that I was possibly unready to "turn a trick" since I'd never actually completed an act of sexual intercourse, but I decided not to worry about it since two hundred dollars would be enough (excluding the tax) for the vinyl jumpsuit at Skullduggery.

So Zack went off and Mr. Larry walked me to his car, a pink and gold 1962 Rambler convertible. On the drive to Mr. Larry's apartment I was nervous so I didn't say much, but he didn't seem to notice. He just kept chatting away about new hair products, fine French cuisine, and his dogs, Cosmo and Gimlet. It took him forever to find a parking space, and I started imagining what he'd look like naked. Ugh! By the time we reached the door my palms were sweating and I wanted to run, but the thought of how great I looked in the jumpsuit overpowered my fear.

Mr. Larry's apartment was done up in French provincial, Louis-whatever furniture with gold leaf and gilt everywhere. Liberace city. The smell of potpourri was so intense I almost gagged. "Make yourself at home, I'll fix us a little nightcap," he giggled as he disappeared into a kitchenette. I was left to stare at a massive gold-framed nude photograph of the guy who played Wally on *Leave It To Beaver*. At least I think it was him. Whoever it was, the guy was gorgeous. I opened a window for fresh air and sat down on a huge white sofa. I was immediately set upon by Cosmo and Gimlet, who started trying to tear my clothes off.

Moments later Mr. Larry swept (there's no other way to describe it, he *swept*) back into the room with two cocktails on a sliver tray, singing out, "Ta-da!"

"I see you have your dogs well trained," I said while fending off the little beasts who were tugging at my pants.

He set down the drinks. "Don't mind them. Come here, my princesses, time for bed." He unceremoniously tossed the dogs into the next room like footballs, then kicked the door shut. "Now, I've made you a nice martini. Drink up." I tried a sip but it tasted foul. "One gulp," he advised. I was leery, but you have to learn sometime. I gulped.

That's actually all I remember except waking up the next morning in a canopied bed that looked like something one of the Hapsburgs would have slept in. I was wearing only my underpants, the clock said 10, and my head throbbed as if my brain was swelling and was about to squirt out my ears. Mr. Larry again swept into the room, this time wearing a silk dressing gown with an ascot and carrying a tray with freshly squeezed orange juice, toast, a poached egg, and a calla lily in a crystal vase.

"I trust you slept well?" he asked while almost tripping over his lap dogs, both of whom were yapping at his heels and trying to leap up and eat *my* breakfast. It amazes me that people put up with animals who display manners that'd get a human child banished to boarding school.

"I don't feel too good," I admitted, sitting up so he could set down the tray which actually did look lovely. Mr. Larry started opening the heavy gold drapes. "Don't!" I pleaded.

"You really soaked up the sauce last night! Eat up, it'll help. Trust me, honey, I been there."

"What, if you don't mind my asking, exactly did we do?" I winced.

"It was all safe it that's what you're worried about, and it was all fun... Stud!" he giggled.

"I wish you'd go into some more detail." I started to eat the food which did make me feel better. Especially when I noted the two hundred-dollar bills hidden inside my napkin.

"We made beautiful music together three times last night and once this morning! By the way, have you joined the Y.M.C.A. yet?"

"Who said I was going to?"

"I just thought it would be nice for you. You could meet some nice boys and get some exercise. I think young people should get plenty of exercise."

Everyone from hot hustlers to geriatric johns seems to think I'm fat. Maybe I should work out, but somehow I just can't imagine myself in gym clothes. I changed the subject. "Sure is a fancy place you got here."

"Thanks, I decorated it myself. Many of the pieces I inherited from my mother, God rest her soul. Say, do you feel like taking in a movie? My treat!"

"Actually, I have something I have to do," I said finishing the last of my breakfast. "I'm going to that big party they're having for Norvex the alien, and I need some clothes."

"Norvex, such a charming creature," admired Mr. Larry. "You sure you don't have time for perhaps even just a stroll?"

I started pulling on my clothes. "No, but thanks though."

"Well, let me give you my home phone number." He handed me a business card. "Call me just any old time."

"Sure thing," I lied. "And thanks for everything."

After I left I went straight to Skullduggery, and I'm now the proud possessor of one vinyl jumpsuit that makes me look like a million bucks. I guess I'd feel better about the way I got it if I could remember the details of my night of wild passion, but you can't have everything.

Dear Diary,                                                    Sunday, Nov. 3

Anguish! Irritation! Outrage! This morning Dora told me that my charming brother Kyle is going to be one of the celebrity co-hosts at her stupid alien party (which is going to be held at the warehouse where they have Substratum of all places). He gets to meet the guest of honor while I'm passing out canapés to Noe Valley matrons anxious for a close encounter of any kind.

"Why'd you invite *him*?" I asked.

"I'm asking anyone and everyone to participate," she explained. "You don't much like Kyle, do you?"

"I suppose he's all right," I grumbled. "For what he is. Considering."

"I remember when you two were little you used to fight morning, noon, and night. Frankly, it was a pain in the neck. I know all brothers do it, or at least mine did when I was a kid, but you're getting a little old for sibling rivalry. You might want to think about transcending your adversarial self."

"It's just that he and I have totally different values," I explained.

"Meaning what?"

"Meaning he likes stupid all-American things like money, status, and popularity. I don't think he cares about your alien, or the rainforests, or culture, or anything."

"Chester, you're living with a lot of anger," Dora scolded. "You haven't been treated with respect, and you want to hit back at everything that's hurt you. But you could start to ask yourself what acting angry or 'cool'" (she made little quotation marks in the air with her fingers) "really gets you. If it's not helping you grow as a person you need to move on. Anger is fine, you can love your anger, but it's not an answer in itself. You need to channel it into something constructive so you can finally let it go. It hurts me to see you so down on Kyle. Sure, he's a bit of an all-American, but that doesn't make him a monster."

"Not exactly," I admitted. "Only he gets to be on television and worshipped by millions of love-starved girls; he sells disgusting fast-food products and violent computer games to innocent teenagers who don't know any better, while I have to suffer in obscurity."

"If you don't approve of what he does, why are you jealous that he gets to do it?" she asked.

Damn, I hate being psychoanalyzed. Before I could admit that Dora might have a point she revealed her ulterior motive. "I don't want any scenes between you two at this event. This event is not *about* scenes and anger and who got a bigger piece of pie. It's about something much *larger.*"

"Yeah, like your credulity."

"What's that supposed to mean?" She pursed her lips waiting for my answer.

"Are you really one hundred percent sure they're aliens? I mean, it's pretty funny that they got away with the prank for so long, but come on!"

"I have no doubt whatsoever. I suppose I have no hard evidence, but the Committee does have access to certain restricted information. Plus, they strike me as sincere." Dora crossed her arms and added, "Kyle believes in them."

"That figures."

I went to my room to brood. So I'm not supposed to mind that I get to be a servant while he gets to be a celebrity. Well, I know one thing. Not only am I doing my catering work in a black vinyl jumpsuit, but I'm dying my hair blue. Maybe I'll never be as cute or hot or sexy as Kyle, but when people see us together they're going to look at *me*!!!

Dear Diary,                                          Monday, Nov. 4

Daphne called up today in tears. It seems she and Klaus broke up after having an argument about capital punishment. It seems he thinks it's okay to off people sometimes while Daphne thinks life is inviolable.

"Daphne, you're better off without someone who doesn't share your basic world view. Dump him," I advised.

"But he's really great in a lot of ways. And remember he got you your fake I.D. Besides, did you find out about the basic world views of those boys, Zack and Franklin?"

"Boys like Zack and Franklin don't have world views."

"Though I admire the courage it takes to become a sex worker in our erotophobic society I can't help but think those two aren't the best companions for you. Why don't you go to the local Gay-Lesbian-Bisexual-Transgender-Questioning youth rap group, or a political meeting or something?"

"I don't 'rap' and I don't have any politics," I replied.

"I thought you were a... what was it? A Monarcho–Syndicalist?"

"Well, yeah, but I'm the only one so there aren't any meetings."

"When we're making love Klaus is so sweet, you'd think he was liberal and humanistic, but when it comes to politics or philosophy he changes into another person. He starts talking about Nietzsche and gets all inflexible."

"Beauty's only skin deep, Daphne. I say you're better off without him. Find someone with more character."

"Maybe you're right," she agreed. "It's just that we've only been broken up for three hours and I already miss him so much it hurts."

"Remember when you broke up with Todd? Or Monty? Or Jeffrey?" I reminded her. "You thought it was the end of the world each time, but you got over them. Besides, he was too old for you."

"He's only twenty-eight," she replied huffily.

"What's wrong with a cute little teenage boy? They're always hitting on you, I've seen it. I'd kill for a cute little teenage boy."

"Teenage boys are immature and stupid, it's like dating Beavis or Butthead."

"Well, it's better than nothing," I said.

"I'm not so sure about that. But, Chester," she moaned, "if you could just see the way Klaus looks at me when I take my clothes off."

"Daphne!" I was appalled by even trying to imagine the expression on Klaus's face.

"You can be such a prude sometimes, Chester. Klaus is so at ease with his body, he moves like an animal, like a sexy, muscular tiger, or..."

I held the phone away from my ear till she was done, then I said I had to go to dinner. I hope Daphne finds someone new soon so we can go back to talking about *me* and *my* problems.

Dear Diary, Wednesday, Nov. 6

Today I was about to go in the front door of the Main Library down by Civic Center when I saw Zack and Franklin zipping along the curb on skateboards. I've always gone ga-ga for skate rats. Daphne and I even tried skating once when we decided it would be a great way to meet cute boys, but neither of us could get the hang of it and we had to settle for just watching, which actually got boring pretty quickly. The guys would just go mutely around and around and around doing the same jumps over and over like hamsters on an exercise wheel. Well, Zack saw me and came up to talk, just as if I was a normal young person. That would never, ever, ever, have happened to me back in hateful St. Dymphna where being seen with me would be social death for a skater.

"Hey, I heard from Mr. Larry about the other night. Way to go." Zack punched me on the arm in that way guys have of punching each other on the arm.

"Yeah, it was keen," I said, instantly realizing I sounded dorky. I turned to Franklin who stood behind Zack scowling mutely. "Hello, Franklin. Long time no see."

"Whussup?" he asked, not sounding like he wanted an answer.

"Not much. Hangin' out," I said, being sure to drop the "g" on hanging so as to sound casual and inarticulate. Franklin was dressed like Zack in slacks cut off below the knee, a baggy tee shirt, and a racing jacket, but somehow on him it didn't work. While Zack looked hiply disheveled, Franklin just looked frumpy.

"We just came from the weenie wash," said Zack by way of conversation.

My curiosity forced me to risk sounding like the greenhorn I am by asking, "What's the weenie wash?"

"The bookstore," explained Zack.

Seeing I still didn't understand, he elaborated. "You know, the dirty bookstore, the glory holes. You stick your dick through the holes in the side of the video booth and some guy on the other side sucks it. Get it? A weenie wash."

"I get it!" I said, laughing weakly. Shocked though I was, I tried to act as if nothing could be more natural. Don't these guys worry about getting their penises cut off by some pervert collector?

"Wanna go up to Polk Street with us?" asked Zack.

"Sure," I replied. My social life is blossoming beyond my wildest dreams in this magical city by the bay! Franklin, however, didn't look too happy with my invitation. I realized he has a crush on Zack, who will hopefully discover my inner qualities and realize that Franklin, though perfectly nice, would be all wrong for him. As we walked Zack began telling me about some guy who'd given him five hundred dollars for shaving his body, the man's, not Zack's. Zack didn't even have to take his clothes off.

As we approached the sleazy part of the street with the bars and drugged-out teenage runaways Zack tied his jacket around his waist and stuffed his shirt in his back pocket, though it couldn't have been over sixty-five degrees out. He must be real warm-blooded. Franklin said he wished he had some pot and Zack complained that he too needed some "weed" but was broke. I didn't ask what happened to the five hundred dollars he'd supposedly just made for fear of offending him. After all, he's the only male friend I've had since third grade.

Suddenly a convertible with a slimy-looking yuppie pulled up beside us. "Whussup?" asked Zack sauntering over to the side of the car like he was born doing it. Franklin beamed admiringly.

"Hey, Zack, my man! Need a ride?" asked the driver with a nasty looking grin on his face. He was wearing a pastel mint green '80s-style sportscoat with the sleeves pushed up to reveal his hairy forearms. All at once I knew fashion fear. Zack apparently *did* need a ride and barely remembered to wave goodbye to us before driving off. I was left alone with Franklin.

"So what'll we do now?" I asked.

"Dunno," said Franklin. "Wanna get some coffee?"

"Okey-dokey," I replied, cursing my choice of words as I spoke.

As we walked towards a nearby cafe (San Francisco has two on every block) I decided to pump Franklin for a little info. "So, did you go back to Substratum that night I saw you there?"

"Nah, I ran into a friend of mine and we went over to his house." How popular he is, I thought to myself jealously, even if he does have a drug problem and horrible taste in music.

"Your friend Mittens seems nice."

"Mittens? Oh, you mean that midget chick who's always got all that Pokémon shit with her? I don't get her. I mean, what is her drama?" How mean Franklin can be, I thought to myself.

We ordered capuccinos. "So, Franklin, just how well do you know Zack?" I tried not to sound jealous.

"We're pretty tight."

"He seems like a real cool guy." Again I sounded dorky.

"He's all right, I guess." Franklin looked uncomfortable and began stirring his coffee nervously.

"Does he do a lot of crystal? I mean, is he on it all the time?"

"He's not a full time tweaker, but he and Miss Chrissy are pretty well acquainted."

Miss Chrissy, I knew from various anti-drug billboards and print ads, was crystal. When he and I are wed, I will send him off to the Betty Ford Center first thing. The only thing my husband is going to be addicted to is my love.

Suddenly Franklin got the look of a hunting dog spotting a rabbit. "Creep!" he barked.

"Who, what, where?" I asked, turning around. He pointed to a man in his forties in a brown leather bomber-jacket, newish jeans, aviator sunglasses, and a long cream-colored scarf. He looked like someone you'd see in an old photo from Studio 54. "Doesn't anyone on this street know what year this is?" I muttered to myself.

"That guy picked me up once, you know, a trick..." he stopped as if uncertain whether to tell me more.

"And, and... ," I encouraged.

"I was at his apartment and I asked for the money up front."

"Naturally," I said. Franklin shot me a look that said, 'How do you know?' "I've read a lot of novels," I explained, wondering if Zack had told him about Mr. Larry and me.

"So MissThing says her friend is coming by with some money in about fifteen minutes and we ought to get started. *Okay!?*" It took me a moment to figure out who Franklin was talking about because of Franklin's verbal tick of sometimes saying "she" or "her" when he's talking about guys. "I should have left then, but I said 'We'll wait.' Normally I'm pretty mellow, but after fifteen minutes of her trying to paw me, and not even offering a beer, I looked him straight in the eye and go, 'I'm leaving now and you gotta pay me.' And she goes 'I don't have any money!' and I'm like '*Hello?!* You do not bring me to your apartment and tell me you don't have any money. I'm gonna have to take something.' And she's like, 'My friend must have been delayed.' *Okay!?* So I search the apartment, which is like just a bedroom and a kitchen. I mean, this guy is not exactly loaded. And the creep is getting all threatening like, 'You'd better not take anything, I can have you killed.' And I go, 'It costs ten thousand dollars to have someone killed. If you could afford to have me killed then you could *certainly* afford to pay me a hundred bucks!' In the kitchen there was this toaster, and my old toaster had this weird thing of going up in flames which burns the toast. So I go, 'I'm taking this!' and I unplug the toaster and start to leave. Before I could get out the door he puts on this sad face and goes, 'Please, don't take that toaster, take this one.' And he pulls *another* toaster out of a cupboard. So I say I'll have to test it first, and he's like, 'Go ahead.' So I find some bread and sit there watching it toast. All the while he's still trying to talk me into fucking him, saying his friend never stands him up and he'll have the money in a few minutes. Finally the toast came out okay, so I took the second toaster home."

"Gee, Franklin, that bites," was all I could think of to say.

"Well, I did get a toaster out of it." He seemed pleased with himself.

"Yeah, but the whole thing was so Kafka-meets-*Monty Python*."

"Whatever."

"You know, I too have had experiences in the world of male prostitution." He looked shocked. I guess Zack had kept mum. I then told him about my night with Mr. Larry, though naturally I had to improvise the parts I didn't remember because of alcohol blackout. He was even more surprised and impressed than Daphne'd been when I told her.

Dear Diary,            Thursday Nov. 7

Daphne called this morning and it seems her world-shaking crisis is resolved. Klaus said he could see her side of the issue and they made up with an enormous orgy of love. Lucky her. I'm starting to feel like one of those best-friend type gays from mainstream movies and T.V. whose only function is to listen to the sexy girl's dating problems and offer sensible advice while presenting a wholesome, acceptable image of male homosexuals to the general public. To avoid that loathsome fate I spent the day dying my hair midnight blue with streaks of turquoise and black.

Dear Diary,            Friday, Nov. 8

After dinner I called Zack. I suppose I shouldn't go around telling other people's business but I did mention Franklin's miserable hustling experience. "It was like a cross between *Monty Python* and a Kafka-esque nightmare," I concluded.

Zack went nuts. "I love *Monty Python!*" he said, before reciting all his favorite routines. He must have memorized every episode. I like the show myself, but listening to someone repeat it word for word is not my idea of fun. When we're married and living in a small house with a white picket fence and two kitty cats, I will have a word with him and ask him not to do that. Since we're still courting though, I kept mum. I mean, he really is cute. Fortunately he paused for breath after singing the Spam song and I managed to jump back into the conversation.

"So tomorrow I'm going to meet the space alien, Norvex." This unfortunately reminded him of a trick he'd turned with a paleontologist which he began to recount in staggering detail. To get him off the phone I improvised a shrill buzzer-like noise and told him I needed to get my laundry out of the dryer. But he really is handsome, and I'm sure he's a great lover seeing as he gets paid for it and all. I wonder what I like doing in bed?

Dear Diary,                                                    Saturday, Nov. 9

Dora spent the afternoon centering herself (meditating in the living room while snacking on whole-grain Fig Newtons) so she could be in the proper frame of mind to receive wisdom from the aliens. "Tonight may well be the first time since he's come to Earth that Norvex will be communing with minds *really* interested in learning from him," she explained.

At five Daphne arrived, smiling and looking radiant, no doubt fresh from a lovefest with Klaus. She was wearing all black (short cocktail dress, patent-leather corset, fishnets, thick-soled combat boots) and dripping with silver jewelry. Her snow white hair was cut in a flat-top, only a little longer and with wisps over her ears.

"You look great! *Tank Girl* meets *Weetzie Bat,*" I said, truly awed by her style.

"Thanks, Chester. Hi Dora." She grinned. "I'm so excited. I just can't wait to meet Norvex!"

"That's wonderful, dear," said Dora, untwisting herself from her lotus position. "You believe he's an alien, don't you?" she asked, shooting me an accusing glance.

"It doesn't really matter to me one way or the other. I just think it's so wonderful the way he's brought the issues surrounding sexuality and exchange economy into the realm of popular discourse."

"Where'd you read that?" I asked.

"If you're implying that my observation was unoriginal, you're wrong, although I will admit that I've discussed the whole thing with Klaus. He's a Foucaultian."

"Is Klaus your young man?" asked Dora.

"Yup!" said Daphne happily.

"We've got to find someone for Chester here," said Dora, motioning in my direction.

"I'm on the case," said Daphne. I hate it when people talk about me in the third person.

"Oh, look at the time," said Dora, glancing at the clock. "I've got to go change." She bustled quickly to her room.

"My, isn't Klaus brainy." I was getting really sick of hearing about Klaus.

"I think your new friends have infected you with a strain of anti-intellectualism," Daphne sneered.

"Have not," I shot back.

"Have too."

"Have not!"

"Have too!"

"So you and he sit around discussing philosophy?" I asked. "I thought he was a druggie."

"He's an extremely complex person. Wait, look at his picture." She dug a small glossy out of her purse and handed it to me.

"Handsome, in a conventional sort of way," I admitted as I handed it back.

"He asked me to marry him, but I said I wouldn't take legal vows till they let same sex couples get married, too."

"That's noble and all, but aren't you getting kind of mushy? What about your plans to become a sex worker and lead a life completely free of patriarchal bondage?"

"Maybe later."

Just then the doorbell rang and Dora ran through the living room in a bizarre white gown that looked like the robes you'd see on Bible figures in a children's book.

"That'll be Mr. Okamura. Where did the time go? Could you zip me up, Daphne?"

"Sure thing. This is a beautiful dress."

"Thank you, it's silk. A friend made it for me. I'll see you both tonight and don't be late. We need you!" She flew out the door looking uncentered, and maybe even sort of panicked.

"Dora seems so nice. Very woman-centered," observed Daphne following me to my room.

"Is that what it is?" I stepped over the piles of clothes, CDs, and other junk blocking the doorway.

"You wouldn't know it to look at him," Daphne sighed, "but I think Klaus has a very feminine soul."

"Klaus, Klaus, Klaus!" I was infuriated. "What about me? Do you like my new hair?"

"Sure, but I don't think you'll be turning too many tricks like that. Rich gay men who buy hustlers for sex tend to like the more collegiate sort of look," advised Daphne, though how she knows I can only imagine.

"I wasn't planning on making a career of it!" I objected. "Do you think I could though, I mean, if I really set my mind on it?"

"Honey, you can do whatever you want to," she said as I squeezed and squished myself into my new jumpsuit.

"Ready to knock 'em dead?" asked Daphne.

"Yup."

"Super! I'm just going to fix my makeup one last time, then we're off."

That was forty-five minutes ago. So here I sit, writing in my diary, awaiting my destiny.

Walking out of the elevator into the lobby Mr. Finley and I were immediately confronted with the spectacle of our host, a wizened looking old soul in a floor-length white dress that put me in the mind of a film I'd seen about Aimee Semple McPherson.

"I am Dora Julian. On behalf of all Earthlings, greetings and blessings," she orated, nodding her head regally as the other hotel guests milling about the lobby stared at her with alarm. "Allow me to present Mr. Okamura." She gestured to a man in a white suit with a video camera. "He's a documentary filmmaker, and will, with your permission, be recording this meeting-of-worlds for posterity."

"Please, record away. Nice to meet you both," I said quickly, looking past her. "May we go right away? I'm rather hungry. You will have some appetizers, won't you?"

"The event will be catered, and if you require nourishment, by all means let us hurry. The limousine awaits without." Ms. Julian spoke slowly and carefully, as if she was imparting the sacred wisdom of the ancients, and had the annoying habit of smiling at me knowingly, as if we shared some amusing secret.

After a short ride we were deposited before a nondescript building, in front of which was a scene reminiscent of a Hollywood opening. Velvet ropes held back a sea of paparazzi, reporters yelling questions, and what can only be described as "space fans" screaming as if we were pop stars. "Quite a turnout," I observed.

"Not everyone on this planet is as unevolved as you might think from watching the news," she said as we entered the building. "Many people have been heartened to hear of a world ruled by wisdom rather than base material considerations. You have shown us another, a better, way."

The last part of her flattery was almost drowned out by the applause of several hundred guests in semiformalwear milling about the room which was gaily festooned with streamers and balloons. A gaggle of people from the Interplanetary Friendship Committee (all identified by name-tags) rushed to greet me. "May I get you a drink?" asked a Claire Morgan, as Dora shot her a nasty look.

"I've been meaning to try some of your hard liquors. Veeba says that something called a Cosmopolitan packs a real wallop, which I gather is a good thing." I smiled. Finally, a real party. "May I try one of those?"

"We'll go to the bar," said Dora, dragging me by the arm, as Claire, Mr. Finley, and a whole entourage trotted along a few paces behind us. The cocktail proved mouth-wateringly delicious, and I drank it rather quickly as Ms. Julian introduced me to a bewildering array of semi-famous playwrights, quasi-renowned artists, up-and-coming designers, overexposed actors, and deservedly obscure poets. Despite their usual role as skeptics, it was Earth's bohemian, artistic, and intellectuals who more often than not believed us to be actual space aliens, while the bulk of the population, usually gullible to the point of idiocy, believed us to be frauds. Most curious. Many of the local politicians also showed up, which surprised me. Back in New York, the power chieftains often made a point of slandering me to curry favor with the bigoted and ignorant masses of voters to whom they are beholden for office. San Francisco turned out to be quite different in that the local establishment was a credulous and fun-loving bunch who seemed intent on making up for the rest of their planet's boorishness, an immense and ungratifying task I'm sure.

After an hour of brief introductions to these well-intentioned types, it became clear to me that someone somewhere (doubtless Ms. Julian) had decided I was not to be monopolized but more or less evenly divided amongst the crowd. All four hundred guests would be able to say they'd a nice chat with me. Unfortunately, it was the same small talk with everyone. Yes, I was enjoying my stay. No, Zeeronians didn't build the pyramids. Yes, San Francisco is a lovely town. No, we can't communicate with whales.

I ordered a second Cosmopolitan from a passing waiter which I gulped down while Ms. Julian steered me towards a sculptor who proceeded to relate to me in grueling detail the terrible trials of producing art that people didn't want to see. I fear that at that point I began to feel sorry for myself. Here I was a zillion miles away from home, abandoned by my girlfriend, and surrounded by well-meaning but largely tedious strangers. Then I spotted the thoroughly revivifying sight of a young man wearing a skintight black jumpsuit, looking for all the world like Diana Rigg as Mrs. Peel from *The Avengers*, except that he sported blue hair and silver wraparound sunglasses. While balancing an enormous tray of appetizers on one hand he was saying something I couldn't hear to a radiantly handsome lad in a sportsjacket. Suddenly they became engaged in a heated argument. I interrupted the sculptor to ask Ms. Julian who they were.

"Those," she said in a tone betraying more embarrassment than maternal pride, "are my ex-husband's sons, Chester and Kyle." She approached the boys, whispered something to them, and then brought them over to meet me. The younger boy looked familiar somehow.

"Norvex, my name is Kyle Julian. I'm a big fan of yours!" said the beauty in a charming but practiced sort of way. "How are you enjoying your trip?"

The smiling creature in front of me seemed conceited and disingenuous. He was performing. "Oh, it couldn't be more splendid," I replied airily.

"I heard you're interested in television. Me too. In fact, I'm an actor on one of the top-rated shows for teenagers, *Hangin' In There*. Have you ever seen it?"

So that's where I'd seen him before. Unbeknownst to me, alcohol, in addition to making one feel woozy and giddy, can instill a sense of recklessness. In my case, I'd been robbed of my manners without my knowing it.

"I'm afraid I have, but don't despair, perhaps your next show will be better." Kyle dropped his big phony smile, Ms. Julian looked away, and Chester lit up like a sun.

"Thanks, sure, yeah. Hey, you enjoy your trip, okay?" he mumbled, walking away. Chester looked right at me in a strange way. As I gazed back at him, something happened. To be exact, my heart went *zing!*

"Hi, my name's Chester, and I think you're super," said the lad with a winning smile that could only have come straight from the heart.

"Glad to know you," I replied in my most flirtatious voice. Ms. Julian sighed loudly and tried to spirit me away from the boy with the firm hand of one who has lived all her life at social functions.

"You must come and meet Sudsy Mudsy, the famous hippie clown." As I've mentioned though, the alcohol had disinhibited me.

"Do please let go of my arm, I'm quite capable of finding my own way around the party. Perhaps you would be kind enough to fetch me another one of these," I held my empty glass aloft, "while I speak with this delightful boy here." She grimaced but made off with my empty towards the bar.

"Uh," said Chester, blushing and clearly at a loss for words.

"May I try one of those?" I asked, pointing at a green mound on Chester's tray. "What are they?"

He found his voice. "Tahini kelp-balls with sesame seeds. They're not as bad as they might be. So why'd you agree to come to San Francisco?"

"I was invited, and I needed to get out of New York. It's a bit trying on the senses with all the noise and dirt and what not," I said, reaching for a kelp-ball from the tray.

"I'd love to go to New York. It's so much more sophisticated than here. Not that San Francisco is so bad. Where I come from though..." He shuddered.

"Where do you come from?" I said, wiping my mouth with the back of my hand.

"A boring nowhere about three hundred miles to the south which I'm sure you've never heard of," he replied. "I was shipped here to stay with Dora to get me out of the way."

"You sound happy about that."

He nodded his head. "I am. Now I don't have to go to school and get things thrown at me."

"I'm so glad." I smiled at him.

"Hey, there's Daphne." He waved across the room. "She's helping me serve hors d'oeuvres. Ugh! She's giving a cranberry-salsa toastette to Kyle. I wish she'd spill the whole tray on him."

"If she did he'd have to take off that horrible outfit," I mused.

"You're real sensitive to clothes on Zeeron, aren't you?" he asked, cocking his head to one side winningly.

"Absolutely. We have a saying on Zeeron that translates roughly as 'Good clothing is the root of good conduct.' "

"Wild," said Chester. "I've been to this space before. There's a club here called Substratum. It's really cool, though the music sucks, and the people are kinda weird, and it's too hot and crowded." Dora Julian reappeared.

"Here's your drink. Now, I'd like you to meet..."

"Perhaps in a minute, Ms. Julian." I glared at her and she retreated.

"What's that?" Chester asked, pointing at my cocktail.

"A Cosmopolitan."

"Mind if I try it? Dora made me promise not to drink, but a taste wouldn't hurt. I've never tried one before."

"I should caution you, it contains alcohol."

"Well, duh." He swallowed half the rather tall glass. "It tastes like High C! Wow, I really liked that. Thanks." He started doing a spontaneous dance to the background music.

We talked for a few minutes, although I remember little of what we said because I was intoxicated not only by the drinks, but by Chester himself, who with his vivacious insouciance, reminded me a bit of Veeba. After a few minutes of listening to him, his nonstop prattle became fascinating. I don't remember everything he said, but I do remember that he told me he shared my enthusiasm for madcap, screwball comedy and suggested that I'd probably like Margaret Rutherford's *Miss Marple* films. "Maybe we could go see one sometime?"

I suggested.

Just then Ms. Julian returned carrying a tray of vegetables. "Chester, could you take this over towards the tables against that wall, I don't think those people have been offered anything in a long time. He grudgingly went off to do her bidding, although he gave me a parting glance that set my heart on fire. Ms. Julian then firmly took hold of my arm and redelivered me to the center of the party. "I can't imagine what Chester's been telling you. He's been staying with me because he doesn't get on with the children at his school. Do the kids on Zeeron give their parents such grief?" She contorted her face in a mock display of discomfort which may have hidden a bit of real hostility.

"Fortunately, our world doesn't have familial relations, but actually, he seemed perfectly sweet." My eyes followed Chester across the room.

"Look, there's Jane Zaeb!" said Dora trying to catch her attention with a wave.

"Could I please, *please*, not meet her?" I begged.

"She's a fascinating person," said Dora, fixing me with a hard, scrutinizing glare. "Have you heard her sing?"

"Yes, but I'm afraid I can't bear folk music. When I hear people that mournful and sincere I just want to lie down and expire. Zeeronians prefer upbeat happy music, you know: The Captain and Tennille, Bananarama, The Monkees, The Spice Girls – or better yet, nice peppy show tunes."

"Really?" she asked, sounding disappointed. "Sometimes the truth is painful. Does that mean one should ignore it?"

"No, but you can always play The Glad Game," I responded.

"Pardon?" asked Dora.

"Perhaps you're unacquainted with your Earthly masterpiece, *Pollyanna*. It's a Disney film in which Hayley Mills plays a poor girl who always looks on the bright side. She makes a game of finding reasons to be happy, The Glad Game, and teaches everyone in a troubled small town how to open their hearts "

"Well, we all create our own realities," said Dora.

"Nonsense," I said, with a bit more vehemence than I intended. "Pollyanna didn't create any reality, she just decided to be cheerful instead of whining, moaning, and singing folk songs."

"Let's discuss this another time, shall we?" suggested Dora peevishly. From that point on she became a bit colder and less familiar, focusing narrowly on the task of guiding me around and initiating small talk. Off in the corner I could see Chester, theatrically serving the hors d'oeuvres like a butler in an old movie, bowing at the waist and gesturing above them seductively with his hand. I made a mental note to ask Mr. Finley if there were any butlers left on Earth and to make a point of seeing one if in fact there were. Watching Chester throw kelp balls in the air and try to catch them in his mouth I couldn't help but contrast his exuberant frivolity with the solemn portentous and pretentious chatter of the rest of the crowd. "How awful it must be to live on a grim planet like Earth but be blessed with the happy-go-lucky sensibility of a Zeeronian," I thought to myself.

Finally Ms. Julian declared it was time to have a toast. Champagne was brought out and a local spoken-word artist made a long-winded and only slightly coherent speech about interplanetary friendship. We drank. I immediately decided I liked champagne even better than Cosmopolitans. It tickles one's nose and produces a certain delightfully irrational giddiness. When I took a second glass from a passing waiter, Mr. Finley, who'd been lurking in a corner suddenly charged up to me.

I fixed him with a steely glare. "Ah, the inevitable Mr. Finley! To what do I owe the dubious pleasure of this visit?"

"I hesitate to bring this up," he replied cooly, "but the quantity of alcohol you've imbibed could prove discomforting."

"I have not yet begun to tipple! Leave me be, you bilious, babbling, bureaucratic booby!" He scowled, making ugly lines in his forehead, but returned to his corner.

"Blue-green algae paté?" asked a small voice. I spun around to see the girl Chester had identified as Daphne. As I took one she smiled at me lasciviously. "I want to personally thank you for challenging our society's repressive, puritanical, sex-negative mores."

"Don't mention it," I said mechanically as Dora and a man in a fedora elbowed her out of the way.

"Norvex, I'd like you to meet the mayor!" Dora announced triumphantly. "Mr. Okamura, are you getting this?"

The man began shaking my hand vigorously when suddenly there was a loud boom and the lights went off. The mayor was dragged away by security guards as the crowd panicked and began madly dashing this way and that. Ms. Julian was knocked over by an obese man, and as she tried to get up, several more people tripped over the poor woman. I stood stock still, my terror mitigated somewhat by my drunkenness. "What a useful invention these cocktails are," I thought to myself. As the lights flickered on and off I noticed Mr. Finley running towards me, then lost sight of him in the crowd. Suddenly, I felt a hand on my arm and was pleased to see it was Chester's.

"C'mon," he commanded, dragging me into what looked like a coat check room. Actually it was a coat check room, but one with an exit. "This way," he said as he ushered me out into the street. A taxi was waiting at the curb and Chester shoved me in as several police cars arrived on the scene. "Brannan and Second, please," he told the swarthy turbaned cab driver.

"Oughtn't we tell someone where we're going?" I asked. "And where *are* we going?"

"This club, Ghastly Chambers. It's supposed to be fun. Gee, that was so weird back at the reception. I wonder who shot at you?"

The taxi was lurching in the traffic and I began to get sick to my stomach. I also developed a peculiar feeling of dread mixed with exhilaration. "You know, I'm not allowed out by myself," I began to explain.

"What?" asked Chester looking at me warily, as if I was perhaps a bit dangerous.

"The government keeps an eye on me. A Mr. Finley chaperones me everywhere. I wouldn't be surprised if I'm routinely tailed by other watchdogs too."

"You're paranoid." He sounded disappointed but not surprised.

"Not at all. I'm an alien, I have access to important technology. Your government certainly isn't going to let it fall into the wrong hands. Nor do they want to risk having something untoward befall me which could precipitate an intergalactic incident. The Zeeronians wouldn't take kindly to anyone who did me harm."

"You mean you're like... on the level about being an space alien?" Chester seemed astonished.

"Certainly! I don't do this for everyone, but here, look." I showed him my three dimensional, wallet-vids of Zeeron. For some reason it was important to me that this enchanting young lad believe in me.

He lifted his sunglasses. "Wow, these are pretty rad. They're like tiny home movies on cards."

"Exactly. That's me climbing the ladder into my house, that's a dance in the courtyard of the Institute where I teach, that's Veeba and I making love, that's my pet, Umgornis 5, licking her paw..."

"You have cats like we do?"

"Not exactly. Ours have three eyes and two tails, as you can see."

"So are the people who found the launchpad in Russia and accused you of being frauds really evil space aliens like you said?"

"No, we devised that story to make ourselves seem even less credible so that people would leave us alone."

He handed me back the cards. "You know, they can do a lot of stuff with holograms and videos these days. Maybe this is some new digital computerized thing..."

"Say no more!" I pushed the Zerk button on my necklace and trans-dimensionally shifted, disappearing momentarily. "I trust you believe me now?" I asked once I'd returned.

"Guess *so*," he said, "how'd you do that?"

"It's extremely complicated. It involves... trans-dimensional shifts."

"Wow." He looked a bit stunned. "Kyle was right. I was telling him he was stupid for believing you were really an alien."

"You really shouldn't let your little brother bother you so. He has problems of his own."

"Are you *insane*? What problems? Having too much money? Being too good-looking?"

"Child actors don't end up very well as a rule," I explained. "They usually fail to develop either their personalities or talents, then they age and just as they lose their looks they decide they want to be appreciated for who they are as a person or for their all-too-frequently nonexistent acting skills. Meanwhile everyone on the planet will offer them drugs, drink, and debilitating flattery. Wasn't your brother in a motion picture with Patrick Damon Donnelly?"

"Yeah, *Go For It! 2.* You don't miss a trick. Are you sure you're from another solar system?"

"Studying show business from Earth has been my life," I said. "Anyway, Patrick Damon Donnelly..."

Chester knew the story. "Was found dead in a sleazy motel..."

"After consuming special k, heroin, and cocaine. He had everything going for him, but he felt so out of touch with reality..."

"He *was* out of touch with reality," corrected Chester.

"Granted. But he also *felt* so out of touch with reality that he started slumming it with male hustlers. In no time he was turning tricks on Santa Monica Boulevard as a Patrick Damon Donelly lookalike and scoring drugs to do with his fellow prostitutes." I'd followed the story with great interest due to the fact that I found Mr. Donelly exquisitely handsome, a fact I thought it wise not to mention to Chester.

"My heart bleeds. He had millions of dollars, and millions of adoring fans but he couldn't be happy. Well, boo-hoo-hoo."

"He was treated like a performing monkey from the time he was eight, tap dancing for dollars in front of hotels, spending his days in casting calls instead of school. His parents' love was totally conditional."

"Sometimes I wonder if my parents love me at all," declared Chester solemnly.

"Now it's my turn to say my heart bleeds." I'd no sooner uttered the words than I regretted them, but to my surprise Chester just giggled. Sometimes adolescents need only be teased about their self-pity to snap right out of it. I decided not to apologize. "So your brother could easily end up as another casualty of fame and fortune. In a way he already has."

"Pardon me if I save my sympathy for the lame and starving." He looked out the window. "Could you pull up right there by the curb?" he asked the driver. "We'll just hang out here for a while, then you can call Mr. Finley and tell him you panicked when you heard the shot and ran away. They can't get mad at you for that. It's supposed to be their job to keep crazy people away from you and they blew it." The cab stopped in front of an unprepossessing warehouse covered with indecipherable graffiti.

I paid the fare, feeling as usual that I was seriously endangering my health by touching the grubby, ugly paper bills that are the Earthlings' units of exchange. Chester took my hand and led me towards the door. "Uh-oh. This doesn't look right," he said.

"I.D.!" barked a gigantic doorman wearing his cheap black suit without panache.

"What's going on tonight?" Chester asked him. "This doesn't look like Ghastly Chambers."

"Spinning Wheel. DJ Phooey. Space-hop. Macrobiotic cocktails," said the doorman mechanically.

"We're already here, let's check it out," suggested Chester gamely. He showed his I.D. and was waved through, but when I tried to follow I was stopped in my tracks by the doorman's arm.

"I.D.," he grunted.

"He's totally old!" complained Chester.

"Look, I'm 126, but my passport is at home."

The doorman pointed to the curb. "You can catch a cab over there."

"Come on!" said Chester, leading me around the corner. "Let's walk for a while." Just then a couple came out a side exit. My young guide grabbed the door before it closed and ushered me in. The place was packed with animated young people, machines poured smoke into the air, and bright lights flashed. Following Chester's lead I pushed through the sweaty crowd, marveling at how alien Earthlings smelled - sickly, almost putrid, and yet somehow appealing in a base, animal sort of way. We made our way to a bar overcrowded with patrons desperate to forget their unpleasant lives through the marvel of cocktails. Chester ordered, and after an eternity of waiting, during which we couldn't converse due to the loud music, we were served. Taking a sip of his drink Chester winced with pain. "These drinks taste like rancid orange juice with rubbing alcohol," he observed, screaming at the top of his lungs so I could hear.

"Let's not drink them," I suggested.

"What?" he yelled.

"Let's not drink them!" I shouted.

"We already paid for them!" he said, as if that had anything to do with anything.

"Do you suppose there's anywhere less crowded and noisy to stand?" I asked.

"Look, there's a chill-out lounge." He led me through a door into a room where softer ambient music was playing (although one couldn't appreciate it due to the boom, boom, boom of the bass coming from the main dance floor). About two dozen youngsters lolled about on bean bags looking ostentatiously relaxed. I collapsed next to a girl in brown velour who was fondling a skinny boy in overalls. Chester squeezed in beside me.

"Do you have discos and clubs and stuff on Zeeron?" he asked.

"Certainly, thousands and thousands. Possibly millions. Most Zeeronians go out every night of the week but one. On Recharge Day one stays home to mend outfits and do beauty treatments. Though of course our week has only six days, and our days only twenty-three-and-a-half hours."

"Wow, you go out every night?"

"Not I, personally. I'm afraid I only hit the town every other day or so due to my busy schedule." Fearing I sounded like a stick-in-the-mud I changed the subject. "You know, you have a highly Zeeronian sense of style. It's quite becoming." I stared into his green eyes and noticed there was a mole next to his left eyebrow he was trying to hide under his foundation. He also suffered from acute acne. My heart went out to the young glamourpuss beside me, trying to present flawless skin on a world almost devoid of adequate makeup and/or dermatological treatment. I was seized by an uncontrollable urge to kiss him, an urge I succumbed to. Pure delight! It wasn't a moment before our osculation was interrupted by the girl sitting next to me.

"Aren't you that space alien dude?" she queried.

"No, he's not!" said Chester, kissing me again. She returned to her conversation.

Suddenly Chester stopped. "What about Veeba?"

"Veeba, yes, well Veeba and I haven't been spending too much time together. Also, you might remember Zeeronians have practiced free love since your people lived in caves and hunted mastodons with spears. We needn't worry about her."

"Oh." He looked relieved. "So you're a teacher on Zeeron. You don't seem like a teacher."

"That's not surprising. On Earth every teacher is forced to be half jailer because of compulsory education. On Zeeron nothing is compulsory."

"But people still do things, that's *so* cool!" he gushed.

"I take it you're a student?"

"At the moment I'm not in school." He looked at me coyly. "I'm doing a little modeling till I go to college next fall. Do you have models on Zeeron?"

"Not exactly," I explained, "though we do have posing artists whose craft consists of doing things with elegance and hauteur."

"That's all they have to do? Just be elegant and haughty?"

"Nobody has to do anything on Zeeron. Labor performed for money on Earth by grudging and desperate wage slaves is done on Zeeron for the love of it. It's a much better system, people don't try and foist what one doesn't need upon one just to make money. Even better, people don't get overworked and cranky. You'd be surprised how much of the misery in primitive societies is due to your barbarous system of wage labor."

"No, I wouldn't."

"We Zeeronians are indeed a lucky bunch, a people singularly lacking in pain, frustration, and existential misery."

"You sound homesick," said the boy, putting his hand on my knee.

"I think you're right, I am." At that moment, out of the corner of my eye I thought I saw Mr. Finley moving through the crowd on the other side of the doorway, but I convinced myself I was simply paranoid. "Perhaps we'd better go back to the party, people will be looking for me."

"That party was stupid," muttered Chester bitterly.

"I would have preferred more dancing," I admitted.

"Let's!" shrieked Chester, leaping up and grabbing me by the hand. We pushed our way into the other room and as I gyrated, he twisted. It felt marvelous and I realized I hadn't been getting nearly enough exercise on Earth, partially due to the fact that heavy breathing in that polluted atmosphere is guaranteed to make one nauseous.

One can tell a lot about a person from watching them dance. Chester's self-consciously kooky theatricality contrasted sharply with the dancers around him who were affecting an unaffected pose. His ostentatious uniqueness made for a charmingly spirited act of defiance against his low-status in the terrestrial pecking order. After a while we returned to the ambient lounge where I sat on a broken sofa already inhabited by several heavily intoxicated youngsters. Chester sat on my lap. Special feelings stirred between us and we began to kiss, more slowly this time. He tasted sweet, salty, and delicious. I realized I was more than just a little infatuated, which set off an alarm in my head.

"Chester, you're awfully nice, but we live in different worlds, literally, and if we were to get mixed up together we could both get hurt."

"But you're so handsome, and you're smart, and you've got good taste," he replied winningly, running his hand up my back. "And you like me! Let's not worry about tomorrow, let's have a little fun tonight. Can we go to your hotel?"

My good sense was overrun by hormones. "Mr. Finley is liable to be there and I'd rather not spoil the lovely feelings I'm having right now by seeing his face," I replied. "Let's go to your place."

Chester fairly pushed me out of the club and into a taxicab. We spent the ride to his home kissing, tongues and all. In no time we were in his room which was positively squalid. Dirty clothes rested in mounds upon the floor while open but empty dresser drawers yearned hungrily for clean garments. Cartons from a local restaurant perfumed the air with the scent of rotting, mediocre take-out food. The unflattering overhead light cast eerie shadows. "Sorry about the mess," said my young host pulling me onto his unmade single bed and kissing me tenderly. Eager as I was to ravish Chester, I felt obliged as his senior to reprimand him for his slovenly ways. I pulled back.

"I know it must be hard not owning a robo-maid and having to clean up for yourself, but this room..." I was stopped dead by Chester's soft smile which rendered me speechless. He stood up to turn off the light, then struggled out of his jumpsuit. As I removed my clothes, a nude Chester opened his one small window, and his pleasingly fleshy figure was lit fetchingly by moonlight.

"I think you're beautiful," he whispered, kissing me on the lips.

"You can guess what I think of you," I offered, nuzzling and then kissing his neck in the hope that he'd do the same to me. Instead he lay flat on his back and stared at me moonfaced. I ran my hand down his chest and belly, which made him squirm.

"God, I'm so fat," he said unhappily, drawing a sheet over himself.

"Don't be absurd, you're delectable," I said, pushing away the sheet and running the tip of my tongue from his right nipple to his left, and then down to his bellybutton.

"I could be a lot thinner..." he began, but I looked up and shushed him. For the next few moments he was quiet, then he started again. "You, you're not fat." To silence him I gave his mouth something else to do.

The Earthlings, although their erotic technique is often hobbled by their sexual repression, more than compensate for that with the fierceness of their unfettered barbarian passion. At least Chester did once he'd gotten over his self-consciousness. Unfortunately, because of Earth's filth and disease, one must fornicate with plastic devises covering the genitalia. At first I was uneasy with the "condom," but once I began to think of it as an article of clothing I relaxed and was happy to be well dressed even while making love. We were writhing away in ecstasy, when we were startled by a loud bang on the door.

Chester interrupted his screams of pleasure to shout, "Go away, I'm busy!" at the unidentified knocker.

"Open up, now!" demanded a male voice, continuing to pound on the locked door.

"Get lost!" retorted the sassy child.

"Perhaps we'd better see who it is," I suggested as someone shot the lock off with a gun and the door burst open. Two policemen clamored into the room and loomed over us menacingly. In the hallway behind them I saw a distraught Dora Julian and an even more distraught man in an ugly tan suit accompanied by a woman in a hideous floral dress that was inches away from being a mere housecoat. They all stared at Chester and me, mouths agape, while the curtains blew romantically in the breeze coming through the window as if nothing had gone wrong.

"Dad! Mom! Dora! Are you *insane*?! Get out of here!" shrieked my frightened paramour.

The frumpy woman screamed at the top of her rather powerful lungs while the man in the tan suit exclaimed, "Oh my God!" in a tone that on Zeeron would be reserved for natural disasters. "What do you think you're doing?!" he demanded of us.

"Sir, I think that should be quite obvious," I replied as calmly as I could.

"Get away from my son!" he ordered, pushing into the already overcrowded room as one of the law enforcement officials began taking pictures. On Earth not only do primitive taboos concerning intercourse between people of the same sex carry great weight, but Chester's youth actually made the action *illegal*. The photos could be used to get me in a lot of trouble. Even so I remembered to smile for the camera, although I'm afraid Chester looked terribly put-out and shocked.

"Mom, Dad, all of you, *leave*!" commanded Chester firmly, if hysterically, as Mr. Finley and three more police officers arrived, winded and out of breath. Squeezing into the crowded room my exasperated guardian/warder rolled his eyes upwards in the direction of "heaven," the mythical residence of the Earthlings' sky god.

"I demand you arrest him!" the man, whom I surmised was Chester's father, implored Mr. Finley. "My son is seventeen, this is illegal!"

The harpy in the housecoat pointed at me. "I hope they lock you up!"

"I assure you I did nothing to coerce your son into bringing me here," I protested.

"Now, Beverly, I've tried to tell you he's from another world. They have different ways there," said Dora Julian, by far the most composed of the lot. "And Chester is old enough..."

The harpy interrupted her. "Shut up, Dora! We ask you to take care of Chester and what happens? The police call us up and tell us he's missing and potentially the subject of an alien abduction." She turned to Chester, "Well, this... this is worse!"

Chester's father joined in. "Johnson, arrest that pervert, he was *molesting* my child!" The largest of the goons put his hand on my arm and jerked me out of bed. I began dressing, which wasn't easy since he didn't let go.

Mr. Finley, who'd been surveying the unfolding catastrophe with alarm, snapped into action. With great authority he flashed a badge and took command of the situation. "United Nations Command for Law Enforcement. I'll handle this. Chester, get dressed. Mr. and Mrs. Julian, Ms. Julian, please come with me. Johnson, don't let them out of your sight."

Chester and I dressed surrounded by G-men.

"I'm really sorry about this, Norvex," said my forlorn lover. He looked to be on the verge of tears.

"Don't worry. I know sex with boys under eighteen carries stiff penalties on your planet. One is locked in a cage with violent criminals, fed inedible slop, and denied adequate entertainment for years and years. But you see, I have diplomatic immunity."

At that moment, Johnson handcuffed me. Before I could protest, he maneuvered me out of the room and out the front door where the media and the police awaited. Chester followed, un-handcuffed, but held on either side by his mother and father. The look on his face was one of shock, but there was a healthy glint of defiance in his eyes. Suddenly he wrestled free of his captors, ran up to me, turned to the press and cried, "One for the cameras!" Then, all I can say is, there was something in that kiss!

Dear Diary,                                         Sunday, Nov. 10

Why must I endure the bazookas and grenades of outrageous fortune? I finally find Mr. Right, and not only does he live on the other side of the universe, but my parents won't let me see him! At the moment I'm locked up tight in a psychiatric hospital for "observation." Dad's the one who's totally insane! The whole ride over here he was telling me that I'm not old enough to "see" anybody, let alone extraterrestrials. For just about the first time ever, and despite her having been close to hysterical earlier, that woman he's shacked up with was kind of sympathetic. She said that she knew it was hard for the young to wait for love, but that I should have because Norvex is going to go home to his own galaxy and leave me here, brokenhearted. I told her he loved me and would never do that, but what do I know? Once I was checked in and given some ugly pajamas and a sleeping pill they left, slobbering guiltily about how they love me.

This morning I was woken up at the crack of dawn by an orderly who looked like a sumo wrestler. He gave me a greasy breakfast that I'm sure had more calories and saturated fat than any breakfast should have, but which I ate anyway to calm my nerves. When I was done eating the orderly came to take my tray away and I asked for a phone to call Daphne but he wouldn't give me one which made me irate. I almost said something really rude, but I thought of Mr. Larry and told him to "Get the heck out!" instead. Not long after he'd gone Dad, Drusilla, and Kyle came trooping into the room acting obnoxiously cheery and hopeful.

"What am I in here for? And why can't I call Daphne?" I demanded.

"We went through this last night. You're in here for your own protection, and the doctor thinks it would be better if you didn't call Daphne for a little while," said Dad in the calm tones reserved for excitable nut cases. "You don't understand now, but what the alien did to you was horrible. The doctor said you might not realize it yet because you're in shock."

"What Norvex did to me was not horrible, and the only thing I'm in shock about is your reactionary, homophobic reaction," I screamed angrily, if redundantly.

"Yes, it *was* horrible," Dad said again. "I don't know how they do it on Zeeron, but sexual assault is a crime here on Earth and we intend to see that he pays for what he did."

"Get real!" I yelled back. "I'm the one who hit on him! I think you'd better start asking yourselves what it might be like to have a Zeeronian in the family, because I intend to marry Norvex just as soon as I can get him to pop the question."

"I think we'd better go, we're making him hysterical," suggested Drusilla. She and Dad turned to leave.

"We'll get the doctor," said Dad.

"Oh, I see how it is. Space aliens are all very fine *in space,* but you wouldn't want your son to marry one. Bigotry, plain and simple!" The door closed behind them leaving Kyle whom they'd forgotten.

"Gee, Chester, this really sucks. Mom and Dad are being way harsh."

"What's with you?" I asked.

"Look, you made the front page." He pulled out a newspaper from under his sweatshirt. Under the headline, Alien Sex Fiend Nabbed in Tryst with Teen!, there was a picture of me and my new boyfriend kissing for the cameras outside Dora's. Normally I hate photographs of myself, but the blurriness of the newsprint hid all my blemishes, so I think I looked pretty good.

"Would you do me a favor?" I asked, hoping Kyle's sudden and unprecedented friendliness was sincere.

"Depends what it is."

"Call Daphne and tell her where I am and that I want to formally ask Zeeron for political asylum. Tell her that Norvex is a great guy, and that I want to marry him and get off this crazy planet."

Kyle's eyes bugged out, and I think I detected a little newfound respect for his older brother, which is as it should be. "Okay," he said as the door opened to admit a nurse who demanded I take some happinutrin pills to calm me down. I think they're making me sleepy. I sure hope I dream about Norvex. Am I in love?

During the airplane ride back to New York, Mr. Finley explained in ghastly detail what exactly had transpired the previous night. "A small Montana-based, religious cult calling itself Christian Soldiers decided that you're an agent of the devil, or possibly a demon yourself, sent to Earth to announce the coming of the anti-Christ."

"But whatever gave them that idea?"

"It was based on their interpretation of what they called 'hidden scriptural prophesy.' Anyway, they infiltrated the catering company that staffed the bar at your reception and saw to it that all the ice cubes were made with holy water, which they thought would induce a spontaneous exorcism once it got into your system, or at least badly burn your mouth causing you to reveal your true identity. When you drank your cocktails and nothing happened they got into a squabble amongst themselves over the theological implications and one of them shot at their leader, whom he decided was the real satanic agent. Once the gunman was wrestled to the ground they flickered the lights to distract security so they could make a getaway. We caught them, of course, and for several hours we thought they'd kidnapped you and were covering it up. After a time, the doorman from the club across the street told us he'd seen you leaving in a taxi with someone who could only have been Chester Julian."

"He's not exactly inconspicuous, is he?" I smiled, thinking of Chester's blue hair.

"We contacted every cab driver in the city and finally talked to the one who'd dropped you off at the boy's house."

"I bet you felt awfully silly for not having looked there in the first place," I speculated maliciously.

"The Julians didn't press formal charges only because I gave them the impression that crimes committed by extraterrestrials are handled by the United Nations. They're sure to make trouble if you're seen roaming around free though. They're extremely angry, as you no doubt ascertained. Also, since the press caught wind of this it's likely to become a political issue, and believe me, no politician is going to want to look soft on pederasty. It might be necessary for you to 'do some time,' as they say."

Scared although I was, I played indignant. "Mr. Finley, could you have possibly forgotten the awesome powers of destruction at my disposal? My fellow Zeeronians would not hesitate to use their vast arsenal of weapons on Earth should anyone get any ideas of punishing me. I might also mention that on Zeeron we discovered millennia ago that when we abolished punishment crime actually *diminished*. You might want to try it yourselves. I mean as soon as you eliminate poverty and mental disorders and all that."

Mr. Finley smiled wanly. "Your rooms have been bugged since you arrived, and Veeba let on to her friend Fabrice that your military might is a hoax."

I gave in to self-pity. "Oh, I wish I was back on Zeeron, back in Braxo City, back in my own bed..."

"I'm sorry about all this, I really am. All diplomacy aside, I think Zeeron sounds wonderful, and you and Her Excellency are a lot of fun. I'll put in a good word in for you wherever I can. Oh, by the way, I know Veeba doesn't know how to make a trism. Does Runchka?"

"No," I said glumly, "though s/he can turn one on and off."

"I don't suppose you..."

"I wouldn't know one if I tripped over it. Our machines replicate themselves, only a few mechanical artists bother learning how things work."

"That's something of a relief. There are people so anxious to get their hands on the secret of perpetual motion they might resort to unscrupulous means."

"Like kidnapping, then hypnotizing or torturing us?" I suggested.
Mr. Finley smiled sadly and nodded.

"How charming!" I said with what I fear was an acidly bitter grin.
For the remainder of the trip I sat in stony silence, enraged at the
Earthlings, irritated at Veeba, and frightened for myself. As our car
drew near the hotel I saw that there was once again a crowd of protesters
being kept at bay by policemen and barricades.

"Veeba and Runchka are being brought here presently," Mr. Finley
informed me as we entered the suite.

"What do you plan on doing to them?" I asked in a disagreeable
tone.

Mr. Finley, whose face was normally impassive, looked embarrassed.
"The district attorney seems to want to try and prosecute them for
conspiracy to corrupt a minor."

"Jolly good fun!" I said, patting him on the back with a manic
joviality that clearly made him nervous. While Mr. Finley sat in the
living room, talking on the phone with the U.N., I collapsed on the
bed in my room and, despite my terror, soon mercifully passed out
from sheer utter exhaustion. Worrying really takes it out of me.

Sometime later I was awakened by Veeba, barging into my bedroom
unannounced. "Hi, love," she sang out, turning on the television and
sitting next to me on the bed. "Seems you've gotten into some mischief."
On the screen before us appeared Chester's father, his face mottled red
with anger, calling for my castration. His image was replaced by an
anchorwoman explaining that since the United States government
regarded us as citizens of the United Kingdom, but the United Nations
still insisted we were extraterrestrial diplomats, legal complications were
guaranteed. As she spoke a mugshot of Chester flashed on the screen.
"Oh my, you *did* have a nice time at the party, didn't you!" said Veeba,
poking me in the ribs.

"I suppose I did," I admitted as the anchorwoman began relating
the story of a baby harbor seal pup who'd been saved from certain
death by charitable animal lovers.

"I like her hair," observed Veeba. "Yours, however, could use some help." She ran her fingers through my tangled chartreuse locks.

Before she could offer a style suggestion, Mr. Finley came into my room. "I'm afraid you're going to be put under arrest any moment," he declared flatly.

Veeba was indignant. "Mr. Metzenbaum, I saw the boy's picture and he's quite adorable. Why are you mad at Norvex for doing him?"

As he explained the situation to her I could faintly hear the angry chants coming from outside the hotel. I rose to look out the window and saw a giant banner emblazoned with the slogan No Special Rights For Extraterrestrial Gays! being held by some ferocious looking xenophobes.

The phone rang ominously and Mr. Finley answered. "Uh-huh... Uh-huh... No, of course. I see... I see... I see... Right away." He turned to us with a look of pity.

"Don't make that face!" cautioned Veeba.

"The New York City police don't know you're really aliens, so I'd suggest you cooperate with them fully. I'm terribly sorry about all this, I can't tell you..." He was interrupted by a knock at the door. In a moment several heavily armed personages stormed into the room with vicious intent plainly visible in their eyes. They were followed by the press, cameras flashing. I pressed the S.O.S. button on the necklace Klajo had given me back on Zeeron as a man read us our rights. A burly policeman then handcuffed Veeba and I as she protested shrilly.

"Norvex is the one who made love to that boy! Why are you punishing *me* with this ugly and impractical jewelry?" she shrieked.

Mr. Finley explained the situation to her once again, but I somehow think she failed to fully grasp the terrible danger we were in. It was as if we were playing a party game that she found tedious, but would go along with for just a little while longer because her companions insisted. Mr. Finley did manage to make the police agree that the hostile crowd would be cleared far away before we were taken to the police station so at least we wouldn't be set upon by vigilantes before we could meet our cruel and wretched fate at the hands of the ignorant and brutal authorities. While the police dispersed the outraged denizens of the metropolis, Runchka, who'd been gathering wildflowers in Mexico, was led into the apartment on the arm of a government goon. I didn't even say "Hi" because I was simply too depressed.

"Greetings. It saddens me that we have met with misfortune, Norvex," said Runchka, looking truly downcast. I smiled at him/her, but could still think of nothing to say. I get like that when I'm overwhelmed.

Veeba, making a great show of her glumness sang out, "I suppose if I'm to go to prison I'd better freshen my makeup. Mr. Finley, would you get my lipstick? It's right next to the lamp by my bed." By this time one would think he'd had enough time to grow used to our Zeeronian priorities, but he made no move to accommodate her. Veeba repeated, in a suspiciously slow voice, "My lipstick... it's right next to the lamp... in a blue container... you can't miss it."

Runchka, who had not yet been handcuffed suddenly perked up. "Oh yes, Veeba... your lipstick. I shall bring it to you forthwith!" S/he darted into Veeba's bedroom.

"Hey!" shouted the cop who'd been holding him/her.

Runchka returned from the bedroom wearing a tiny smile which baffled me. Then I saw why. What s/he was holding was not lipstick at all but pleasant partyizer which s/he turned on full blast. At once all the humanoids in the apartment were turned into happy zombies by the pale yellow mist from the tube.

"Do take off our handcuffs, sweetie!" Veeba requested of a handsome young officer who immediately complied. Once free I used my necklace to contact Gropvak and asked it to land the ship on the roof of the hotel.

"Be there in twenty-four minutes on the dot, Mr. N. You know, I haven't had much to do up here, it's been pretty lonely..."

"Please hurry and be careful, they may fire exploding missiles at you. Dodge them." I rung off.

Veeba's tolerance for pleasant partyizer is truly monumental, and the spritz which incapacitated the Earthlings barely affected her at all. In a fit of playful malevolence, she undressed our persecutors and initiated an orgy. When three more policemen entered, the sight of their captain and several colleagues involved in a daisy chain sent them reeling, until they too were put under by the rapture gas. As we hastily packed our bags I heard some startling news from the television, which had never gotten turned off. "My name is Daphne Van Vechten, and I'm a personal friend of Chester Julian's. We of the Chester Julian Defense League protest his persecution by the agist, homophobic, anti-alien, and sex-negative authorities. We demand he be immediately released from the psychiatric institute where he's being held against his will. This is a violation of Chester's civil rights, and a blow against the rights of all youth." I recognized the speaker as the canapé server from the fateful reception who'd thanked me on behalf of Earth's libertines.

"Oh, how awful!" said Veeba, stuffing a few cans of sparkling hair mousse into a travel bag. "We must help him, mustn't we?"

"I should think so!" I replied, anger cutting through my pleasant party mood.

I went up to the roof to await our craft and gazed at the street far below where a mob of fat ugly Earth monsters waved their meaty fists at us in anger. Suddenly they froze in fear, then dispersed at top speed. I turned around and discovered why. Our spacecraft was hovering a few feet above the roof of the hotel with Gropvak's sternly pretty mechanical face peering through a porthole as her four hands waved in greeting.

"Sorry it took so long, Mr. N, they sent that shuttle thing after me and I had to lose it," Gropvak explained through the open hatch from which it was lowering a short retractable ladder. Loading up all our booty was a big job, but several policemen and reporters under the influence of pleasant partyizer came to our aid, lugging wigs, books, plants, and so on. Before boarding the craft myself I asked the still-enraptured Mr. Finley an important question.

"Mr. Finley, if someone from Earth were to visit another planet, say, for instance, Chester were to come to Zeeron with me, what would happen if he tried to return to Earth?"

"Chester, such a nice boy. You two made a cute couple. But we wouldn't know if anyone who'd been to another planet was a spy. He could be carrying alien pods in his body, or a micro-camera in his eye, for all we know. Even if they let him back on the planet he'd have to stay locked up."

"But you know we haven't any weapons, how could we pose any threat to you?"

"You don't, but what about the others? The Felkusians or the Mithribians? Earth's security forces are terrified of aliens. Only reason you weren't destroyed the minute we found out you were defenseless was 'cause we were scared you might have friends who could harm us."

"I suppose one can't be too careful," I agreed, removing his arm from around my shoulder. "Thank you so much for an enjoyable visit. If you're ever in the Andromeda Galaxy feel free to drop in." I caught myself. What was I saying? This man aided in my arrest! "But call first, okay?"

Once in the air we all sighed with relief. "I'm really quite tired of this place," said Veeba.

"I as well," I admitted. "Nonetheless, I have an errand to run before we head home. Set course for San Francisco if you would, Runchka."

"I think somebody's been bitten by the love bug, as they say on this insect-infested world," teased Veeba.

"Jealous?" I asked, hoping just a little that she would be.

"Not particularly, I'm bored to tears with you. Yet I can't help worrying. If you bring this boy home you'll never be free of him."

"What makes you think I want to be?"

"He'll follow you around like the local creature known as a puppy dog. He won't know anybody, not that you really do either, locked away in your university or institute or whatever it is. You're really taking on quite a project."

"So what? Aren't I entitled to a project?" I asked. Veeba shrugged. As we sped across the planet I suddenly realized I had a problem. I was a wanted man and everyone would recognize me from the television news. Since the spaceship had been seen by Earthlings in New York, word would be spreading quickly that we were authentic extraterrestrials. Would the U.N. let everyone know we were defenseless as well? Also, I'd have to find out where they were holding Chester before I could spring him. There was so much to consider, so little time, and so much danger. To buck up my courage I donned a silver lame body-stocking with shiny white thigh boots. Like all Zeeronians I feel more confident when well dressed. No sooner had I changed than I saw the foggy peninsular city of San Francisco through the porthole.

"That outfit is screaming out for something," cautioned Veeba, scrutinizing my ensemble.

"I'm in a bit of a rush...but what did you have in mind?" I asked.

"Let's see," she continued scrutinizing.

"I am in a *hurry*!" I reminded her.

"White goggles... and what about white gloves? And perhaps this nice white cap. Now just put on this blue eyeshadow and some nice white lipstick. Much better!"

As usual she was right, the outfit did really sparkle with her additions. I have a terrible habit of under-accessorizing.

"Where to?" called out Runchka from the cockpit.

"I was just coming in to tell you. Dora Julian's. I think it's near Dolores Park." I turned to Gropvak. "Could you ring Ms. Julian for me?"

A few lights flashed on Gropvak's chest. "No answer," it responded after a moment.

"Try Daphne Van Vechten."

A whirring sound emitted from its head. "No Van Vechtens listed in the San Francisco directory. You want I should call someone else?"

"I can't think who just at the moment. Give me Dora's address and I'll try going to her door, perhaps she's just not answering the phone." Giving Runchka instructions to hover, but under no circumstances to land, I climbed down the ladder into the park where several almost nude men were sunbathing despite the chill air. I was going to ask one of them for directions to Dora's but they all fled in terror before I had an opportunity. Walking a few blocks I found and entered a small corner grocery store.

"Could you tell me how to find 558 Norton Street?" I asked politely.

"Going to a costume party?" asked a grizzled man in a blue apron.

"No."

"Pretty fancy get-up you got there." He eyed me up and down.

"Thank you."

"Look like one a them aliens."

"I suppose I do. Have you any idea which way Norton Street is from here?" I asked again.

"You in show business?" He wiped his nose with the back of his hand.

"Not right at this moment. Can you, or can you not, tell me how to find this address?" These Earthlings could be so infuriating.

"Jeez! Cool your jets, man. You come in here in a friggin' freaky outfit like that..." He continued on in that vein but I didn't stay to hear the rest of his blather. Fortunately, upon exiting the store I noticed a donut shop I'd seen from the taxi the night I went home with Chester, and from there, managed to locate Dora's apartment building which was just around the corner.

I rang her bell to no avail and was dispiritedly heading back towards the ship when an unpleasant voice shrieked, "It's him!" I turned to see an angry-looking man and woman, both wearing identical khaki pants with ludicrous beige synthetic pullovers. The woman pointed at me and began a tirade about child molestation while the man threatened my person with physical violence. I sprayed rapture gas in their direction, but wasn't sure it got to them as they were a good three yards away from me. Panicked, I ran up the block and ducked into the first store I saw. The second I entered, my olfactory system was assaulted with the odors of various soaps, oils, and sachets so powerful they almost knocked me out.

"Can I help you?" asked a preternaturally perky blonde girl behind the counter.

"Just browsing," I said, trying not to breathe too heavily. How did she stand working in such a melange of stinks?

"Hey, wait a minute," she scrutinized me, "aren't you that creep who pretended to be an alien and then molested that poor teenage boy?" I took out the pleasant partyizer to spritz her, but with lightning reflexes she knocked it out of my hand. "Freak!" she screamed as the tiny canister fell to the floor and broke open. I covered my face with my hat, not in the mood to become any happier. Fortunately, the clerk got a large whiff. With a beatific look on her face she began skipping around the store, joyfully singing, "I love you, you love me, we're a happy family..." Although in mortal danger on a hostile alien world, I couldn't refrain from angrily exacting some revenge, and set about dousing her with scents from a nearby aromatherapy display. Rain. Orange Blossom. Kiwi. Coconut. Pine. Rose. Vetiver. After a moment I got a hold of myself and stopped. I was going native, becoming as barbarous as my hosts! The clerk clearly didn't mind being turned into an odoriferous monstrosity though, and in fact began scenting herself with even more vials. Gardenia. Vanilla. Patchouli. Exiting the store I ran back to the park, ignoring the glares and stares of passersby, and found that there was now a small crowd of curious Earthlings staring at the ship in rapt wonder. Amongst them was a jolly-looking police officer with a walrus mustache. I tried to rush towards the ladder without being seen by him but was entirely unsuccessful.

"Whoa there, buddy!" he bellowed with an inane grin, while blocking my path.

"I am *so* sorry I can't stop to speak, officer, but we're running late," I said quickly, looking for a way to get past him.

"You're the phony alien, right? Why aren't you in jail? And what's that, and how is it... hovering... floating... staying up there?"

"I'm out on bail," I lied, as suddenly I recalled the solution to countless difficulties on my favorite television show *Bewitched*, "and this ship is actually a balloon we're testing for an advertising campaign! Absolut vodka is going to use me in a print ad, Absolut Alien."

"Yeah?! I love those Absolut ads," said the enthusiastic guardian of public order.

"Being a celebrity certainly has its perks! We do need to get going though, as the designers have to make some adjustments to the ship, paint Absolut on the side and what not. We'll be back with the camera crew tomorrow. Why don't you come by, say around eleven? Perhaps you could be in the crowd scene!"

"That'd be great!" said San Francisco's finest, stepping aside with a friendly grin.

"Ta!" I climbed up the ladder into the ship at top speed.

"Veeba, I do wish Zeeronian civilization had taken time out from dressing well and throwing memorable parties to invent phasers and transporters like on *Star Trek*."

"I thought you did quite well down there," said Veeba, giving me a peck on the cheek. Now that I'm going to be romantically involved with someone else she seems much friendlier.

"Mr. N! I called all the information operators on Earth and found the Van Vechten girl's number," announced Gropvak.

"You're marvelous! Call her immediately!"

Someone picked up on the first ring. "Who is it?" asked Daphne, her voice emanating from Gropvak's mouth.

"Norvex 7," I replied into Gropvak's ear.

"OHMIGAWD!" screamed Daphne. "You've got to help. His parents committed him! He's locked up! He wants to marry you! Wait!" I then heard someone grab the phone and get on the line.

"Mr. Norvex, I'm so glad you called. I'm Mr. Larry, a friend of the dear boy's, but you can call me Larry. Now, we've simply got to do something for this child. He's been taken to a mental health facility, that's what they call the nut house these days, a mental health facility, but it's still a looney bin, and his parents, well, they're upset, terribly upset about him, and you, and I think it's terribly unfair, and the press has been truly awful. This morning's headlines were just *awful*. So when I got a call from Miss Daphne, I drove down here to meet her and figure out what we could do for the boy. We were thinking of lawsuits and all that dreary stuff, but of course little Chester wants to be with you, and go back to planet Zeevon."

"Zeeron…"

"But, you see, we didn't know where to find you, we thought you'd be in jail, or something awful like…"

I interrupted, "I am temporarily free, but about to head for my home planet. As for taking him with me, I have to think about it. This is his world, shabby and idiotic although it may be. No offense."

"None taken, dearie, nobody knows the shortcomings of this planet better than I do. Why the stories I could tell you would..."

"Could you put Daphne on the line?" I guessed that Mr. Larry had been drinking alcoholic beverages, an activity which I knew from personal experience diminishes one's capacity for rational decision-making.

The breathless young voice returned. "Look, I spoke with Chester's brother Kyle. He saw Chester, and he wants political asylum on Zeeron." She paused and added, "And I think he's in love with you."

"Love? We've only just met! And there is quite an age difference, I'm a hundred and nine years older than him. In eighty years I'll be ready to settle down and retire but he'll be a swinging ninety-seven. I'll want to stay at home and knit sweaters, he'll want to go out dancing all night. Anyway, what does he know about love? He's only seventeen."

"*I'm* seventeen, and seventeen isn't too young to know about love," declared Daphne.

"Well, I remember being seventeen. Vaguely. Well, maybe not, but I remember *remembering* what it was like to be seventeen. One falls in love at first sight, but it's something one can get over. And advanced as he is, Chester is still of this world." I was about to dismiss the impossibility of we two, with our vastly differing backgrounds, ever finding happiness together when my arms recalled his embrace and my lips recalled his kiss. I sighed. "Okay, where is he and how do we spring him?" Together, Daphne and I devised a plan.

Using Daphne's directions, Runchka located the Van Vechten house a few hundred miles down the pretty California coastline. Parking the saucer in hover mode several yards above the front lawn I could see Daphne waiting on the porch, looking quite darling in a lacy black dress with patent leather platform boots. She stared at our ship with awe in her heavily mascara'd eyes. "Hello!" I called out as I opened the ship's hatch and lowered the ladder.

"Hi Norvex! Why don't you stay up there and we'll join you," suggested the sensible girl as a chubby gentleman in a loud checked sportscoat and a lavender neckerchief emerged from the house sipping from a martini glass. I nodded my assent and Daphne scampered up the ladder, calling out for Mr. Larry to follow her.

"Be there in a second," he hollered, dashing back into the house. Daphne pulled herself into the ship and took a deep breath. "Wow!"

"Do you have it?" I asked. In response she showed me a small 'ray gun' commonly manufactured on Earth as a children's toy. Mr. Larry emerged from the house carrying a pitcher.

"Your ship is like, really something!" gushed our guest looking around the saucer which was uncomfortably crowded with artifacts. "I'm really glad you're going to help Chester. Frankly, I was worried he'd never find anyone to, you know, *like* him. You do like him, don't you? You sounded so ambivalent."

"I'm reasonably certain that I do. That is to say, I don't really *know* him, but all my instincts tell me he's a marvelous young man."

"Yeah, he's great," Daphne agreed. "You know though, I thought you and Veeba were, like, an item. It always looked that way on T.V."

"We are, or were, but Zeeronians aren't especially monogamous," I explained.

"Neither are Earthlings so much. At least not gay guys. One thing's been bothering me though." She tilted her head, and asked, "If it doesn't work out, will he be able to come home?"

"I'm afraid your government would be too paranoid to allow that."

"Hang on, I'm coming," bellowed Mr. Larry, huffing and puffing as he slowly climbed the ladder, still holding the pitcher.

"If Chester left and returned, he'd be kept under lock and key. Even if he got out, your planet's tabloid press would eliminate all personal privacy, following him around like some latter day Jackie Onassis or Princess Di."

"He might like that," observed Daphne.

"Almost there!" Mr. Larry cried out, turning pink with exertion.

Veeba, who'd been changing into a stunningly elegant opalescent gown with silver strappy sandals emerged from the walk-in closet. "Hello, Daphne, so pleased to meet you. I'm Veeba."

As she gazed on the other worldly glamour that is Veeba, Daphne's eyes lit up. "Hi, Your Excellency. I recognize you from the news."

"Made it," announced Mr. Larry, finally heaving himself aboard, panting like a dog.

"Let me take that from you," said Veeba, removing the pitcher from his feeble grasp. "Smells lovely. Martinis?"

"Why, yes!"

"Brilliant. I'll fetch some glasses."

"Veeba, we're about to rescue a prisoner on a barbarian planet a zillion trillion light years away from anywhere. His jailers will have personality disorders and lethal weaponry. I don't believe this is an appropriate time to serve cocktails."

Veeba patted my hand. "Getting nervous, are we?"

"Perhaps," I confessed.

"All the more reason you should have one of these." She handed me a glass. "Daphne, darling, here's yours. Now why don't you come with me and you can tell Runchka where to go." The girls scampered off to the cockpit.

"Wait!" bellowed Mr. Larry, finally getting his breath back.

"Sorry," said Veeba, returning to pour a martini for him.

"Cheers," I mumbled, taking the pitcher from Veeba and setting it on a stack of authentic commemorative plates.

"Bottoms up!" Mr. Larry toasted, taking a noisy slurp from his glass as he surveyed our craft's interior. "As you've no doubt guessed, I'm Mr. Larry." He examined the ship with a connoisseur's eye. "My, my, I must say, your accommodations here are lovely. Not much space, but I like what you've done with it."

"Thank you," I said as we both took a seat on the sofa facing the porthole. "It's usually not this cluttered, but we're taking home quite a few souvenirs. Look out the window," I suggested. We were flying slowly and low to the ground, and pedestrians were fleeing in terror as we passed.

"From this height people look like hamsters," observed Mr. Larry.

"I hope the Air Force doesn't show up."

"What could they do to a super space-age flying saucer like this one?"

"Shoot it out of the sky. We don't actually have any weapons or defenses."

"Oh." He finished his martini with a single gulp.

"Fear not, if need be we can fly away faster than the speed of light. I just don't want to leave without Chester."

"To tell the truth, I'd prefer to be back on solid ground," admitted Mr. Larry looking queasy. "I've never cared for flying."

"You know you're welcome to come with us to Zeeron. There's not much room, but the trip is only three weeks. I think I've decided it would be inhumane to leave anyone on this planet."

"No, no. I'm too old to change my ways. I've got my salon. I'm a hairdresser, you know."

"But that makes it all the better! On Zeeron you'd be a leader, a prominent and influential citizen. People would bow and curtsy and address you as Your Excellency."

This piqued Mr. Larry's interest. "Do you have martinis on Zeeron?"

"We could have the computers synthesize whole swimming pools full of them if you wanted."

"No, no, no, I've had enough already. Well, maybe one more." He held out his glass for a refill. "And I'll be fine here on Earth, but thanks for offering."

"We've arrived," announced Veeba, coming back into the room with Daphne in tow.

"If only we had some real weapons," I mused, opening the hatch. "We're almost out of rapture gas."

"Say, why not take my hairspray? It'll freeze anything in position," offered Veeba, fetching me a thin canister from her vanity.

"Why, thank you, I'm sure it will come in handy. Well, Daphne, we'd better hurry before they send for reinforcements. Wish us luck, everyone!" I lowered the ladder.

"To your health!" toasted Mr. Larry as Daphne and I climbed down onto a carefully manicured lawn in front of a dull tan box of a building surrounded by neatly manicured shrubs.

"Do you still have your toy gun?" I asked.

"Check," she replied heartily.

"You're quite the brave one, aren't you?" I complimented as we arrived at the hospital's glass doors which, without warning, swooshed open. A receptionist, who, in her crimson Dior knock-off blouse, bore more than a passing resemblance to a tart from an old B-movie, sat at the front desk filing her long red nails. Looking up to see us she screamed and set off a loud alarm. Apparently we were not unrecognized. Daphne ran down a corridor at top speed and I followed.

"Where are we going?" I demanded, not, I thought, unreasonably.

"I don't know," she admitted over her shoulder.

I stopped dead in my tracks. "Don't you think it would be wise to ascertain the whereabouts of our prospective emigrant before we become winded and get caught by security guards?"

"That was a rhetorical question, right?"

As she spoke a pair of hefty guards in unremarkable navy blue uniforms with truncheons came quickly waddling towards us. We set off down another corridor at a rapid clip, passing dozens of unmarked doors, any of which might have had Chester behind them. As we reached an intersection I collided with an efficient looking nurse in a white polyester dress who'd been half walking, half running around the corner. I was knocked down, but fortunately Daphne was there to help me up with one hand and with the other point the ray gun at the nurse, who let out a high-pitched shriek which pierced even the loud ringing of the alarm.

"Take us to Chester Julian's room, and don't make another sound or we'll vaporize you!" screamed Daphne. Our terrified captive consulted a chart she was carrying and motioned for us to follow her. After a series of twists and turns through the beige institutional corridor we arrived at Room 356. As I tried the door the nurse knocked the gun from Daphne then grabbed my arm and flipped me through the air. My body hit a wall and slid to the floor, which had an unpleasant artificial lemon smell.

"Haiyaaa! Don't move. I know capoiera, ju jitsu, and kung fu!" she bragged, assuming a menacing position: knees bent, arms held up like weapons. From my position on the floor I spritzed her with Veeba's extra-hold hairspray. Getting up slowly, and in great pain, I was gratified to see that she was frozen stiff.

Daphne took the canister from me and examined it. "Do you think Veeba has any more of this stuff? I have problem hair."

"I'm sure Veeba will give you some. Now, how are we to get into Chester's room?"

"Oh, Nursey here has some keys, let's try them out." The door opened on our second try.

Chester sat on a thin bed staring out a window which gave him a view of a perfectly manicured lawn and a freeway overpass. "Norvex! Daphne!" His face lit up like a sun when he saw us, though I could see there'd been tears on his cheeks.

"Did somebody here want to escape?" I asked. For an answer I got the best kiss I've ever gotten on any planet, in any galaxy. Our happy reunion was interrupted almost immediately by several uniformed guards bursting noisily into the room. I grabbed my companions and tried to Zerk us out of harm's way, but pressed the wrong button, and instead sent another S.O.S. to Zeeron. Fortunately our attackers were denied the opportunity to riddle us with bullets by Daphne who froze the lot of them with Veeba's hairspray. A moment later we were all three running at top speed to the hovering craft outside.

Once in the ship I rushed into the cockpit and instructed Runchka to fly the saucer to the North Pole, out of harm's way. I returned to the main room to discover Veeba in charming hostess mode. "Chester, I've heard so much about you, all of it delightful." She handed him a martini.

"Hi Veeba, I mean Your Excellency, I've seen you on T.V. Wow, my heart is beating so fast, this is so exciting!" The boy's body was positively vibrating with excitement.

"Just call me Veeba," offered Her Excellency magnanimously as she rested a hand on his shoulder in a calming sort of way.

"Hey, Mr. Larry!" Chester's eyes almost popped out of his head.

"Dear boy, good to see you! My word! You've changed your hair again!"

"I think it looks okay," said Chester self-consciously.

"Mr. Larry and I formed the Chester Julian Defense Committee," explained Daphne. "We weren't just going to let you rot in that place."

"Thanks," smiled Chester. "What now?"

"What exactly do you want to do with yourself?" I sat down on the sofa and patted the seat next to me, indicating for him to join me.

"I think you should change before anything," said Veeba looking at the hideous hospital gown the Earthlings had given Chester in an effort to break his spirit. "I'll fetch you something of Norvex's." She disappeared into the closet as Chester sat down next to me.

"Daphne tells me you'd like to come to Zeeron and that..." I was suddenly unaccountably shy.

Daphne helped me out. "You said you'd like to marry Norvex."

"Well..." He looked flustered.

She continued, "What an adventure - Zeeron! But, if you leave, what'll happen to me, all alone here with no best friend?" Daphne suddenly looked terribly small. "But don't think about that, just do what's best for you. But, I don't know, there's no place like home."

"That's sort of what I was counting on," explained Chester.

"If you'd care to hear my opinion," said Veeba, returning to hand Chester a light blue metallic jumpsuit with neon yellow fringe, "you don't seem mean or bossy enough to make it on this planet."

"Thanks, Veeba, I'll change in a minute. Um, Norvex, I'd never see Earth again if I went with you, would I?"

"Your government is terrified of extraterrestrials. It could get sticky." I smiled, inadvertently remembering how everything got sticky the last time we were together.

"In other words, no," said Chester, looking around the ship with wonder in his young, young eyes. What was I doing picking up a waif from a barbarous planet I'd come to visit for purely scientific reasons? Gossips would claim my trip was merely a pretext to troll for alien booty. But then, I reasoned, you can't please everyone. I took the boy's hand in mine, knowing I desperately needed to say something.

"Chester, we don't know each other terribly well, but I think we've connected on some deep aesthetic level. I like your clothes, you like mine. We have fun together. We're sexually compatible. All that may not seem so extraordinary, but in fact it's quite rare. And..." I thought quickly, "*you're cute!* Adorable. And we could have lots and lots of fun together. I'll see you're not bored on Zeeron. You won't have to worry about money because there isn't any, and you can live with me, and I can implant a computer chip in your cerebral cortex so you'll speak Zeeronian."

His eyes showed that he was flattered that I wanted him badly enough to make an effort, but there were still reservations. "It all sounds kind of fun... say, do you really like all that corny old T.V. and cheezy pop music?"

"Yes. We Zeeronians don't suffer as much as you Earthlings do so art with darker themes tends to strike us as a bit overwrought. I warn you though, you'll spend your life alone if you sit around waiting for someone who shares all your opinions and prejudices."

"Well, I watch *Daria*, so I guess I'm not so totally above television. It's just weird is all."

"A lot of things on Zeeron will seem weird to you. It's not like you're going to the Planet of the Apes, yet few people will share your points of reference. No one will have grown up in a family, used money, had to live without sex, contracted illnesses, or endured celebrity roasts and award ceremonies. You will be an oddity... or *novelty* rather. But still, people immigrate all the time, so don't worry about fitting in."

Runchka emerged from the cockpit and tried to help out. "Please allow me to introduce myself. I am Runchka Bezoo of the planet Felkus. If I may be so bold as to interject... according to my calculations your planet has a 86.41 percent chance of experiencing a major ecological catastrophe. Deforestation, excessive fossil fuel consumption, global warming, and the toxicity of your air and water are growing..."

I interrupted. "Chester, I don't want you to come with me because you're afraid of staying here, not that you don't have reason to be. I want you to come because it will be an adventure, because it's the best option for your future, and because I want you to be with me."

"But, but..." Chester blushed and grasped for words.

Veeba had at it again. "Most Earthlings are neurotic and ignorant, not that it's their fault. After all, they've grown up on an irredeemably barbarous world. Oh." She glanced at me, suddenly aware she was contradicting my academic thesis. I nodded for her to go on. "On Zeeron, millennia of deflating sarcasm have eradicated the barbarous impulses towards self-righteousness, avarice, megalomania, and melodrama. We're honest without being earnest, bemused not bitter. We don't mistake cynicism for wit, nor militancy for sincerity. Open your eyes, Earth is a cesspool of complacency and conventionality, get out while you can!" She collapsed next Mr. Larry who'd been staring owl-like at her tirade. "Don't ogle me that way, you sodden sodomite, pour me another martini!" she barked.

Mr. Larry complied with her request, and as the Earthlings say, put his two cents in. "Dear boy, I know you're hanging around with Zack and Franklin, and probably having the time of your life. Everything is fun, fun, fun, and you can have sex all the time with all the men you want…"

"I have never *once* in my life consummated a sexual act with another human being!" protested Chester shrilly. "Not while I was awake anyway."

"But you won't be young forever, and once you're grown, being a flaming nelly queen, and let us be honest, that's what you are, can be quite a drawback. Effeminacy is acceptable amongst the cute and young, but for men of a certain age, well, the best one can hope for is to be the comic relief. The world of gay men is one big meat rack, and once meat is past its expiration date, that's it. You'll grow lonely as you sit looking out the window, watching Adonis after Adonis prance by, oblivious to your sweet disposition and warm heart, and eventually you'll become so desperate for a shred of human affection that you'll have to buy the attentions of desperate strangers, some of whom try and steal from you, half of whom are on drugs, and most of whom display about as much tenderness as an inflatable sex doll!" Tears of self-pity welled up in Mr. Larry's eyes. "Now if I'm not mistaken, on this planet Zeerom, being a queen isn't an issue. Am I correct?"

"Absolutely," I concurred. "Machismo died out in our eighth millennium. And I might add that as a rule we all age rather gracefully."

"Go!" screamed Mr. Larry. "Get out while you can! Flee! Flee!"

"You're sure you wouldn't like to come with us?" I asked him.

"No, I'm fine," sniffled Mr. Larry, refilling his glass.

"Hmmmm," was Chester's enigmatic response to all this.

Runchka piped in. "It may also be advisable to recall that our advanced technology allows everyone to lead what by your standards would be an indescribably luxurious lifestyle. You would never have to work or clean up after yourself."

"He doesn't exactly wear himself out with that now," I interjected, recalling his slovenly room. "There are some big advantages to the technology though, not that I blame you for this, but the foundation you use…" Chester looked panic stricken. "On Zeeron we could clear

up your skin right away. Runchka, a demonstration if you please." S/
he found his/her doctor's bag, removed the implement that had cured
Veeba's blemish and went to work. In a minute it was done. Veeba led
Chester to the ship's flattering full-length mirror. We all followed, eager
to see his reaction.

"Gee!" said Chester and Daphne in unison.

"I don't have zits anymore, and no blotches, or pock marks. I look
like a movie star!"

"You look really good!" concurred Daphne.

"You always looked like a motion picture star to me," I lied.

"Wonnerful, wonnerful," said Mr. Larry teetering about unsteadily.

Chester looked at me, at Daphne, then burst out with his decision.
"What the heck, let's go to planet Zeeron!"

"Good move," said Mr. Larry. "Now, if you don't mind, could you
take me back to San Francisco? Just drop me off at the Triple Peaks, it's
on the corner of Castro and Market."

"Runchka, if you please," I gestured towards the cockpit and s/he
went inside. I turned to Chester and just smiled.

Chester, however, turned to Daphne. "Are you coming?" he asked
pleadingly.

"Dooo come along, Daphne!" purred Veeba.

"Oh, oh, oh!" Daphne looked panicked. "I'd love to, but, I don't
think I'd better. I mean, my mom is here. And I've got Klaus, and... I
just don't think I'm ready."

"Change your mind!" suggested Veeba.

"Daphne!" cried Chester with real panic in his voice.

"Daphne, coming or staying?" I asked gently.

"Staying," she said, sounding a bit ashamed of herself. "You know,
I could get a cable access T.V. show, and you could watch it on Zeeron,
couldn't you?"

"Sure he could!" I encouraged.

"It's not the same," Chester lamented.

"You still want to join us?" I asked him, slightly afraid he'd say no.

"I said I was coming, didn't I?" he snapped. Teenagers on Earth are
petulant by nature so I ignored his bratty tone.

"Merely giving you the option, darling," I replied.

"You sound like an old married couple," observed Veeba disgustedly.

"Can we be one?" asked Chester.

"One what?" I asked.

"A married couple?" Chester replied, staring into my eyes. "Zeeronians do have marriage, right?"

"Certainly. People marry each other all the time, but it's not the same as here. Zeeronians can marry whom or whatever they want with no particular obligations. I myself am married to three co-workers, my robo-maid, Veeba, and a delightful-smelling drugnutz bush near my house."

"I love you, and I want you to marry me," Chester said solemnly.

"Do you hear what I'm saying? Marriage means completely different things in our respective cultures. On your world a wedding means monogamy, child rearing, and community property. On ours it's a pretext for a party celebrating two people's or things' affection for each other."

"We can iron out the differences later. C'mon, do you want to?"

I knew I should refuse, but when I looked into his eyes all I could think was, "Yes!" which is what I said. "But I think you should propose in a more fitting manner," I added.

Chester got down on one knee and took my hand as is the custom on Earth. "Norvex, will you marry me?"

My heart was pounding wildly. "Yes again," I replied. Chester rose to his feet and kissed me on the lips passionately.

"Congratulations!" said Daphne.

"You really snagged yourself a prize," said Mr. Larry to Chester. "And *you!*" he said turning to me and winking luridly.

"I'd be honored to perform the ceremony," offered Veeba.

"On Zeeron it's customary for hairdressers to officiate at weddings," I explained to my fiancé.

"How long does it take?" asked Daphne.

"However long or short you want," replied Veeba.

"I'm his best friend," said Daphne, "I want to attend. Why don't you do it right now?"

"Is it okay, Norvex, can we? Daphne can give me away!" Chester was being just adorable – jumping up and down with excitement, grinning from ear to ear.

"Fine with me," I assented. "Veeba, start the ceremony, and make it short. Gropvak, could you play the Zeeronian wedding march?"

"Sure thing, Mr. N!" it replied, starting the lovely music.

"Do you, Chester, take Norvex to be your husband, so long as he's fabulous and your relationship is oodles of fun?" asked Veeba.

"Absolutely! Yes! Totally!" he replied.

"And do you, Norvex, promise the same in reverse?"

"Yes."

"Right then, kiss, kiss. You're married. Have a ball," concluded Veeba, ending the ceremony.

As we were congratulated all over again by our Earthling friends, Runchka emerged from the cockpit. "We're hovering over the bar you requested, Mr. Larry." I opened the hatch and lowered the ladder, deriving a bit of malevolent satisfaction from watching the Earthlings below run for cover.

"Thank you," I said to Mr. Larry, "for all you've done."

He began down the ladder. "Don't mention it. Have a safe flight!" he called out as we all waved.

"I shall take us to the Van Vechten estate," declared Runchka returning to the cockpit.

Daphne began crying and Chester's face went ashen.

"I think this is goodbye," I said to her as gently as I could.

"Why won't you come?" Chester asked her, taking her hand in his awkwardly. She just turned her face away. After a quiet, uncomfortable moment that seemed like an eternity I was lowering the ladder in front of her home.

Chester watched dolefully as she climbed down towards the green lawn. "Say goodbye to my family for me, okay? Especially Dora, I'll miss her. And say goodbye to your mom, I'll miss her, too," Suddenly tears welled up in his eyes. "But, Daphne, I'm going to miss you most of all. Think of me when you look at the stars!"

Here we sit, on the long ride home. Veeba's been reading the works of Quentin Crisp, Tennessee Williams, and Jackie Susann. Just now I heard her muttering, "Brilliant in spite of it all," an impressive accolade given what the Earthlings had just put her through. Runchka's hands are full tending to the plants that crowd our cabin, giving each the correct quantity of water, reading to them, making sure they get enough light. I rather believe s/he and Veeba have been little more affected by our voyage than they would've been by a short vacation to Buxmort, the planet of pleasant beaches.

Chester is busy, busy, busy with educational holographs learning all about his new home. "Gosh!" and "I can't believe it!" fall from his lips regularly during each passing hour. I think he's finally grasping the advantages of living on a civilized planet like Zeeron where he'll have more opportunities than he ever dared dream of on barbarous old Earth. Still, culture shock would seem to be inevitable, and to ease the transition I've been watching Earthly television shows with him. We snuggle up in front of the holograph player and nibble ozgruch and popcorn. I strongly suspect that in the long run he'll adapt well to his new world; youthful resilience will keep him from being overwhelmed.

As for me, my reputation as an Earth scholar is assured, and as an agreeable bonus, I've picked up a lover. Not bad for someone who wasn't sure he'd even come back alive. Still, my journey was every bit as stressful as it was successful. Seeing billions of sentient beings wallow in misery and ignorance has left me more unsettled than I'd anticipated.

It's especially hard to think of the more intelligent and sensitive ones, the Chesters and Daphnes, having to spend the rest of their lives in such a dismal milieu. Furthermore, the mystery that propelled me to Earth remains unsolved. How could such stupid people transcend their idiotic surroundings and create works of such genius? I may never know. Finally, although I'm glad I visited Earth, I have no desire to ever return to that benighted world. If I ever go looking for my heart's desire again, I won't look any further than my own backyard!

**25**

Dear Diary,                                                    Monday, Nov. 9

Here I am on my way to planet Zeeron in a flying saucer! The ship is incredible, though to hear Veeba gripe you'd think we were hurtling through space in a garbage can. We've got soft flattering pink light, comfy sofas, artificial gravity, and a robo-maid who does all the cooking and cleaning. Best of all, when I go to sleep at night, it's with *my husband*!

At first I couldn't believe I'd really left Earth. I can't say I miss my family much, or Zack and Franklin at all, but it drives me crazy that I can't pick up a phone and call Daphne. Actually though, I got over any regrets about moving to Zeeron last night when were watching T.V. The lead story on *Infotainment Tonight* was me. "Today, teen actor Kyle Julian's older brother, Chester Annesley Julian, became the first Earthling to emigrate to another planet when the seventeen-year-old boarded, apparently of his own volition, the Zeeronian spacecraft. The three Zeeronians, who contrary to many reports, were indeed extraterrestrial visitors, were forcibly expelled from our planet by order of the United Nations over charges of espionage and statutory rape..." Right away Norvex started in on how awful it was of them to "besmirch" our love affair, and "cast ugly, untrue aspersions" on his character. I think he's worried how the story will play on Zeeron.

Actually, I was angrier than him. Here I am making history and Kyle still gets mentioned before me! As if that isn't bad enough, they interviewed him and the reporter asked why he thought I'd left, like how could anyone be anything but perfectly satisfied to live on Earth. Kyle looked straight at the camera, oozing phony sincerity. "Chester was always a special person." Hearing myself referred to in the past tense was weird, but as far as Earth's concerned, I'm history. "He was always searching for something *more*. Even as a child we could all see something, like, *different* in him. I'll be playing him in an upcoming television mini-series on this network. It's going to be called *Out of This World...*" I didn't hear the rest because I threw a nearby cocktail shaker at the screen, smashing both into a million pieces.